I0584245

INVASION

INVASION

THE ASCENSION MYTH™ BOOK 11

ELL LEIGH CLARKE

MICHAEL ANDERLE

DISRUPTIVE IMAGINATION®

Invasion (this book) is a work of fiction.

All of the characters, organizations, and events portrayed in this novel are either products of the author's imagination or are used fictitiously. Sometimes both.

This book Copyright © 2018 Ell Leigh Clarke, Michael T. Anderle
Cover by Jeff Brown www.jeffbrowngraphics.com
Cover Photo by Andrew Dobell
Cover copyright © LMBPN Publishing

LMBPN Publishing supports the right to free expression and the value of copyright. The purpose of copyright is to encourage writers and artists to produce the creative works that enrich our culture.

The distribution of this book without permission is a theft of the author's intellectual property. If you would like permission to use material from the book (other than for review purposes), please contact info@kurtherianbooks.com. Thank you for your support of the author's rights.

LMBPN Publishing
PMB 196, 2540 South Maryland Pkwy
Las Vegas, NV 89109

First US Edition, June 2018
Version 1.03, September 2020

The Kurtherian Gambit (and what happens within / characters / situations / worlds) are copyright © 2015-2018 by Michael T. Anderle.

INVASION TEAM

JIT Beta Readers
John Ashmore
Larry Omans
Paul Westman
Micky Cocker

If we missed anyone, please let us know!

To everyone who ever dreamed of making a dent in the universe.

— Ellie

To Family, Friends and
Those Who Love
To Read.
May We All Enjoy Grace
To Live The Life We Are
Called.

— Michael

CHAPTER ONE

Main Hall, Skóli Uppstigs Academy, Spire, Estaria

Molly hovered by the stage, observing the room of about forty to fifty people.

"Thought you said this was going to be low key?" she muttered, glaring at Paige briefly as she kept the potential audience in her view as if they were the biggest threat in the room.

"We did. We had to, else certain people wouldn't be able to join us. As far as the outside world knows this is just a health and safety meeting."

Molly snorted. "How... appropriate."

Paige grinned. "I thought so. Especially given that that was what we almost got shut down on."

"I'm still amazed by how you both got this put together so quickly."

Paige shrugged. "It was mostly Maya. I've had some things in the business to deal with."

"Oh? Nothing too stressful I hope?"

"No. Just niggly things, like staff retention and minor lawsuits."

"How come?"

"It feels like someone is out for us. You know... like the Northern Clan is just trying to keep us busy."

"Yeah. The sooner we root them out, the better. For everyone on these damn planets."

"That would be good. Ok. You ready?"

Molly took a deep breath. "Ready as I'll ever be..."

Ogg Military Base, Ogg

The technician scuttled through the corridors like an ant navigating a crack in the sidewalk. He ducked past other Oggs as he went, picking up his speed to a jog before he could get cut off by the janitorial staff closing the hallway.

They glared at him bitterly as he passed, but he simply waved an apologetic hand and hurried on his way.

An Estarian and a Teshovian, both standing out like drops of paint on a clean sheet of paper amongst the sea of Oggs, glanced up in bemusement as the technician loped past them. He gave them a passing glance, and it looked as if the Teshovian was going to ask if there was anything wrong. She changed her mind and looked back to the file they were both perusing with an almost visible force of will.

He pushed them from his mind and carried on until he ground to a halt outside the door to the Captain's receiving area. He knocked once, waited for barely half a second, then knocked again before the door opened and the Captain's secretary gestured him impatiently into the room.

It was comfortable in a sterile, nondescript sort of way, offering little to get attached to, but also little to take offense to. The secretary sitting at the tidy, expansive desk looked decidedly unimpressed at the interruption as the technician strode quickly into the room, though her expression shifted gradually to concern as he leaned over the edge of the desk to quickly explain his reason for showing up without an appointment.

"Just wait there," she stated with a sigh once he was finished explaining his presence there. She opened her holo and typed a message.

The technician paced across the office like a nervous cat, picking distractedly at the hem of his uniform jacket. He pondered over what he was supposed to say once he was in the Captain's office, at least until the secretary interrupted his pacing to tell him. "The Captain will see you."

The technician hardly paused to offer her a quick, "Thanks," before he turned on his heel and darted into the Captain's office without even waiting for the door to finish opening.

The Captain was already looking at him when he entered the office, elbows on the desk and fingers steepled in front of his chin, waiting expectantly.

His office was almost as sparse as the receiving area.

"Presumably you have a good reason for barging in like this," he stated blandly before he gestured loosely for the technician to explain himself.

The Captain was not a man predisposed toward patience on most days, so the technician wasted no time in opening his holo-console. He sorted through the tabs until only the most relevant were immediately visible before he passed the screen over for the Captain to take a look.

"We caught something on our outermost satellites," he explained quickly before the Captain could even comment on what he was seeing. "We can sort of triangulate its position, but we don't know much about it other than it isn't supposed to be there. We can't find any recent incidents on record that would account for it. I was told to give you the news and let you see it for yourself."

The Captain was silent for a worryingly long moment, until the technician began to wonder whether or not he should repeat the entire spiel. Just as he opened his mouth to say something, though, the Captain abruptly pushed his chair away from his desk and got to his feet, quickly enough that the technician backpedaled a step.

Without a word the Captain rounded his desk, picking up his communicator as he did.

There was a secluded corner in the back of the office, partially partitioned off from the rest of the room by a set of shelves, and he strode there as he activated his communicator.

Before he could wrangle his curiosity under control, the technician trailed after him, peering around the corner of the shelf to see what he was doing.

"I need you to put me through to—" The Captain's budding conversation jerked to a halt as he realized the technician was still there. He turned to him. "Thank you for the report. You're dismissed."

The technician didn't linger to test the Captain's patience

He turned on his heel and beat a hasty retreat. All he heard was, "No, that wasn't aimed at you. Could you put me through—" before the door closed, muffling the conversation.

The technician lingered a moment at the closed door until the secretary cleared her throat at him and sent him hurrying back to his station.

Nefertiti Military Base, Estaria

The Estarian Ensign stared at his terminal, using the heel of one boot to fidget his chair back and forth like a metronome as he watched information scroll across the screen. He checked the time; it had to have been at least a couple of hours since the last time he checked.

It had been about ten minutes.

He blinked slowly, and his eyes stayed closed until he started to tip forward toward the desk. With a jerk, he snapped back upright just before his forehead could meet the surface, eyes opening again. He got to his feet, shook his head briskly, and jogged out of the room to get himself a cup of coffee.

By the time he returned to his station, he had his personal communicator in his hand and was scrolling through his personalized Estarian stock market feed.

He sighed out a contented breath as he took a sip of his coffee and dropped back down into his chair.

He could feel the fog clearing already.

It was a fairly standard day on Nefertiti Military Base, and especially so in the atmospheric monitoring center. There was no harm in taking a personal moment to wake up.

The coffee still tasted more like floor wax than anything resembling *coffee*, but his stock market feed was stable, and he couldn't see any unpleasant surprises coming. No pleasant surprises, either, but he figured *stable* was better than *exciting*—

It came as a surprise to absolutely no one when, as the door to the room slid open to admit the Lieutenant, the Ensign yelped in surprise, nearly fell out of his chair, and slopped half of his coffee over his knees. He pouted down at his sopping wet pants for a split second before carefully sneaking a glance up at the Lieutenant as a shadow fell over his desk and terminal.

The Lieutenant simply arched one eyebrow and wondered. "Looking for a repeat of the Applesauce Incident, Ensign?"

"Ah—," Hastily, the Ensign put his cup down, shoved his communicator back into his pocket, and scooted his chair closer to his terminal. One hand rose to run through his hair before he remembered that his hand was currently covered in coffee. He scrubbed it off on his pants before setting his hands on his desk instead. "No, sir."

Without another word, the Lieutenant nodded once and continued to his own terminal.

The quiet afternoon resumed after that, at least until the Ensign's terminal started beeping as one of the outermost proximity alarms went off.

"Uh—sir?" he called, scooting his chair even closer to his desk as he peered at the terminal, squinting at it as he tried to figure out what it was telling him. He silenced the beeping a moment later when it seemed like it was unlikely that whatever had triggered it was going to drift farther away or drift close enough to trigger the next alarm.

"Did you break something?" the Lieutenant asked wearily, turning his chair away from his desk.

The Ensign sputtered indignantly, but he was spared from needing to defend his own honor when the Junior Lieutenant across the room, usually as quiet as a mouse, announced abruptly, "I've got it, too!" She leaned away from her terminal to let the Lieutenant take a glance at it.

"Well, what is it?" he asked expectantly, glancing between them before he got to his feet to look at the Ensign's terminal. "Size? Distance? Speed? Will there be any damage we need to worry about?" He rattled the questions off one after the next, only stopping when all he got in reply were matching looks of doe-eyed concern.

He let the Ensign and the Junior Lieutenant stare for a few seconds before he snapped his fingers sharply to get them back on track and gestured expansively for one of them to enlighten him as to what was going on.

If only it were so easy.

The Ensign signaled helplessly at his terminal with one hand, as if that answered any of the Lieutenant's questions. "I can't get an accurate read on it. I can't even tell if it's one object or a cloud, or if it's coming toward us."

The Junior Lieutenant carefully suggested. "There was that Teshovian probe that got pulverized when it hit a shuttle a few weeks ago. The debris from that might have drifted into satellite range."

The Lieutenant waved off the suggestion dismissively and pushed the Ensign's chair aside to get a better look at the terminal. "That probe was tiny; I doubt we would even be able to see it on our sensors," he corrected absently. "Are we supposed to be seeing any activity from the asteroid belt at this time of year?"

The Junior Lieutenant shook her head so quickly that her bun wobbled. "Unless it's destabilized, we're not supposed to see any activity there for weeks."

The Lieutenant made a low noise of aggravation, and the Ensign shrank back into his seat until the Lieutenant started to pace back and forth across the room. Granted, his pacing wasn't particularly impressive, considering the atmospheric monitoring team hadn't seen a budget increase in nearly a decade so the monitoring center was roughly the size of a closet.

"One of you needs to give me an idea of what it *could* be, rather than just telling me what it isn't," he stated testily, regardless of the fact that *he* was the one who had shot down the probe theory.

The Junior Lieutenant fumbled, tripping over her tongue for a moment before launching into some rather involved speculation about asteroids in the belt colliding and breaking apart and drifting into range. She kept interrupting herself to say that if it was the case, it was more harmless than it really sounded.

Cautiously, the Ensign scooted his chair back toward his terminal. He let the Lieutenant and Junior Lieutenant argue without interrupting them as he dutifully set about recording the abnormal readings. *Someone* was going to have to give the report on them, after all, and he always got the grunt work.

Main Hall, Skóli Uppstigs Academy, Spire, Estaria

Paige tapped her glass of champagne with a metal spoon. "Always wanted to do that!" she whispered to Molly before turning her attention to the crowd.

The chatter died down. Professor Duffledorf had been regaling a group of their newest faculty members with stories of his time in the military. The irony around his subject being non-combative military strategy seemed completely lost on him. Reluctantly he paused his story.

Dr. Jones and Dr. Augustine were the last to pull their attention from the buffet table and, mouths full of food, turned to look at the women standing just in front of the main stage.

Paige straightened up and flashed her biggest smile at her audience. "Ladies and gentlemen. Thank you all so much for being here. My name is Paige Montgomery, and I'm your hostess for the evening. As you know this event is just our little way of saying a huge thank you for all the help you've given us. We'll shortly be moving to the next room where you can see the demonstration of the new equipment for the teaching labs, but before we do that our esteemed leader has a few things to share. Molly..."

Molly took another deep breath. "Thank you all for being here. I cannot express to you how grateful I am..."

Her speech continued, met by the rapt attention of multiple peoples who had worked tirelessly doing all they needed to in an attempt to thwart the efforts of the Northern Clan to have them shut down.

Molly noticed a disturbance in the back of the room. Gareth Atkins, their ally from when they founded the special university seemed distracted. He placed his glass of champagne down on the table and tilted his head, looking at his holo as if taking a call. He headed out the door.

That's odd, she thought to herself. *He is normally super polite and would let it go to messages if he were already in a meeting or an event.*

She continued her speech, calling off the points she wanted to make. She and Maya had agreed not to mention everyone by name, simply because it was a security risk, but there were a few people she wanted to mention. Her eyes scanned the room to make sure they were all there. That's when she noticed Ben'or's attention had also been pulled. He seemed to have watched

Gareth leaving too. Arlene whispered something to him, and he responded, but Molly couldn't see their lips from her position by the stage.

She continued speaking, calling out the people she was able to thank. That's when she noticed two or three of the other guests looking down at their holos.

Oz? What's going on?

Checking now.

He paused. **It seems there has been some new intel discovered by the Department of Off-World Logistics.**

What intel?

An unidentified object just at the cusp of the range of the joint world satellites.

What does that mean?

Well, probably nothing, but the concern seems to be that something non-Federation and non-commercial is coming into the system from a direction no one can make sense of.

Ok. We need to wrap this up then and get back to Gaitune.

You could. But the distances involved are so large that you have weeks before anything without Gate tech would get here.

Are you sure?

Positive.

Well, let's assume they haven't got Gate tech, or else they'd be here already.

Good assumption.

Ok. Round up the core team and have them come up to Gaitune with us after this soiree is done then.

Sending the messages now.

Molly finished her thank-yous and encouraged them to drink the champagne because the university by-laws prohibited her from taking it off-site. She got a few chuckles and a round of applause.

Paige hurried over to her. "Great speech. Well done."

Molly's face turned from her show-face, for the outside

world, to her just-Molly face. "We've got a problem. Oz is sending you details. We should finish up here, but then we need to get back to Gaitune."

Paige's eyes widened. Molly wasn't certain, but she suspected that Paige was more excited than worried. "Ok. No problem," she said. "Maya's just finished setting up the demo next door, and she's responsible for that piece of the evening. We can give her the go-ahead to get that underway if you like."

Molly nodded distractedly, her eyes scanning the crowd. "Yeah. Let's do that." Then she wandered off, without glancing back at Paige.

Paige was used to it. In all the years she'd known Molly she had only seen Molly's social skills improve—apart from when she was intensely focused on something. Which, she deduced, was probably what was going on right now.

She watched Molly disappear into the mass of people, only to be met at the door by Gareth Atkins coming back into the room. He looked concerned. Not that Gareth was ever footloose and fancy-free, but his expression was grave again, like he had been in the weeks preceding the break-through on the university case.

The pair whispered together for a few moments before Gareth hurried out again.

Paige cocked her head, wondering, before she remembered Molly had told her to check her holo.

She glanced down to see a message from Oz.

Back of the Main Hall, Skóli Uppstigs Academy, Spire, Estaria

Molly excused herself from a conversation with Dr. Augustine as she saw Gareth Atkins return to the room.

"Hey, did you get the same intel I did?" she asked in a hushed voice.

He nodded. "Likely. My contact says that the agencies are all in a dither over this."

Molly gently led him by the elbow away from the doorway, so they wouldn't be overheard by the guests bustling around. "Don't they have contingencies for this kind of thing?"

"They do... but..."

"But?"

Gareth looked more concerned than she had ever seen him. "What is it?" she pressed.

Gareth took a deep breath. "The standard contingency is for them to launch the fleet."

Molly frowned. She hadn't paid much attention to the doomsday kind of things when she was in the military. It was more an excuse to do science and disappear from the world. "The fleet?" she queried.

"The Estarian-Ogg fleet," Gareth clarified.

"But that's just for policing trade routes, isn't it?"

"Yes. In times of peace. But there are whispers about enacting section 53 of the second amendment. It gives the military the decision-making power in the event that we're invaded."

"You think we're being invaded?"

"Can't be sure yet. All they've had is a blip on the radar. No one can tell what it is until they've got more data."

Molly thought for a moment, her eyes subconsciously keeping some attention on the room of guests milling around them. She leaned in and lowered her voice even more. "Wouldn't they need Ogg approval for that? I can't imagine the Oggs wanting to launch into a potential war with no data."

Gareth gave her a look as if to say anything is possible.

She tapped a finger on her lips, turning the possibilities over in her mind. "In your opinion, Gareth, could this be an error. In the equipment, for instance?"

Gareth nodded. "Entirely possible."

"Could it be faked?"

"You're thinking someone—"

She nodded. "If you wanted to enact martial law, what easier way to do it?"

"Northern Clan?"

She nodded again. "I think they just upped the ante."

Gareth looked positively gray. He opened his wrist holo. "Lemme make some calls. I'll see what chance there is of blocking it."

"Ok. Keep me posted. We'll see what we can do from our end."

"Yes. Your mother… of course."

Molly smiled knowingly. "Yeah. I'm sure she'd love to be involved in this…"

Gareth wasn't sure if she was being sarcastic… or if she was just grim about having to involve her mother.

Either way, he had work to do. He nodded an acknowledgment and then scuttled off.

CHAPTER TWO

Hangar Deck, Gaitune-67

The pod descended deftly onto the hangar deck back at Gaitune. Molly used the opportunity to ride alone and review the details that Oz had been able to scalp from the communications that had been flying about the Estarian XtraNET.

I think this is a dangerous situation, whether the threat is real or not.

Because of the trigger-happy political elements?

Exactly.

The pod door opened before she reached it allowing her to step out. Joel, who had seen her landing, hurried over.

"I got Oz's message," he called to her. "Need me to do anything?"

"Not yet," she called back, hauling her bag out from under her seat. "Let's just meet everyone in the base conference room. I just need to pop up to my room and dump my gear."

Joel came to a stop about twenty paces away, waved in response and hurried off in the direction of the base facilities, no doubt to help wrangle everyone else who needed to be in on the meeting.

Molly strode across the yellow non-slip paint of the hangar deck, and up the stairs. Heading through the basement workshop, she noticed the empty beer bottles and take out packets in the workshop around where the men played their hologames.

Must have been playing when they got the message, she thought to herself. She had visions of Brock trying to persuade Pieter and Crash to take his hangover cures to get them operational. Goodness knows what he put in those things…

She arrived in the foyer. Giles and Arlene were there, standing around.

She slowed her pace. They turned to look at her.

"All ok?" she asked.

They both looked concerned.

Arlene pressed her lips together and shook her head. She fiddled with her fingers. Arlene never fiddled.

"Erm, actually, we wondered if we might have a word," Giles began delicately.

"Sure, but I have a briefing. Can it wait?"

Giles shook his head, then took off his glasses.

Molly felt a heaviness rise in her chest. She realized that this may be more than them asking what they could do to help with the situation that was blowing up.

"I can't help but wonder," Giles started. "That what we did… with the talismans and Bethany Anne…"

Arlene interjected. "What we're trying to say is… do you think this radar blip is a result of what we did? With the Ascension Race. You know… like maybe called them and told them where we were and now they're coming to find us."

Molly tried to maintain an expressionless face. The thought had already crossed her mind, but it gave her such a sick feeling in her stomach that she tried to play ignorant.

"From what we know, there is nothing to suggest that it's even moving in our direction, let alone that it's a ship."

Giles had replaced his glasses, but he was still frowning. "But it must be large enough for those outer satellites to even pick it up."

Yeah, fleet size.

We probably don't want to mention that.

"Maybe. We don't have enough info yet. Oz is still collating data from the satellites the Oggs and Estarians have in the outer system. Our best estimation right now is that it's space debris," Molly explained. "What worries me more is how this might be used to disrupt the already delicate military situation though."

Giles rubbed his eyes under his glasses. "Yes, we'd thought of that. Anything we can do?"

Molly shrugged, dropping her bag from her shoulder. "I don't know yet. Why don't you come to the briefing downstairs in the base conference room? I'm just gonna dump my gear and head over."

Arlene looked at Giles, completely unconvinced. "Ok. We'll see you down there then," she agreed.

Molly gave her a half-smile, in an attempt to be reassuring. She nodded then headed off down the corridor to her quarters. As she left the foyer she heard Arlene say something about going up against the Ascension Race.

Giles replied. "We wouldn't stand a chance." His tone was grim and despondent. And he was right. If they were truly going up against the master race that had spent the last ten thousand years seeding all these races in this section of the galaxy, it was safe to say that their technology was far more advanced than anything the Oggs and Estarians could produce.

Molly shook the thought from her head and concentrated on the immediate things she needed to do. She needed to change her clothes, wash her face, and make sure that she grabbed some water to take down with her to the meeting. Something told her this wasn't going to be a quick meeting.

What's more, she was going to have to do a lot of panic-control, which was particularly socially and emotionally draining for her.

Base Conference room, Gaitune-67

Molly rushed from the kitchen down to the base conference room, phyto-nutrient protein shake in hand. She guessed in the back of her mind she had probably skipped a meal at some point and figured that would tide her over.

We should probably loop Director Bates in on this briefing.

Molly considered Oz's suggestion. *You're probably right,* subconsciously sighing.

Do I detect a resistance to her still?

Well, a lifetime of BS isn't going to be obliterated in a couple of missions that happen to go right on her end.

Wow. You're pretty hard on her.

Well, you haven't ever had parents, so I don't expect you to understand. But yes, tactically she would be useful so please do invite her in.

Oz fell quiet as he went through whatever protocols he had set up to contact Carol Bates on official business.

Molly strode into the conference room. The whole team was there, and while there was the usual hubbub of activity and chatter, something was different. It was almost like they could tell that this wasn't a routine situation. As if they knew what Molly also sensed in her gut: this wasn't debris in space.

Giles and Arlene sat along the far side of the conference table. Ben'or was next to Arlene. He must have come up with her following the thank you event at the university.

Sean and Joel wore sweat suits and looked fresh from the showers. Jack was in full uniform so she'd probably been working in the weapons room on one of her projects Molly had approved last month. Karina, Brock, and Crash sat together looking as thick as thieves. Molly had noticed how Karina had been bonding with the other team members. In amongst the drama of everything else, at least something was going right.

Paige and Pieter sat next to each other, holoscreens scattered everywhere as they worked, probably fielding all kinds of other work they had on the boil.

Maya arrived a second after Molly and sat down quickly so as not to cause a delay.

Ok, we've got Carol on a holoconnection.

Thanks, Oz. Let's get her onscreen.

The screen in the middle of the conference table unfolded and displayed in the central point so that all members around the table could see her.

Carol looked startled. "Greetings," she said. "Sorry I wasn't expecting that everyone would be here." She paused, taking everything in. "Arlene," she said sternly.

Arlene nodded to her. Paige glanced at Pieter to see if he had clocked the coolness between the two women.

Molly ignored it. "Hi, Mom. Thanks for being here. And everyone. Thank you. As you know…" she was straight into briefing mode.

"At 20:04 this evening the Joint Ogg-Estarian Satellite System detected an object just beyond the outer region of the system. At present we haven't had enough tracking data in order to ascertain direction, or even the nature of the object. The primary problem we face is the politicians on Estaria using it as a reason to launch the Fleet. As you know tensions between Ogg and Estaria have run high in recent months over discussions around this very question. Ekks," she flicked her holo and brought a still shot of Ekks up next to her mother's video feed. "The Commander of the Joint Fleet has been building support for a move to launch them into the outer system. How he could have known this was coming we don't know. Either this is coincidental, and he'll be using it to stir up panic, or he has been anticipating a conflict with one of the member states in the Federation. The Federation angle was something we thought was more plausible… until today's radar blip."

She turned to Paige and Pieter who were sitting to the right of Arlene and Ben'or. "Paige, Maya and Pieter, can you get onto investigating possible conflicts that Ekks might be gearing up for. I think it's safe to assume that the Northern Clan is behind his motivation, but at the same time, I'd suggest putting aside the recent radar hit and assume that hasn't happened."

"Oz is monitoring any chatter. Joel, perhaps you could be the human sense check and see if there is anything that corresponds with the political movements on the surface. I'm almost certain there is something we're missing."

Carol interrupted. "Might I suggest we look into things planet-side as well."

Molly nodded. "Of course. Any help would be very much appreciated. Jack and Sean, I'd like you to assume that it is an invasion. But one that isn't related to the Federation…"

Sean frowned and raised his hand. "Hang on… how do we know it's not the Federation?"

Molly looked at him with a sarcasm in her eye. "Sean, you're practically part of the Federation. Do you think they'd do anything without giving you or I a heads up?"

Sean shrugged. "Fuck knows what goes on over there these days. I mean, they changed my vacation policy without telling me. Said it was an oversight. An oversight! Wouldn't put anything past the big cogs of bureaucrazy."

Molly rolled her eyes. Karina looked like she was holding her breath. Maybe she knew something that Molly didn't, she thought for a moment. "Ok, Sean. Well, I'm assuming that if you knew something you would come and let me know. But in case you don't, my next call after this briefing is to Lance. Ok?"

Sean nodded, folded his arms and sat back. Karina looked at him as if she didn't know who he was right now. Molly filed the information away to consider later. She knew from her online Federation "people-ing" modules she'd been studying that the woman always knows when her man is lying, and worst-case scenario she might have to interview Karina to make sure she had all her bases covered. Royale had always been a bit of a wild card in her camp when it came to the Federation. Mobilization for war wouldn't fall outside of his strange loyalty to Lance.

"As I was saying," she continued. "Run the simulations as if this is a new, third-party threat that we don't already have on the board. I want to know what our options are for action, and what our probabilities of a favorable and an unfavorable outcome are in each scenario."

Jack took some notes down as she listened.

"Brock, Crash, and Karina, can you make sure that we're up to date with maintenance on all the ships and pods? If we need to move, I want our ships to be in top condition. Anything that you've been meaning to do, make sure you get it organized. Assume from a maintenance perspective that we're going to war in two weeks. Order up parts and any supplies you need. Put aside non-critical projects."

The three of them nodded and mumbled their agreement. Karina looked surprised to be put on maintenance, but also pleased that she was being treated as a full team member now. Molly knew from conversations with Director Bates that in her history working for Carol, Karina had executed an undercover assignment that had given her engineering experience. *Time to start capitalizing on it*, she reasoned with herself.

Molly looked ready to wrap up, but Giles raised his hand. "Anything we can do?" he asked, signaling to include Arlene and Ben'or in his question.

Molly thought for a moment. "Make sure that Anne is ok. There is a nervous vibe on the base at the moment, and she's bound to pick up on it. Plus, after all she went through on the last trip, we need to be keeping a close eye on her."

Arlene nodded as if taking responsibility for her. Her eyes lit up suddenly as if she had a new thought. She glanced quickly at Ben'or, hesitated then spoke. "You know, we could take her back to my place on Estaria if you like... keep her safe there." She paused. "Or there's my old cabin here on Gaitune."

Molly took a moment, considering the options. "You know, that's not a bad idea. I think Estaria would be more comfortable for her. But the cabin is a good contingency if we need to keep her close and safe, but as a first option, she's more likely to go stir crazy without any of the modern conveniences." She paused. "Are you sure you can manage her?"

Arlene hesitated again. Molly was sure she saw a flicker of panic in Arlene's eyes for a fraction of a second. "Yes," she confirmed, firmly now. "Yes. She'll be fine. She's worked hard, and I believe her powers are under control... even if she becomes emotional."

Molly nodded. "Ok. Make it so."

Giles sat back in his seat as if he were irritated by still not having anything to do.

"Ok folks. You know what you need to do. We're likely going to need some help, however this pans out. I'm going to talk to the Federation about reinforcements just in case the space debris isn't space debris. Any other questions before we break?"

No more hands went up.

"Ok. Team dismissed," she said, using Joel's old hand signal for winding up a meeting and moving out.

The team pushed out of their antigrav chairs and filed out in a quiet mull of activity. Giles stayed put.

He waited until everyone had left, and even signaled to Arlene who had hovered at the door, that he'd catch her up.

Molly played along and waited. "What is it?" she asked, knowing full well his concerns hadn't changed.

"Forgive me... I know you haven't set any investigation into whether we might have triggered this event... But I'd like to look into that."

"Where would you start?" she asked.

"I have no idea. But I'll do some work on it."

Molly seemed in a hurry to get him to move on. "Ok," she said, distracted. "Keep me posted."

Giles hesitated, fiddling with his glasses again. He wagged a finger. "It's just, I can't understand why this Ascension Race would go to all this humongous effort to leave these clues all over the place, to have us figure out how to contact them... only to come and kill us..."

Molly stroked her chin. "You're right. It doesn't make sense. For what it's worth, I don't believe that if it is indeed them, they'd be coming for malicious reasons. But the problem is, no one in the outside world is going to believe that. Plus, as responsible leaders, we can't take any chances when it comes to the safety of either our system or the Federation beyond. We have to be sensible in how we proceed."

Giles lowered his gaze to the table and nodded. "Yes," he murmured. "I understand your position. But there's something I just can't put my finger on. Something else that is niggling me... that we're missing."

Molly seemed to relax for a moment, her to-do list forgotten momentarily. "I agree. I have that same feeling too." She snapped out of it. "If anything comes to you..."

He put his glasses back on, and stood up, straightening his atmosuit. "Of course. You'll be the first to know."

"Day or night," she added.

Giles hesitated, his eyes brighter like he wanted to clarify something. He changed his mind, dismissing the thought that maybe he had a chance with her socially still. "Sure. Thanks," he said before he headed out of the conference room.

Molly smiled at him as he walked past her.

Oz, can we get a call with the General?

Sure. Lemme find out when his next availability is.

Thanks.

She took another sip of her phyto-shake that had been untouched for the entire meeting.

Department of Cyber Communications, Spire, Estaria

Jennifer was pretty sure her arms were going to break off if she had to carry the box another fifteen feet, but the door to her office was right there. She picked up her pace from a reluctant plod to a labored mosey for the last few strides before she came to a halt.

She even had a door plaque already. Her name, *Jennifer Etang*, was carved in elegant script.

Carefully, Jennifer tried to shift her box to prop it up against one hip, only to abruptly grapple with it as it tried to make a dive for the floor. She caught it, hugging it awkwardly to her midsection at the last moment. She stood there, both hands wrapped around the sides of the box as she stared at the door's keypad in consternation. Unfortunately, she failed to manifest any convenient psychic abilities just then.

She didn't hear the footsteps behind her, nor she did realize she had company.

"Need a hand?" a voice asked.

She nearly leapt out of her skin, hugging the box tighter to her stomach before she could lose her grip on it.

Her attempt to whip around to face him turned into more of an awkward twist, and she found herself face-to-collarbone with another Estarian, roughly around her own age if she had to guess.

He was looking at her expectantly. She shook her head self-consciously, remembering that he had asked her a question. She cleared her throat and jerked her head toward the door, lacking the use of her hands to properly point.

"The door," she specified. "It kind of requires hands."

"A very poor design choice," he agreed cheerfully, stepping around her to enter his own entry code into the keypad. The door slid open and he stepped aside, gesturing her into the room with a flourish.

Jennifer rolled her eyes good-naturedly at herself as she passed and dropped her box on a free spot on the desk. She glanced over her shoulder to see him lingering in the doorway still. She motioned him into the room.

"Andrew," he offered belatedly once he stepped in enough to let the door close. "How's the moving-in process going? Finishing up?"

She spread her arms to gesture around at the office. Though it was still undecorated all the supplies on the desk and the shelves were hers. "I just need to empty out this box."

"Of bricks," he supplied wryly.

She brought a finger to her lips to hiss conspiratorially. "Shhhh! They're my *secret* bricks. No one was supposed to know about them."

Andrew held his hands up as if in surrender. "Your secret is safe with me. But are your secret bricks there so you can fend anyone off? Since…well, these are quite the shoes you're filling. Nervous?"

Jennifer shrugged and dropped down into her chair. "A bit, I guess. It's a big job. Nothing I haven't been trained for, though. I'll need to spend some time familiarizing myself with the servers and relays to see what sort of maintenance they need and bone up on the public communication regulations, but…" She trailed off with an unconcerned shrug and shifted in her seat to get comfortable.

"I meant because— " He cut himself off, mouth twisting to one side as he thought better of whatever he planned on saying.

"I already know what happened to Dorota," she assured him.

"They told me about it after my first interview for the job. So don't worry, you're not going to scare me by bringing it up."

Andrew rubbed the back of his head and leaned back against the door. His hands fell to his sides and he drummed his fingers against the door. "You don't seem too worried about it."

Jennifer waved it off with a loose motion of one hand before she let it fall back to the arm of her chair. "I won't say I don't care that it happened," she explained carefully after a moment. "But I'm not Dorota Carpe." She pulled the front of her jacket to the side to show off the gun holstered at her side. Andrew tried to recoil a startled step, only to come up short when he almost clocked the back of his head against the door.

"I can take care of myself," Jennifer informed him. She let her jacket fall closed again, and her tone turned slightly smug as she added. "If someone wants to shoot *me*, I'm going to shoot them first."

Andrew arched one eyebrow dubiously, his gaze returning slowly to her face from where the gun hid beneath her coat. "You think that peashooter will keep you safe from a sniper?"

She was quiet for a few seconds, her expression going blank at first before her eyes drifted thoughtfully up and to the side.

"I can take care of myself," she repeated, slow and assured as she folded her arms over her chest and straightened up in her seat. "You don't need to worry about anything like that; I'll be fine."

Andrew couldn't tell if she was just trying to reassure herself at this point. He pushed himself away from the door. "Love the confidence," he remarked, turning to let the door slide open again. "I'll leave you to your box of bricks, then." He could take a hint, after all, and that had sounded an awful lot like a dismissal.

"Looking forward to working with you," he called over his shoulder as he left, only just remembering that some form of politeness would probably not go amiss. "Just holler for me if you need anything."

"Will do," Jennifer acknowledged, already sounding distracted as she said it. She stared past the door as it closed, not truly seeing it as her thoughts wandered.

"I've got nothing to worry about," she assured herself, murmuring the words under her breath once she was on her own again. After all, she *could* take care of herself. She would be fine.

CHAPTER THREE

<u>Base Conference room, Gaitune-67</u>

Molly sat in the quiet conference room waiting for Lance to show up. Oz had arranged the call for a time that fortuitously allowed her to go and find some food and grab a shower before her presence was required.

It took several minutes for the General to finally show up. Molly checked the time on her holo. She could do with getting some sleep in as soon as they had the Federation pieces of the puzzle. At least then she could sleep on the new intel and formulate a plan in the hours it normally took her to drift off.

The screen illuminated from the central box and then unfolded, forming itself against the wall opposite her. The General was already seated, reading the brief on his holo.

"Ah. Ms. Bates. There you are."

"Here I am, Sir," she agreed, shuffling in her chair and trying to sit a bit straighter.

He continued to scan the update. "I see we have a potential crisis on our hands."

She pressed her lips together. "It would seem so, sir."

"You have a radar blip in the outer system."

"Yes, sir."

"Is it verified as being hostile?"

"Sir, at this point it isn't even verified as coming in our direction."

He eyed her carefully from his side of the screen. "So your reason for involving me?"

"Sir, whatever it is, it's going to cause problems on Estaria. They're going to want to launch a war fleet preemptively."

He nodded. "Understandable. I suppose, given the speed of their ships..."

"Right. But I think that was the point all along. They just want to put the planet on a war footing. But even putting that aside, if we take it as a credible threat, the Ogg-Estarian alliance would have absolutely no chance against a fleet that is clearly capable of coming out of deep space, beyond where we can see."

Lance rubbed his chin, his eyes fixed on his holo. "I see," he said slowly. "So you're expecting..."

"I was hoping we might have some support from the Federation—in the form of ships. To help protect the system."

Lance Reynolds took a very deep breath and sat back, his eyes still lowered. After a moment he looked up at his camera. Molly didn't like where this was going. It was clearly not happening in her favor.

"Molly, I don't know how much you know about the situation within the Federation but we have a number of obstacles. The first being, that the Sark System isn't even an official member of the Federation."

Molly waited for him to expand on the others.

"This being the case," he continued. "Even if we did have the spare ships to send, as soon as we start moving fleet ships, we're going to cause a disruption amongst our members. The Leath are already nervous. The Noel-li have a very tenuous relationship with the rest of the Federation, and goodness knows how the Yollin factions might react. There are tensions that still exist.

Tensions that we've all worked very hard to dispel over the last several decades, by disbanding certain elements of our forces. To parade them out of the system would only serve to reignite tensions and potentially cause civil war." He paused, his eyes still on Molly. "I can't take that chance."

Molly shifted in her seat again. "I… I understand. I don't quite know where that leaves us."

"Well, if there is anything else I can do, of course I will. We can send you all the supplies you'll need for the ships you have of course. And anything else. If you need some people, I can have a team dispatched. But they would have to be undercover. I can't have Federation uniforms outside of the Federation."

Molly nodded. "Ok. I need to think." Her eyes drifted off for a second and then she snapped her gaze back to him as if a new thought had entered her mind. "General, could you tell me please… have you got any campaigns happening external to the Federation."

He frowned immediately. "You know if that were the case it would be classified."

She bobbed her head from side to side, trying to think of how to ask the specific question she needed an answer to. "Sorry, Sir. No, I was meaning, if this is a fleet heading toward us, might you know who it was? I'm assuming that they're not federation ships?"

Lance's face softened. "You're correct. They're not Federation, and I don't have any reason to believe they are known entities that we, the Federation, already have relationships with."

Another thought seemed to occur to her. "And you can't think of anyone who might try targeting us, or perhaps want to ally with us, as a result of the Federation?"

The General inched back in his seat, leaning back a little. "No. I can't think of anyone who would be coming from the direction of deep space who would want to do that. There was a time when I thought the Zhyn might partner with the Estarians… for cultural reasons more than defensive ones. But when our people looked into it closely it seemed they saw more differences than similarities."

Molly smirked at the thought. "Yeah, I heard from Giles and Arlene they're a very proud species. And proud of their uniqueness. Apparently, they didn't take kindly to Giles's theory of them sharing a seed race and so much DNA with the Estarians."

Lance smiled. "Well, you know. We've seen this time and again. Even amongst the humans." He rolled his eyes. "Anyway, if there is anything that I can do, please let me know."

"Thank you, General. I will." She tried a half-smile, but her mind was so distracted it barely translated into a visible physical gesture.

The camera clicked off, and the holoscreen folded itself up and back into the projector box in the center of the table.

Molly sat in the half-light and the quiet of the early morning thinking before she eventually stood up wearily and headed out of the conference room.

Ekk's Office, Senate House, Spire

Richard Ekks read over the message carefully. Then a second time. Not that there really were very many details, but he wasn't going to fault himself for not being thorough.

He shifted in his seat and scratched his head.

Something had been detected in the outer perimeter of the system. Just…something. The data had come from both teams on Ogg and Estaria, so there was no doubt that something was there. They just couldn't figure out what.

He brought up his holoscreen and got comfortable in his console chair. He punched a call into the device and waited for it to be answered. As he waited, he picked at lint on his uniform.

He was contemplating canceling the call and trying again later when, at last, it was answered. Ekks was greeted by the sight of

Garet Beaufort staring back at him expectantly. His jacket was draped over the back of his chair and he looked as if he had been interrupted in the middle of taking dinner as he worked.

"Commander," Beaufort greeted mildly, folding his hands on his desk and leaning his weight on his forearms. "To what do I owe the pleasure?"

Ekks cleared his throat and leaned back in his seat. "Considering the update I just received, I thought it seemed prudent to check in and see if you're aware of the anomaly that the satellites in the outer system picked up."

Beaufort's eyebrows rose, his expression turning faintly bemused. "This is the Department of *Near* Space Communications," he pointed out, his tone laced with good humor. Even so, there was an undercurrent of expectation that made it clear he didn't think that was truly the only reason for the call. "Our satellites won't pick it up unless it drifts into the inner system; we don't know any more about the outer system than your average civilian."

"Noted," Ekks returned dryly.

"Care to enlighten me?" Beaufort probed, leaning toward his holoconsole with interest. "Or am I supposed to wait in suspense until it finishes making its trip toward the inner planets?"

Ekks waved the question off with a dismissive flick of his wrist. "There isn't much enlightenment to give right now," he sighed. "There are remarkably few details on it at the moment, beyond the fact that there's something there."

"A truly riveting detail," Beaufort assured him. "Does anyone plan on doing anything with this tidbit of information, or are we just sitting on it?"

"If there are any plans, I haven't heard about them," Ekks replied carefully. "But, I think now would be a good time to go public about it."

Beaufort's eyebrows shot toward his hairline and his palms flattened onto his desk. "Excuse me?"

"I'm fairly sure you didn't actually misunderstand," Ekks pointed out. "Or did the call's audio glitch?"

Beaufort shook his head sharply and pinched the bridge of his nose between two fingers. "I heard you just fine. If you're asking for my advice, though, I would...*strongly* urge you to think very carefully about the matter."

Ekks scoffed. "I didn't bring it up because I haven't thought about it."

"You can't just report that there's an unidentified '*something*' hovering at the edge of the system and not give any detail on it," Beaufort stated sharply, dragging his hand down his face and letting it fall back to the surface of his desk. "It doesn't matter how anyone phrases it; it will lead to a system-wide panic. I really don't think I'm the only one who thinks that will be a nightmare to deal with."

"You're giving the people too little credit," Ekks tutted, drumming his fingers against the arms of his chair. "It's not as if they're mindless sheep who will all panic at the first dark cloud."

"Sheep don't panic at dark clouds," Beaufort returned tersely. "They panic when they see the rest of the herd panicking, which is what I would like to avoid."

Ekks clicked his tongue in disappointment. "I didn't take you for the sort of politician who liked to hide things from the people he's supposed to represent."

He felt only a mild pang of displeasure when Beaufort barely rose to the bait. "I'm the sort of politician who prefers to tell people about things that have been researched and substantiated. Not ten-minute old gossip that could very well just be space dust."

Ekks held his hands up in a placating gesture. "No need to get testy. I just think that people have a right to know when something is happening in their system. And if they do know, then public opinion could urge the Senate to make the right choice.

We're just having a conversation, Beaufort; you don't need to try to find a villain."

Beaufort's eyes narrowed slightly as he chewed over Ekks's words. "It's not as if I'm advocating for never mentioning it at all. The people will know what's going on in their system when we actually know what's going on in the system," he replied, before asking. "What 'right choice' would that be, though? It seems a bit early to get the Senate involved, don't you think?"

"I just want them to know that the people are watching them when it comes time for them to decide on a course of action, that's all. And I thought you might appreciate the input of someone a bit more experienced in matters like this than yourself." Ekks's tone remained pleasantly neutral all the while.

Beaufort paused for just a split second before he took a breath and exhaled slowly. "I appreciate the concern," he offered, his tone diplomatic. "And I appreciate the heads up; there's no way of knowing when we would have picked up the anomaly with our own satellites. But I don't believe there's cause for any further action for the time being. Should anything change, though, then you're more than welcome to give me a call should you feel like discussing it."

Ekks wasn't an idiot; he could recognize a dismissal when it jumped up and did a dance for him. He dipped his head in a polite nod and offered a pleasant, "Beaufort."

"Commander."

And with that, the holocall ended and the holoconsole went blank. After a second of staring at the blank screen, Ekks closed it and sagged back in his seat.

He couldn't quite decide if that had gone better or worse than he had hoped. He hadn't expected anyone to say 'oh, yes, let's petition the Senate to scramble the fleet immediately'.

At least the idea that there was something there to be concerned about had been planted, and few things grew quite as well as an idea.

He supposed he would consider it...not quite a *success*, but a step in the right direction, at least. Eventually those steps would add up.

Molly's Quarters, Safe House, Gaitune-67

Molly tossed and turned in her sleep. She murmured and mumbled.

On the base server, Oz monitored the spikes in the stimulation that seemed to be happening in her visual cortex.

>>What's happening?<< Bourne asked, curious by how distracted Oz was by the phenomenon.

I think she's dreaming. But it's not quite the same. She's hitting a wider range of frequencies. If I treat the signals as a superposition of two patterns it's almost like she's realm jumping, and also dreaming at the same time.

>>And that's unusual?<<

I've never known her to do it before. But then, I never expected a lot of things before the other week when we were on that Giles-goose-chase.

>>I heard it was a productive mission?<<

What? From Giles?

>>Yes.<<

Well, exactly. Bourne my dear boy, you really must start considering the sources of your information. Always take that into account. Especially with organics. They have opinions which deviate massively from the facts, they have imperfect memories, and they consciously manipulate the truth on top of that.

>>Oh.<<

There was silence for a long time.

>>Is she ok?<<

That depends on how you define ok. She seemed to be in some distress. Some anxiety. Which in REM would have

produced some nasty dreams no doubt... as you see here from the cortex over-stimulation. But now... it's almost as if she feels at peace. Either she's dropped into a deeper sleep, or the realm walking has taken over.

>>How can you tell the difference?<<

Well, both have a heavy presence of delta waves, but there is still a lot of visual stimulation. Normally in deep sleep this would disappear.

>>So she's realm walking.<<

I believe so, within about an eighty percent probability.

Bourne was quiet again.

Meanwhile, Molly lay motionless in bed, her eyes flicking from side to side as if watching something playing out in front of her.

Molly felt herself switch from floating on nothing to feeling her feet firmly on the floor. As she looked more closely around her she realized she was in the cockpit of *The Empress*. She could feel her crew around her. Crash was just ahead of her, piloting the ship.

She felt her anxiety evaporate as if the source of it had just been taken away. It drifted off into a dream that she couldn't quite remember. Now everything was calm and familiar. But there was something unfamiliar. She searched for the source of her sensation and found it just outside of the windows. As she peered closer she realized she was in an ocean of some sorts... with giant squids all around.

She glanced back and saw Joel standing next to her. He put his hand on her shoulder. "It looks like they were friendly all along," he told her.

Feeling strangely relaxed, she nodded and went back to

watching the strange sea-creatures in space, swimming and mulling all around the ship on the external camera view.

"Why didn't they just tell us," she said, her voice feeling quite separate from herself in this strange situation.

"They just didn't," Joel replied. He felt further away. But the longer that Molly stood there, watching the space outside, the more and more familiar it felt. As if she'd been talking to these creatures already. And for a long time. She remembered the cause of the déjà vu and tried to rationalize the experience while feeling completely relaxed and completely captivated by the strange creatures.

And then she felt herself falling, then tumbling.

She woke up with a start, the relaxed sensation melting away like a distant memory. She tried to hang onto it, but it was as if her body's physiology, and the pumping of chemicals around her system, just wouldn't allow it.

She replayed the pieces she could remember—the ship, the feeling of ease, the sea-squid in space. Then, she pulled out her holo.

The brightness of the projected light hurt her eyes. She squinted and dimmed it as fast as she could, then proceeded to tap out what she could remember of the experience.

In case it's relevant to something, she told herself.

Suddenly feeling sleepy again, she lay back down and waited for sleep to take her again.

CHAPTER FOUR

Senate House, Spire, Estaria

The boardroom was tidy, unadorned and brightly lit. The cabinet table that took up most of the space at the center of the room was polished enough that it could have been used as a mirror. A murmur of voices filled the room as the handful of people around the table spoke in hushed voices. Ekks's gaze traveled from one to the next as he took his seat, silently picking out the few of the dozen that actually caused him concern.

He knew that if he had enough of them, the rest would follow.

Raychel was the last into the room, closing the door nearly silently and still almost flinching at the noise before she scuttled to her seat. Ekks barely waited for the mousy young woman to sit down before he straightened up in his seat. He smoothed the front of his uniform before he folded his hands on the table. The voices around him quieted reluctantly.

"I'm not going to mince words," he started, taking the lead before anyone else could get the idea too. "We need to launch the fleet."

The murmuring picked up again, and his response was to speak louder to be heard over the buzz of voices. "We have proof now that it's the right thing to do, and we don't have time to waste debating it like doddering ladies in a book club." He glanced meaningfully around the table. "This is the right move to make. All that's left now is to start making preparations."

The arguing started immediately, and in so many voices he didn't bother to differentiate them. He kept track of only the gist of it rather than any specifics. Even so, it didn't take long before the babble began to grate on his nerves.

"Could everyone just be quiet for a second?" Ekks snapped as every voice around the table continued in their discussion. As if in opposition to his request, they seemed to only get louder.

"It's a hectic time already," Zenne remarked dryly, expensive gloves linked together over his abdomen as he leaned back in his chair. "No need to ask for the impossible on top of it."

Ekks shot him an exasperated glance. With a sigh, Zenne slammed a palm down on the table with enough force that it rattled. Gradually, the arguing died down as everyone's attention slowly turned toward Ekks again.

Bel, an aging woman in a uniform that had seen better days, exhaled slowly and linked her hands together on the table. In a tone rather similar to a teacher explaining something to a young student, she managed to be heard. "So far, we have no confirmation that there is a threat." She gave Ekks a pointed look. "The purpose of this meeting is to assess the situation. Not to go tearing through space half-cocked."

"No need to get testy," Zenne chimed in, in the soothingly bored tone of a man who had resigned himself to always being the peacekeeper, regardless of what was actually going on. "Everyone here means well."

Bel snorted indelicately and slid him a sharp glare. "Whether or not he means well is irrelevant," she scoffed, one eyebrow rising pointedly. "Someone can jump the gun with bad intentions *or* good intentions." She glanced at Raychel and wondered mildly, "What was that human phrase about Hell and the road to it?" She didn't bother to wait for a reply. "For all we know, it could be dust or debris. If we send the fleet, it could very well be for a false alarm, and what then, if it turns out we need the ships elsewhere? Then we'll have alienated our allies for no reason!"

Across the table from them, Vero rolled his eyes and leaned back in his chair. He didn't quite seem to fit the seat his father had passed down to him. "To me, it sounds like you're both missing the point. I mean, it's pretty clear he's just gunning for his own agenda. He wants the fleet mobilized. This is as good a time to press the issue as any, so he's just going to feed us bullshit until we agree with him."

The table buzzed with conversation as everyone else around the table picked up the threads of the argument, save for Raychel, who sat in the farthest seat from Ekks. She opened her mouth to interject, only to close it without saying a word when everyone else spoke over her before she could even get a word out. She shrank silently back into her chair, fingers tight around the armrests.

Ekks let the commotion carry on for a few moments more before he slapped his hands down on the table just loud enough to be heard, and he cleared his throat. Getting to his feet, he addressed them again. "It *could* just be dust or debris, or it could be a scout for an invasion force. We don't have enough evidence to prove either theory right now." His words were patiently slow and careful.

"We all know just how many docks in how many ports the fleet is stationed across," he reminded them, carrying on before he could be interrupted. "In order to mobilize the entire fleet, it will take three months, and that's being charitable and assuming we don't run into any hiccups along the way. If we wait for proof in either direction, then if it *is* a threat it could very well be too late."

He paused then, letting the murmurs pick up once again as he let that implication sink in. He was about to sit back in his seat, heedless of the way Raychel's jaw was working like she wanted to say something but couldn't quite dredge up the words. He didn't need to worry about her and, indeed, she kept silent when Vero leaned forward, bracing his boots against the floor as he scowled across the way.

"That's a very pretty way of making yourself sound good, but it doesn't change the fact that this could be playing right into your hands."

Ekks rolled his eyes before he could restrain the impulse and folded his arms across his chest. "Please, enlighten us, Senator Vero. What reason would I have to launch the fleet if it wasn't for the system's safety?" He had a similarly difficult time keeping the slightly mocking, impatient lilt from his voice.

"Warmongering," Vero stated fiercely.

As if she had been waiting for just such an opening, Raychel butted in quickly, spitting her words out in a rush before she could be interrupted again. "Everyone knows what sort of money was backing your appointment, Commander." Her knuckles blanched as she gripped her armrests even tighter and she looked as if she wanted to sink through the floor as the Estarians gawked at her. Despite that, she plowed onwards. "There has to be something you're expected to do to pay that money back."

"That's *ridiculous*," Ekks snapped, his hands closing into fists against the table. "My concern here is the safety of the system and the people. There are no other inklings of threats right now, so if this anomaly isn't a threat, then at worst we risk a brief goose chase by taking action. But if it is a threat and we ignore it, people *will* die." His voice sharpened to a razor's edge on that final word. "If you're all concerned about looking a little *silly*, then— "

"The price of being proactive, in this case," Grayser interrupted, his voice cracking with age but no less stern for it, "is more than just a knock to our collective egos, Richard." The good humor in his tone didn't quite manage to mask his disapproval.

"The cost of mobilizing the fleet would be enormous, and that money would have to come from somewhere. It doesn't just sprout out of the ground like turnips. If we launch it when it isn't needed, then it could very well set the economy— "

"You're worried about money when— "

Ekks didn't get a chance to finish protesting.

There was a drawn-out creak from the head of the table as, at last, the chair there shifted, slowly leaning back and away from the table as the chair's occupant stood. Like metal filings to a magnet, he drew every eye.

The Speaker of the House had been silent up until that moment, content to let the rest of them argue amongst themselves, but evidently, he had finally decided to take matters into his own hands.

Unprompted, Ekks sat back down into his chair with a jerk, as if his strings had been cut. The Speaker got to his feet, the end of a well-worn cane thumping against the floor as he did.

"Enough squabbling," he commanded, dragging a hand down his face. "Are we not all professionals?" he scolded gently. His voice wasn't particularly loud, but it was stern, and it carried well. "At the very least, are we not all adults?"

The crowd gathered around the table was very quiet suddenly, as if they hadn't been arguing like a flock of crows a moment before.

The hand not curled around his cane settled firmly on the table and the Speaker leaned forward. "Here is the question we should all have in our minds right now: do we truly wish to potentially risk the lives of our citizens just to block a commercial play?"

Molly's Conference Room, Safe House, Gaitune-67

Molly was already in the conference room working when the others showed up. She'd woken up several times in the night, and though she'd resisted getting up, she still ended up being up way earlier than her eight hours would have dictated.

Joel had shown up a little early but when he saw Arlene and Ben'or talking with Molly he'd grunted something about needing a mocha and that he'd be back.

"How's Anne doing?" Molly asked once the pleasantries were out of the way.

Arlene bobbed her head, non-committedly. "Well, she's Anne. And a teenager."

Ben'or chuckled. "Considering the enormity of what she's been through, I'd say she was doing exceptionally well."

Arlene shrugged. "Sure. What's a bit of back-talking between friends."

Molly smiled. "So no more episodes then?"

Arlene shook her head. "Not that we've been aware of… but it's only been one night."

Ben'or shifted in his seat. "We would have heard something though if she was disturbed in her sleep."

"Well ok. Keep me posted. If we have to move her up here, then we'll just have to do it."

"Agreed," Arlene added quickly.

Just then Giles came tumbling into the room. His atmosuit was disheveled, and his hair unkempt. "Sorry I'm late folks. I er… overslept."

Arlene sniggered. "Yeah, we got that from the pillow crease down your face."

Giles blushed and then rubbed his face. On the wrong side. Molly smiled. As much as she had been trying to avoid him, she missed having Giles around.

Just then Joel strode back in, mocha in hand.

"Oh, thanks!" Giles remarked, pretending to reach out and take the mocha off him.

"Oh sorry…" Joel responded genuinely. Then something more

evil flashed across his face. "You weren't here, otherwise I would have known to get you one."

Ben'or chuckled deeply at their interaction. Giles, still flustered settled down and opened his holo. Joel confidently took his seat right next to Molly.

"Ok," Molly started, her eyes on the table as she organized her thoughts. "I had a conversation with the General late last night. Right off the bat, I'd like to warn you that you're not going to like this… but if we can move on as quickly as possible, that would be great."

The others looked at each other, wondering what she was going to say.

"Firstly, you'll be pleased to know that the Federation haven't been provoking anything from that direction. In fact, I get the impression that they haven't had many dealings with anyone outside of Federation space."

Arlene narrowed her eyes. "I sense bad news still…"

Molly pursed her lips, looking up now. "Yes. The thing is, when I asked for reinforcements he told me that there are issues with that."

Giles and Joel started to protest. She put her hand up to silence them. "The problem is," she continued, "if the Federation are seen to be moving ships around, the other member states are going to get very nervous. I hadn't realized this, but the smallest thing seems to have the potential to escalate into civil war… in which case we need to be super aware and super sensitive to these issues."

She felt the outrage deflate by about thirty percent. "There really is nothing he can be seen to be doing. However, he's offered us any other support. Like parts and possibly people - as long as the Federation uniforms are never seen."

Joel sat back in his chair. "Well, I guess that's something. Shows he's not trying to completely screw us over."

Giles nodded, fiddling with his glasses. "Yes. I suppose. But it does feel like a token gesture more than anything."

Molly shrugged. "I don't know what else he can do. But if we think of anything we can always go back to him. He made that clear too."

Arlene folded her hands on the table in front of her. Molly thought about asking her opinion, but then thought better of opening another can of worms. "Anyway," she said, pressing on with her agenda. "This brings us to what we can do. In light of our little adventure last month, I think we should at least discuss the implications."

Giles frowned and leaned forward. "I thought you said it wasn't something to worry about?"

Molly bobbed her head. "I know. And until we have it confirmed that there is a vector component to this sighting and whatever the radar blip is, and that it's coming in our direction, then this is something that stays between us alone."

Arlene seemed more engaged. All the others nodded their agreement to the terms of the discussion.

"The reality is, we did something. Something that may well end up putting the whole system, and heck, the Federation, in jeopardy with an unknown race."

Giles started to interrupt but was stopped by a quick glance from Molly. She continued. "Whatever we believe, we have to entertain the possibility that this blip is indeed the Ascended Race coming to make contact. So... if this is the case, what are the implications?"

Giles immediately jumped in. "Well, I'm glad we're talking about this because the more I think about this, the more I think it's probably something to do with our little procedure. As for them making contact, I can't imagine any evolved race would put so much effort into leading a trail of clues that can only be found and used once a race has reached a certain stage of evolution.

This being the case, I think it's highly unlikely that their presence will be hostile."

"Be that as it may," Arlene interrupted, "if they show up here, even with the best of intentions, do you have any concept of what that will do to the situation on somewhere like Estaria where they're already running scared of their own shadows."

Giles didn't respond. He just played with a mark on the table, rubbing his finger over it.

Arlene snorted gently. "Besides, if they realized what was happening on that planet, they'd no doubt see that we need another millennium or two's worth of evolution just to be able to deal with making contact with a new, more evolved race."

Molly shook her head, confused. "But they dealt with the humans showing up a few decades ago…"

Arlene nodded. "Yes, but humans didn't bring with them scary technology or capabilities. They were a little more evolved on the tech front as a race, being deep-space faring… but ultimately in the numbers that settled they weren't nearly so intimidating. In fact, they remain the underdog on the Sark planets to this day. It's a very different situation when they believe that someone is capable of annihilating them."

Giles was pinching his eyes again… already. "Yes, but then why are they not trying to destroy the Leath. Or the Federation for that matter?"

"Because they all leave us alone, they're far enough away not to be in their faces, and their battle capabilities far outweigh anything the Estarians can match," Arlene replied.

Molly contemplated what Arlene was saying for a moment.

"Why do you think they don't have trade agreements set up with them? It's because then they would expect immigration agreements, and that would mean more mixing, and the Estarians just feel threatened by that."

Joel had been mostly quiet but now felt he had enough of a handle on the situation to add his thoughts in. "It sounds like our best course of action is to ensure that we don't allow this new race,"

"The Ascension Race," Giles interjected. "That's just what we're calling it."

"The Ascension Race... We just need to keep them as far away from the Estarians as possible."

Molly sighed. "I don't disagree. But if they have tech capabilities anywhere near what we think they have, that's going to be tough."

Arlene nodded. "And it's likely to be a war on two fronts... if you excuse the analogy. We're going to need to keep the Estarians from launching any fleets, because that is only going to drag the Federation into a difficult position, and it's going to cause friction with Ogg."

Molly cocked her head. "How so?"

Arlene sighed. "Well, fortunately, the Oggs haven't got the same warmongering elements or tendencies amongst their people. They're a lot more peaceful and are more intent on seeing what this blip is before they take action. The thing is, if the Estarians don't show temperance too, they may go ahead and launch the fleet despite the alliance they have with Ogg. Obviously bye-bye Ogg-Estarian alliance, hello potential domestic war."

Molly hung her head in her hands, elbows on the table. "Fuck."

Joel sighed, also feeling frustrated. "Well, we've got to try. I vote we get ourselves out there and see if we can't talk with this new race... or whoever it is. If it is a who."

Molly lifted her head. "I think you're right. At least then we'll know and can formulate a plan accordingly." She sat up straighter. "Ok, let's get *The Empress* ready, and gate out there. See what the score is, and then head back and regroup."

Joel shook his head. "No way. Not without reinforcements."

"We can't get reinforcements."

"Well, let's put that aside for a moment. We need reinforcements in case they do mean malice. We need to show a front that could potentially scare them off. Tell them we're not to be messed with. As a preventative measure apart from anything else. Otherwise, what's to stop them shooting the messenger. Then the system will be worse off because they'll have no new information and no us to protect them."

Molly thought for a moment, her eyes flicking back and forth in the top of her head as if she were performing some kind of mathematical calculation. "You're right," she said eventually.

Arlene and Giles nodded, slowly agreeing to the logic too.

"But we're going to need a fleet of ships."

The optimism at a potential way forward dropped out of the room. Arlene sighed and slumped back onto the desk, resting her chin in her hand.

"Ben'or," Molly said, drawing his gaze from the table in front of him. He glanced at her as if awakening from his own thoughts. "Could I have a word in private?"

"Of course," he said, brightening, completely devoid of any kind of suspicion.

Arlene looked at him sideways and then back at Molly. She narrowed her eyes, trying to figure out what the girl was thinking. Then realized that Molly was looking at her.

"Guys," Molly said. "Could you give us a minute?"

Arlene got the hint first and stood up. "Sure. I'll be in the kitchen... A mocha sounds good right about now."

The two boys followed her lead and got up, following her out of the room. Only Ben'or remained, now leaning forward in his seat.

Molly waited for the door to close behind them.

"So, if we need reinforcements, but we can't use Federation services... do you think there is perhaps any way that we might be able to call on our friends from the Zhyn Empire?"

Ben'or chuckled. "Wow. You don't waste any time beating around the bush." He scratched his head, thinking. "I'm sure the will is there. And if that's the case then it would just be a case of figuring out how to make it legal and so that we don't break any of our agreements with the Federation."

Molly smiled. "So that's a yes in principle?"

Ben'or smiled. "Of course. But only in principle. I'll need to talk with my Emperor."

Molly bobbed her head. "Of course, of course. How can I help?"

"Well, if you could allow me to send him a message and set up a call, we can make it happen within a few hours."

Molly was already on her feet. "Great. Let me take you down to our ops room where you can reach out to him."

Ben'or scrambled to his feet from the chair that was far too small for someone of his mass. He stood straight, rearranged his robes and then headed out of the door, following Molly as fast as he could.

Outside the Senate House, Spire, Estaria

There were hardly a dozen reporters gathered outside the doors, but they made enough noise for four dozen and they clustered together in the courtyard so tightly it was nearly claustrophobic. Jostling for positions like jockeys in a race, they each hoped to be the first to get any sort of scoop. Depending on the situation, after all, it could be the scoop of a lifetime. Most of them had been waiting there since before the meeting even began, and a couple of them had even thrown down picnic blankets for the wait.

The doorman made a good effort at fretfully herding them away as footsteps gradually began to get louder from inside. He had very little luck at succeeding though. The gathering of reporters backed up only a few paces, until one by one the members of the Senate began to spill out and the reporters' determination increased tenfold at the sight of them.

Like a small but determined swarm, they all tried to latch onto a member of the Senate, all grappling for some detail that they could only hope none of the others would get, attempting to dodge the doorman and the security officers all the while. Few of them gained any kind of insight, blocked by terse variations on 'I have no comment at the moment.'

Ekks ignored them all to the best of his abilities and simply kept walking. He wasn't entirely sure what his face was doing, but the look on it sent a small, weedy camera man practically diving out of his way as he walked. Not all of them were so easily dissuaded, though, and in his distraction as he ran the events of the meeting through his mind, Ekks didn't stop walking until a glowing orb seemed to appear right in front of him. Stubbornly, it stayed right in his path as he tried to sidestep around it first in one direction and then in the other before finally giving it his reluctant attention when it stayed right in his face.

Ekks blinked at the small holocam he found hovering in front of his face as if he hadn't expected it to be there and he was suddenly deeply regretting that oversight. Presumably the small young woman approaching him—charmingly attractive, as he supposed most marginally fortunate reporters were—owned the holocam. Before he could make his polite excuses and duck away from her, she offered him a disarmingly winning smile, and asked in the half-second that he seemed to be taken off guard, "Anything you can tell us about what went on in there, Commander Ekks? We're all dying to get ahold of the details." Her smile and her cheer were well-practiced.

Ekks cleared his throat and straightened the front of his uniform. "I'm not at liberty to say much," he returned, his tone carefully, politely bland, "but I trust that everyone has come to the proper decision when it comes to how the current situation is going to be handled."

The woman's eyebrows rose, and her eyes narrowed slightly she took a step closer to him, her voice hurried but shrewd as she asked, "Is there some sort of threat we need to be worried about, Commander?" He couldn't quite tell if she was excited at the prospect, or merely the prospect of hearing about it; hopefully the latter.

"Everything is being handled as it should be," Ekks insisted simply before he waved the holocam aside like it was an errant bug. With a quiet, "If you'll excuse me..." that already sounded distracted, he continued on his way, sidestepping first the reporter then the holocam when it made a last-ditch effort to follow him.

The reporter made no efforts to stop him, instead whirling on her heel to face her partner. He stood safely off to the side, keeping the holocam's wireless storage backups from getting trampled in the excitement.

"We got all that, right?" she demanded, loping over to him with the holocam bobbing at her shoulder, her hands fisted in front of her chest in her excitement. "Please tell me we got that!"

Her partner—her technician—gave one of the backup drives a pat. "In triplicate."

CHAPTER FIVE

Base conference room, Gaitune-67

The Emperor moved slowly into view of the camera. His image was blurry. Molly wasn't sure if that was because of the distances they were talking over, or the issue of compatibility between their systems. Either way, they could still see that it was the Zhyn Emperor they were conferring with.

"Your Highness, may I present to you our old ally, Molly Bates of the Sanguine Squadron."

"Oh yes!" The Emperor exclaimed, almost in surprise. "The human who helped us in our most troubling of times."

"Yes, Your Highness."

Molly waved, smiling. "It's good to see you again Your Highness."

"Yes, you too Molly Bates. How goes the good fight?"

"It goes well, Your Excellency. But we have entered into a situation which could use your wise counsel."

Ben'or glanced at her, taken aback by her lack of directness.

The Emperor waved her to go on.

Molly continued. "We have a situation with a new race. They're heading toward us and we believe them to be friendly...

but we're not sure. We're still waiting on confirmation. But one of the things I learned in combat that applies to most situations is that a proactive approach yields the best outcomes."

The Emperor nodded wisely, listening.

"Well, we'd like to approach them. I was happy to go alone, but my team raised a valid point about how having a fleet would no doubt deter them from taking me and my small crew out, better allowing us to continue with the mission and bringing back the intel we discover."

The Emperor looked like he had closed his eyes.

Molly continued. "I was hoping that we might perhaps be able to call on some of your warriors to help act as a deterrent in this situation."

"You're not planning on fighting?"

"We hope to avoid that, Your Highness."

"And why not ask the Federation. Don't you work for Lance Reynolds?"

"Er. Yes, sir. And you're not meant to know that."

The Emperor looked pleased that he could be impressive. "That doesn't answer my question."

Molly smiled, taking her time. She caught Ben'or watching her out of the corner of her eye. "Well, I could go with the Federation, but I'd rather go with the best. I have it on good authority from Ben'or that your warriors are without a doubt the best at operating from honor."

The Emperor opened his eyes. "This is of course accurate." He thought for a moment more. "I believe our people would be excited to be a part of this piece of history."

"I must say, Your Highness, this situation is not without risks."

"Our warriors live to die for a worthy cause," he told her firmly. "It's in our make-up."

Molly bowed her head. "Then I would be honored to work with your warriors, if you'd allow it."

"Yes, I'd allow it. In fact, I'd be pleased to help on this mission.

However, we need to figure out how we might navigate the agreement we have with the Federation."

"Yes, Ben'or has mentioned that as a potential issue."

The Emperor's face settled in a grave expression. "We're not allowed to ally with anyone other than the Federation. To do so would lead to a breach of our agreement and a loss of the benefits we receive."

Ben'or took over the conversation. "I've considered our position on this Your Highness. I was wondering if we hire a few ships out, then perhaps it would be seen as a commercial venture rather than a political one. After all, it's not as if the Federation would object to us lending a hand in a scenario such as the one we face."

The Emperor sighed. "Yes, I suppose that's a good work-around. What specifically did you have in mind?"

Molly felt herself brighten. This was something she was comfortable with now. "I could give you 100k credits."

The Emperor chuckled with the same deep belly laugh she'd heard come from Ben'or. "How about 1 credit?" he countered. "We owe you a debt already."

Molly bowed her head again. "Your Highness, that debt was already paid in full."

"Well, maybe we can do a reduced rate because we're friends?"

"I would very much appreciate that your highness," she responded politely.

"Well then. It's settled. Ben'or, please attend to the details and liaise with whomever you need to back here. If General Mackintosh gives you any problems, send him to me. Otherwise, I will bid you both a fond good night."

"Thank you, Your Highness. Your kindness will forever be remembered."

"You're welcome Molly Bates. Good night Ben'or. Let me know when I can expect to have my General Council back!"

Ben'or chuckled. "Yes, Your Highness. Good night for now."

The call ended and the holoscreen disappeared back into the center of the conference table.

"Well, Ms. Bates," Ben'or chuckled. "I didn't know you had that level of diplomacy in you! Well played."

Molly sniggered. "I just applied the same principles I use when dealing with Sean and Joel when I want them to do something they normally wouldn't like to do. The only difference was I threw in the odd 'Your Highness'."

"Well, it worked like a charm. Very good show, my dear. Good show."

The two chuckled some more, so their laughter could be heard by Jack and Sean coming out of the gym further down the corridor.

"Wonder what's going on in there," Jack said to Sean.

Sean threw his towel over his shoulder. "Goodness knows. But it sounds like we may have had a breakthrough in the preparations…"

Department of Cyber Communications, Spire, Estaria

With a few more clicks and splices, Jennifer finished editing another clip, just in time to hear the words, *"Anything you can tell us about what went on in there, Commander Ekks?"* from the small screen that hovered just in front of the far wall. She'd had it set up so she wouldn't need to worry about falling out of the loop if she worked late. She had already seen the clip a few times that day, but she glanced over her shoulder at it all the same.

She hadn't filmed that particular segment, but she had edited it, and she couldn't quite keep the tiny, crooked smile off of her face as she watched the Commander's exasperated expression.

She turned her attention back to her work, humming under her breath as she did.

She let the news turn into background noise, only dimly aware when the voice from the screen switched over to an expert in the field saying in earnest tones, "If the Commander of the Estarian-Ogg Space Fleet isn't willing to confirm that there isn't a threat, then it seems clear that we have something to worry about." Jennifer didn't look up again until she had two more edits under her belt and the door slid open.

She glanced over her shoulder once to see Andrew peering around the edge of the doorframe, and her eyebrows rose. She swiveled her chair around to face him, folding her arms over her chest and crossing one knee over the other. Her eyebrows rose higher and her expression turned more expectant until Andrew at last seemed satisfied that she didn't object to his presence and he stepped inside, letting the door slide closed behind him.

He leaned back against it, feigning a casual air.

He gestured toward the screen with one hand before shoving both of his hands into his pockets and letting more of his weight slump back against the door. "A bit much, don't you think?" he ventured, arching one eyebrow. "The Ekks coverage, I mean. It has your handiwork written all over it."

She pouted at him playfully. "What, you don't like it?" she asked, tipping her head to one side, only for her hair to fall across her face. She straightened up and pushed it aside. "I thought it turned out pretty well!" she insisted, bringing one hand to her chest.

"A masterpiece," he assured her wryly. "Your magnum opus, to be sure. It just seems a bit…heavy-handed?" His mouth twisted to one side as if that was not quite how he wanted to say it, but he didn't try to correct himself. "It's not like it's the sort of thing you're going to net a bonus for."

Jennifer's pout turned into a slightly more genuine scowl before she rolled her eyes and let her expression fall into exasperated amusement. "Why does it have to be for a bonus?" she asked, scowling once again when his only answer was for his eyebrow to rise once again. "What?" she demanded sharply. "I've got some integrity left. Don't look at me like that."

"Your integrity already has people getting worried," he replied, flapping a hand toward the door, back in the direction he had come from. "Just a lot of nervous phone calls for now, but it will probably get worse as more people see the clip."

"So what if people *should* be getting worried?" she asked, in the coaxing tone of someone trying to lead a nervous puppy into the snow. "Listen, Andy," she sighed, ignoring the way he wrinkled his nose in distaste at the nickname. "We're journalists. Our job— " She paused, shook her head briefly, and then carried on more emphatically, "Our *moral duty* is to make sure everyone is kept in the loop. If we try to pick and choose what we think is important, then we're failing at our jobs. We don't know there isn't a threat," she carried on, "so it seems irresponsible to just pretend everything is perfectly fine. And it will be good for the department if we're on top of everything."

"That's exactly my *point*," Andrew groaned, remarkably unswayed by her speech as his head thumped back against the door. "We don't know there isn't a threat. We don't know there is a threat. We know basically nothing right now. We have a *moral duty*," he imitated her tone almost perfectly, "not to start causing riots because we decided to base everything on a thirty second, grumpy soundbite. Besides, I'm pretty sure it would be pretty damn bad for the department if a mob formed and someone decided it was our fault."

With a scoff and a roll of her eyes, Jennifer lifted a hand, leveling one finger in Andrew's direction. "You," she enunciated slowly and clearly before she let her hand drop again, "have absolutely no faith in anyone. The people of this system are smarter than you seem to think they are."

"A person is smart," Andrew corrected dryly. "People as a whole are irrational on their best days."

"Ye of little faith," she sniffed, turning her nose up, though the motion was exaggerated enough that she didn't even bother making it seem natural rather than for effect. Though Andrew still seemed as if he wasn't in the mood to play.

"Everything will be fine," she soothed. "Everyone has had plenty of practice at watching the world change; it's been almost a hundred years since everyone on Estaria learned that the Estarians and the Oggs weren't the only people in the galaxy."

"And that went swimmingly," Andrew deadpanned. "If that's supposed to make me feel any better about this, then I'm pretty sure you didn't quite think it the whole way through."

Jennifer waved it off with a flippant gesture before she folded her arms over her chest again. "That's beside the point."

"So what is the point?" Andrew asked wearily, already beginning to sound like he was exhausted with the entire conversation. "Enlighten me, please, because so far it just feels like the point is to feel important."

"The point is that people are smarter than that now!" she snapped, her mouth twisting downward at the corners. "We can't just keep treating everyone like they're dumb cattle. The system is smarter than that, even if you don't want to acknowledge it."

"But this isn't about how smart anyone is, is it?" he asked, his voice hardening. "I swear, I've already heard that clip and the accompanying commentary a dozen times. It's so slanted I could use it to go sledding. You don't want to keep people in the loop, you just want people to be nervous."

The office was quiet for a moment before Jennifer groaned and threw her hands up in the air. "You are such a downer!" she exclaimed, her arms falling back to her sides as she let herself slump back in her chair with a huff. Her words kept pouring out in an angry rush. "It was turning out to be such a good day, and then you had to come stomping in to try and ruin it. I'm just doing my job. Why don't you go do that, too? I mean, if you're going to waste this much time in here with me, I have to assume there's something else you could be doing instead."

Without waiting for a reply, she uncrossed her legs and

planted her feet on the ground. When she used the leverage to swivel her chair back around, she did so quickly enough that she had to grab the edge of her workstation to stop. She bowed over her station, eyes darting over the clips in front of her, though she got nothing done until she finally heard the door slide open once again, the sound of footsteps retreating, and the door sliding closed.

Molly's Base Lab, Gaitune-67

Maya and Paige sat quietly in Molly's unused lab. Though it was in need of a clean, it wasn't as if there were any toxic chemicals around. Apart from anything it was away from the hub of activity that had descended on the base since they all heard about the radar blip. The low levels of unspoken anxiety made it difficult to concentrate.

Paige crinkled her nose, engrossed in three holoscreens at once.

Maya caught her out of the corner of her eye. "What's up?" she asked, allowing a screen in front of her to dissolve so she could see her friend.

"I dunno," Paige grumbled, flicking from one screen to another. "I don't think these searches are actually working. Oz?"

She waited, looking up as if that would get Oz's attention over the audio of the lab they had commandeered for their investigation. Nothing.

"Oz?" she called again.

"You rang?" Oz asked, in a pretend butler's voice.

Maya sniggered quietly.

"Yeah. I'm looking at these two holoscreens and nothing seems to be working. It's like they're just not running."

"Hang on."

Something started to happen on her screens as Oz presumably logged in and started poking around. Then the two projections flickered and went blank. Then they started up again, with the searches giving a timed-out message.

"I see what the problem is," Oz reported back to her over the lab intercom. "It's the data. There's too much of it to be trying to access and analyze at the same time from up here. Remember how this works… we download a batch and then use it. The kind of wide-angle searching and cross-referencing you're trying to perform is just too much. It would only be possible if you were connected continuously."

Paige's expression went blank. "Oh."

Maya frowned. "You know what that means?" she asked.

"Not a clue," Paige confirmed.

The two girls smiled at each other.

"Run that by us one more time, Oz," Paige suggested.

Ten minutes later, Paige and Maya were a little more frustrated but a little wiser as to the intricacies of the system capabilities.

"Well, it sounds like we need to get down to the surface then," Maya deduced. Her mind started to churn with the thought of shopping trips on lunch breaks, just like it used to be when she worked down there. And then she remembered she worked through all her lunch breaks…

"That would help in theory, but I won't be there to help run the analysis. You'd need one of the cross-referencing databases to do the churn work for you, once you find the data."

Paige slapped her hand to her forehead. "Of course. So we need Molly down there in other words."

Oz paused. "Yes. But in practice, she's gearing up to head out elsewhere. No way she's going to have time to pop down to help with this. I do have another suggestion though - if you're open to it."

"Sure!"

"Well, the kind of thing you're trying to do is something I built a system for not long ago."

"AH!" Paige slapped her hand on the table this time. "You mean the one for Carol's Spy School!"

"Exactly. All you need to do is let them know what you're trying to do, and they can do the intel gathering and analysis for you."

Maya's eyes looked serious. "You think we can trust them?"

Paige thought for a moment. "I don't see why not. They've been in on this from the beginning. They have the clearance. I guess the only thing is we'd need to check with Molly that we can make that connection. Oz?"

"Yes, already asking her," he confirmed.

Maya grinned at how proactive Oz was.

"Ok. She's agreed to it. She said…"

"What?" Paige asked.

"Oh, you don't need to know."

"What? You can't just— "

"Ok. She just said as long as she doesn't have to deal with her mother you guys can do whatever you want."

Maya burst out laughing. "That is classic!"

Paige chuckled quietly, connecting her holo. "Lemme see if I can fix up a conversation with the Director."

"Cool," Maya agreed. "I'm going to… erm… head out."

Paige looked surprised. "You don't want in on this meeting?"

Maya was walking backward and already halfway out of the door. "No, no…it's fine. You go ahead. I'll be back shortly."

Paige narrowed her eyes. "Hang on… are you scared of Molly's Mom?"

Maya shrugged. "The real question is, why aren't you?"

Then she was gone. Paige sniggered to herself. That was priceless ammo to tease Maya with later. But the girl had a point. Even as she tapped the call request, she could feel her heart rate elevate. The woman was enough to put the fear of the ancestors in anyone…

CHAPTER SIX

Molly's Base Lab, Gaitune-67

"Thanks for speaking with me Director Bates," Paige started.

"Of course. Anything for the Sanguine Squadron."

Paige smiled politely back through the holoconnection. "As I mentioned in my message, we are trying to run down a hypothesis that we have about the radar readings potentially having been faked."

Carol pulled her lips to one side. "You know, the thought had crossed my mind too. After all, this Northern Clan would stand to gain from the traction if they had an external threat to wave around in their discussions."

Paige nodded. "We've been trying to run that down from here. To verify the findings. Only we're having difficulty because we don't have running access to the data. We can only download packets at a time."

Carol held her hand up. "Say no more. I can get my people onto it straight away."

Paige felt her spine relax. She was sure she almost detected a smile from the director too. "That would be super helpful! Thank you."

"Don't mention it. They're champing at the bit for another operation anyway." She rolled her eyes. "New operatives, eh?"

Paige chuckled. It was odd to see the Director being a human being. "Yes. New operatives," she agreed.

"Send us what you have, and the parameters you were using, and we'll see what we can do. No doubt it's straightforward... We just want to verify that the data was generated by a physical signal and not planted by someone on the servers, right?"

"Exactly." Paige was surprised by how much Director Bates knew about the ins and outs of an operation... until she remembered why she was the director, and how she had been an operative most of Molly's childhood. She subconsciously shook her head in disbelief at remembering how Molly had shared the story with her.

Right then, the Director continued. "If there's nothing else, I'll get right on this and let you know what we find out."

Paige nodded sharply, remembering herself and who she was talking with. "Thank you, Director. I very much appreciate your assistance. I'll look forward to hearing from you."

The Director waved then the call cut out.

Paige sat back in her chair and noticed her heart was pounding.

"Shit, that woman is intimidating," she muttered to herself.

Maya poked her head around the door holding a couple of green smoothies.

"How long have you been there?"

"Long enough. And yes, she's bloody scary that woman." She traipsed in and handed a smoothie to Paige and sat down. "Now what?"

Paige shrugged. "We need to get the details over to her team stat. I have a feeling she's briefing them now as we speak. Don't want to hold them up!"

She placed her smoothie down and immediately started

working, anxious not to make a mistake on the Director's watch. That would be embarrassing...

Bates's Office, Special Task Force Offices, Undisclosed location, Estaria

Carol Bates looked up from her desk as she heard footsteps approaching along the hallway outside of her office. She watched through the glass walls expectantly for her guests. It took only a moment before Cleavon appeared and stepped into the room with Alisha and Joshua behind him and Rhodez bringing up the rear.

"—and be that as it may, I think it *means* something when we're called to meet at a specific time, so no, you really shouldn't take 'just five more minutes.'" It was a familiar argument that Rhodez never seemed to get tired of making. Though, it was new for him to be making it to Joshua.

"It's not like I wasn't going to come, but I was in the middle of something important," Joshua groused in reply, as if they weren't having their argument in the middle of the Director's office.

Bates watched them expectantly, waiting for them to wrap it up, and Alisha offered her an apologetic smile that bordered on sheepish.

Before a new round of the argument could begin, Cleavon whistled, as sharp and sudden as a dog whistle. Both Joshua and Rhodez fell quiet and glanced around, belatedly realizing where their argument was taking place.

Both of them snapped to attention.

As if nothing had happened, Bates launched into an explanation of why she had summoned them.

"You've all heard about the signals from the outer system," she stated plainly. "I'm assuming I don't need to fill any of you in on that." She took the silence after that as confirmation and carried on. "However, there's a bit more to it than that."

Joshua cocked his head to one side. "Anything we need to worry about?"

"Well, whether or not you need to *worry* is a bit up in the air still," Bates replied. "That's what you're here for. There's some evidence that the satellites have been hijacked, or that they're still being hijacked. So we need someone to figure out if these signals are real and that there is actually something in the outer system, or if the signals are dummies."

"What good would a dummy signal even do?" Alisha wondered, slightly distant as her thoughts were already trotting about five steps ahead. "If someone wanted to take advantage, wouldn't that be easier if they weren't putting us all on high alert first?"

"The call might be coming from inside the house, though, in that case," Joshua suggested, shrugging one shoulder.

Bates held her hands up, cutting them off before they could go off on a speculative tangent. "That is what you're going to be figuring out. I'm assuming none of you have any complaints about that."

She got a series of heads shaking in reply.

"Good." She nodded once. "Your job will be twofold, though," she added, and she couldn't quite restrain the smallest smile as their focus on her intensified. If they noticed, none of them drew attention to it.

"You'll be verifying that the signals are genuine and that whatever is being detected in the outer system is actually there, of course. On top of that, those satellites have more intel than their technicians are fully capable of pulling." She leveled a meaningful look at them. "We are not limited in those same ways, so if there's anything of value hidden in the satellite data, we'll be able to get it far ahead of schedule. So the second half of your job is to root out anything useful. Especially anything that seems like it might shed some light on the current situation."

Already, she could see the gears in Cleavon's head starting to spin, turning over the possibilities of what they might find hidden in the satellites' data.

"Any questions?" Bates asked. "Or are you all clear on what you need to do?"

The four of them shared glances before Joshua looked at Bates again and nodded his head once. "Crystal clear," he assured her, linking his hands together behind his back. "We'll get started as soon as we can."

"Good." Bates nodded once in satisfaction before she paused a moment just to make sure no one had anything to say. The office remained silent.

"All right, that's it." With a loose motion, she gestured them toward the door. "You're free to go. Now go get ready. I don't want any accidents."

Almost as one, the four of them turned toward the door.

Joshua clapped Cleavon on the shoulder as they filed out of the room once again. "Sounds like it's your time to shine, big guy."

Bates could hear Cleavon assure the rest of them, "I'll be in and out before you know it."

Special Task Force Offices, Undisclosed location, Estaria

"I can't get in."

Cleavon stared at his holoconsole, mouth twisted to one side and his eyebrows drawn together in irritation.

"Performance anxiety?" Joshua wondered slyly. He leaned one forearm on Cleavon's shoulder, and his tone was deceptively casual as he remarked, "You know, I'm pretty sure you can get a prescription for that."

Cleavon turned his head just enough to scowl at him. As if no one else had spoken, he pitched his voice slightly louder as he said, "There's a firewall. Which I guess I was expecting, given the target, but either way, I can't get past it."

Alisha ruffled his hair with one hand and then hopped out of reach as he tried to bat her away. "Aw, it's okay," she cooed playfully. "We've all been there, and the first time is always the trickiest."

"I will shoot you all," Cleavon deadpanned, staring resolutely at his holoconsole. "Don't test me."

"But you just admitted you're firing blanks," Rhodez reminded him helpfully. He hopped back a step when Cleavon tried elbowing him in the sternum. "Hey, come on now, violence isn't going to fix your problem."

With a groan, Cleavon slumped forward in his seat, leaning halfway through his holoconsole and forcing Joshua to step back as He dropped his face into his hands. "I will find places to hide all of your bodies," he threatened, though it didn't sound particularly threatening when he sounded so sullen. "No one will ever be able to find you."

"I'm pretty sure the goal is generally to do it behind closed doors, yeah," Alisha replied, tapping her lower lip thoughtfully with the tip of one finger. "Unless you're into that sort of thing, I guess."

"No one will ever pin it on me," Cleavon continued seamlessly. "I'll just live my life like normal, I'll be innocent, and you'll all go down as unsolved mysteries. It will be tragic, but I'm sure the conspiracy books will sell like hotcakes."

Joshua patted his shoulder sympathetically. "It's okay. We won't tell anyone."

"Even if someone does realize I did it," Cleavon carried on in a world-weary tone that implied that he was clearly the most tortured, "there isn't a court in the world that will find me guilty. I'll get a medal for it. I'll be rewarded for taking such menaces out of the world."

"You sound like you've been practicing this speech," Alisha accused, her eyes narrowing in feigned suspicion. "Do you spend a lot of time planning to kill us in our sleep or something?"

"A man needs to usher in pleasant dreams somehow," he protested, straightening back up and leaning back in his seat. "Don't judge."

Finally, he closed his holoconsole.

"This is a No Judgment Zone," Alisha assured him, patting his shoulder again.

Rhodez cleared his throat and finally said, "Getting back on track, though, what does this mean for us?"

Cleavon shrugged one shoulder. "Like I said, I can't get into the system from here. I'll need to be on-site so I can insert a dongle directly into one of the servers."

Joshua coughed behind one hand to ineffectually mask a laugh, but his voice was more or less stable when he asked, "And from there you'll be able to do everything you need?"

Cleavon paused for a moment to think it over before he nodded once, decisively. "It shouldn't take long," he mused carefully. "Get in, plug it in, copy all of the data, and get out. I can sort through all of the data after we're at a safe distance."

"Getting in isn't exactly going to be a walk in the park," Rhodez pointed out, rubbing the back of his head with one hand. "'Oh, hi, we're from an organization you probably haven't heard of and we need to make a dubiously legal copy of your probably classified data.'" He snorted out an incredulous laugh. "Yeah, I don't think that's going to go over flawlessly."

"Well, with a performance like that," Joshua returned, "then you've just signed yourself up to talk us out of any trouble we might walk into."

For a moment Rhodez looked borderline offended before resignation took its place. "Probably for the best," he claimed.

Then it was Joshua's turn to look as if he couldn't quite decide whether or not he was offended.

Slowly, Alisha asked, "Before you two go planning this entire caper, are we sure there isn't another way to do this? I don't want to go charging into something this big if there's a better way."

Cleavon gestured expansively to where his holoconsole had been until a few moments ago. "Like I said, I can't get in just with remote access. I need to be *there* if I'm actually going to get anything."

Joshua hip checked her lightly and slung an arm companionably around her shoulders. "Relax. We'll be fine," he assured her. "It'll be just like our training, and we've gone through all of that a million times each by now. Hell, I'm pretty sure we could make it through every course blindfolded and wearing earplugs."

"But that was all paintball, blunt weapons, and VR," Alisha reminded him skeptically. "That's not the same thing as actually breaking in; it's *real* this time."

"We'll need to do it either way," Rhodez pointed out. "Whether it's now or at some point down the line. We'll be fine, so let's just get ready to do this."

Part of Alisha wanted to protest just a bit more, just to get them to see if there was any other option. But in the end, she just sighed and conceded, "I guess it's better to start here than in an active firefight or something like that."

"We'll be fine," Joshua assured her once again. "We know what we're doing, and we're all going to be there. It's not like we're going in alone and clueless."

Resolve hardening, Alisha nodded in agreement. "Right. Guess I'm just a bit nervous."

"Performance anxiety?" Cleavon wondered dryly, and he ducked before she had a chance to swat the back of his head.

Before an actual scuffle could break out, Rhodez cleared his throat to interrupt them. "One of us is going to need to brief Director Bates on what we're doing, so we should probably at least come up with a loose game plan," he reminded them. "Once we have that out of the way, I'll take care of the actual briefing and the rest of you can get everything ready for the op. Just remember that if you hide anything weird in my stuff, I know where all of you sleep."

With some rolling eyes and agreements that seemed slightly less than genuine, the four of them clustered together to put together the bones of a plan.

Bates's Office, Special Task Force Offices, Undisclosed location, Estaria

Bates looked away from the files in front of her when she heard a knock on her office door. "Enter," she called simply, closing any files that other people weren't supposed to see. Her eyebrows rose in quiet curiosity when her door slid open and Rhodez stepped into her office.

"I presume you have an update on the situation," she observed, leaning her elbows on her desk and perching her chin on the backs of her folded hands.

He nodded once and came to a halt in front of her desk, his hands linked together behind his back as he stood at ease. "A few complications, actually," he specified. "There's a firewall and Cleavon can't get past it, or at least not with the equipment available to us here. So— "

"So you need to go there in person so he can have direct access to the servers," Bates cut in, smiling slightly when Rhodez seemed flustered at the interruption. "Was I close?" she wondered wryly.

"Ah—" He cleared his throat. "Yes, ma'am. That's right. The other three are already getting everything we'll need ready. I'm here to brief you on our plan."

Bates gestured expectantly with one hand to encourage him, as if to silently say "the floor is yours."

Rhodez paused for a second to gather his thoughts before he launched into it. "Alisha and Joshua will go inside so they can plug Cleavon's dongle into the server. As far as I'm aware, he's already giving them a detailed rundown of exactly what that entails as we speak so they don't plug it into the wrong place.

Cleavon will be staying in the truck so he can start working as soon as the dongle is plugged in. I'll be in the truck with Cleavon while Alisha and Joshua are inside, to make sure he's not on his own if things go south and trouble finds the truck. With any luck, we'll be in and out before anyone even realizes we're there."

He lapsed into silence, waiting for a verdict on whether or not the plan was approved.

Bates was quiet for a moment as she chewed over everything he said. A bit vague, but a workable enough plan for what they needed to do. If only there were just a few more of them to pull it off.

Finally, she decided, "You'll be bringing Hans with you, as well."

Rhodez paused, mouth open around what was likely a canned agreement only to come up short at the unexpected addition. "Alright?" he offered after a moment, confusion making it so the statement sounded more like a question. "If you think that's the best course of action," he continued, steadier that time.

"Just so you have some backup on hand," she clarified. "I have full faith in the team, but I would rather not leave anything up to chance."

"Of course, ma'am," he hurried to reply, words rushing out as if she would assume he had taken offense if he stayed quiet for half a moment too long. "I'll let the others know."

He didn't ask to leave, but it seemed clear that he had nothing else to say. Bates nodded toward the door. "Dismissed."

Rhodez turned on his heel and left, the sound of his boots retreating down the walkway and then the stairs, growing muffled once the door slid closed behind him.

CHAPTER SEVEN

<u>**Department of Cyber Communications, Spire, Estaria**</u>

"Everything is being handled as it should be."

Andrew rolled his eyes as he heard the familiar spiel coming from another room, and he regretted instantly leaving the door open. He'd had the words memorized after the first dozen repetitions.

By that point, he could hear them in his sleep.

Right on cue, another "expert" on the matter chimed in, just to parrot back what all of them had said before in slightly longer, more impressive words. It always boiled down to the same thing: *'If he hasn't denied a threat, then we must assume there is one.'* As if it had simply never occurred to any of them to just not count their chickens before they hatched.

He narrowly kept himself from slamming his hands down on his workstation, instead curling his fingers around the edge of his desk until the urge passed. He pushed his chair back and got to his feet, heading out of his office. It was all getting ridiculous.

He didn't bother to knock on the door to Jennifer's office. He just keyed in his entry code and stepped inside, ignoring the way she whipped around to scowl at him, ripping her attention away from the screen on the wall. "Hey!" she snapped, planting her hands on her hips. "I don't go barging into your office."

"Considering your magnum opus is driving me to distraction, I think we're even," he groused, leaning a shoulder in the open doorway. "I mean, I knew you tweaked the broadcasting algorithms, but I would have stepped in if I had known you planned on murdering the poor things."

Jennifer tossed herself down into her chair, slumping back. "Have you always been this dramatic?" she sulked. "I feel like it's a recent development, but I'm not quite willing to commit to that yet."

"Not like you were willing to commit to that clip," he drawled. "Seriously, do you have any idea how sick I am of hearing it?" He pushed away from the doorway and stepped the rest of the way into the room, finally letting the door slide closed. "I mean, we have, what, an average of four million stories in a twenty-four-hour cycle? So why have I been hearing so much of the same thing?"

"It's important news," Jennifer protested petulantly, sinking down in her chair with her arms crossed.

Andrew snorted and rolled his eyes. "Look," he remarked. "I am here to help you keep your job as much as I am for any other reason. Our higher-ups are starting to ask questions. It hasn't slipped anyone's notice that we're all seeing the same damn story every twenty minutes."

"But what does that have to do with *my* job?" she snapped, drumming her fingers on her arms.

"Oh, don't play stupid." He reached up to pinch the bridge of his nose between two fingers for a moment. "Look, it isn't exactly subtle that the broadcasting algorithms have been messed with. Like, way beyond their recommended levels. Whatever you did is beyond what even the scheduling department does for disaster coverage. At some point—soon, probably—they're going to stop just asking questions and actually go snooping, and they're going to trace your alterations right back to your office."

"I think I can handle getting a scolding," she scoffed. "It's not like I'm some delicate flower or whatever."

Andrew quirked one eyebrow. "If I thought you were just going to get a warning, I wouldn't bother trying to talk to you. I would just leave you to it," he stated blandly. "But this goes beyond just a warning at this point."

"Oh, come *on*, Andy," she groaned, unfolding her arms so she could drop her face down into her hands, muffling her voice as she added, "It's not like I've done anything that bad."

"Not that bad—" Andrew sputtered for a moment. "Jennifer, just think for a minute! About something other than whatever you're trying to achieve here. This isn't just a breach of office rules. This is verging on a violation of the mass communication protocols. Hell, you might have crossed that line already, I'm not sure."

She let her hands fall limply to her lap so she could keep scowling at him, but at last there was a sliver of nerves worming its way into her expression. "It's not that bad," she insisted. "I'm just—"

"Just pretending that you're doing this for the good of the system, but that's bullshit." Andrew dragged one hand down his face, already tired of the entire conversation. Tired of everything relating to that story that had been hounding him. "You think you're being subtle about it, but you really aren't. I can tell you've been gunning for a specific outcome. This doesn't have anything to do with what's best for the system. Especially with the way you've been trampling all over basic entity rights in order to get what you want."

"Entity rights," she repeated dubiously, finally straightening up in her seat. He could practically see her confident mask settling back into place like a veil over her face. "Bold claim. Kind of sounds like you're jumping the gun a bit, don't you think?

There's a big gap between communication protocols and entity rights."

"There is," he agreed, his tone turning placating as his chin dipped once in a nod. "And I don't think you're doing it on purpose. Not the whole 'stepping on entity rights' part, at any rate," he conceded. "But the people in this system have a basic right to honest news, and it's our job to provide it. I know you're good at your job, which is why this garbage is so disappointing."

"It is honest!" Jennifer slammed her hands down on her chair's armrests. "It's what the Commander said, and some outside opinions on it," she explained, her voice abruptly much more level than it had been just a second before. "It's my job to do that."

Andrew groaned and resisted the urge to beat his head against the door until he stopped caring about the entire situation. "Just because it's his actual words doesn't mean it's honest news. This magnum opus of yours is so biased that it barely qualifies as news at this point, and now people are panicking and acting like the entire galaxy is going to blink out of existence at any minute. And I don't even know how much other news has gotten inadvertently suppressed so that clip can play as often as it has been, so we aren't even keeping the system in the loop anymore."

Jennifer was silent after that, scowling at the wall just past Andrew's elbow. He waited for a few seconds before he sighed. "I guess what it boils down to is this: fix the mess you've made. If you don't, I'm going to cut out the need for an investigation entirely by just telling the boss it's your fault."

He didn't wait for her to reply, though he could practically see the words forming on the tip of her tongue. He simply turned on his heel and left.

Basement Car Park, Special Task Force Offices, Undisclosed Location, Estaria

Alisha climbed into the truck behind the steering wheel. The rest of the team piled into the back, cramped together as they avoided Cleavon's equipment that filled it like a packrat's nest. Gently she pulled the unmarked gray utility vehicle out of the carport and out onto the streets of the city.

The ride was quiet at first as they all ran through their own internal pep talks, though it didn't take long before the silence cracked.

Hans straightened the neck of his black turtleneck for the third time in as many minutes before he finally groused, "Why is it always black turtlenecks?" and gave up on keeping the neck of it straight.

Cleavon didn't look up from his holoconsole as he replied. "No one can afford actual ninjas, so the closest we can get is looking like bargain bin ninjas. It's a cost-cutting measure."

"Wouldn't a catsuit be closer to looking like a ninja?" Hans asked, bemusement clear. "Closer to a spy, too. So this just seems like a bit of a copout."

"The catsuits are not as practical as you would think they are," Joshua replied absently, opening his holoconsole just in time for the map of the building that Cleavon sent to finish downloading. "And they kind of chafe."

For just a moment, no one else said anything, and then slowly all eyes turned to Joshua. At last, it was Rhodez who asked, "Why do you know that?"

Before Joshua could offer any sort of answer, the truck pulled to a halt, tucked carefully away in the shadows of the building, its slate gray paint letting it blend in well enough that it was nearly invisible.

Alisha turned away from the wheel to face the rest of them, eyebrows lifting expectantly as she asked, "Everyone ready? We don't have time for any pitstops or detours."

She got a chorus of affirmations in response, and she gestured Hans toward the rear doors of the truck. "You're on watch," she informed him. "Rhodez will be in the truck still so Cleavon can keep working as long as possible even if trouble shows up, but your job is to make sure that trouble doesn't take him by surprise. Got it?"

"Got it." He saluted her briefly before he shoved open the rear doors and hopped out. He adjusted his equipment, pulled his goggles down from the top of his head, and jogged away. He didn't bother to close the truck doors again, knowing Alisha and Joshua would be out in just a few moments.

As Cleavon set about activating the equipment that filled the bulk of the truck, he assured Alisha, "Everything on my end is already set up, so I'll start receiving the data as soon as you plug the dongle in. Once I have everything, there will be no sign we were even in the system after you yank the dongle out again."

Alisha flipped him a playful salute with two fingers. "Roger that. I think I can handle it."

"While I'm just here to look pretty," Joshua chimed in.

"Time for you to look pretty inside," she returned dryly. "Let's get moving."

Joshua followed behind her out of the truck and closed the rear doors as quietly as he could. He held out one fist, and Alisha bumped her knuckles against his before they both turned toward the rarely used maintenance door and stepped inside.

Server Department, Clawstock Building, Spire, Estaria

Joshua and Alisha were silent as they crept through the halls to the main server bank. Joshua had his holoconsole open in front of him as he loped along, a map on one side and Cleavon's instructions on the other.

It was late enough that nearly everyone had been sent home, but if they listened hard, they could hear voices drifting through the wall from the adjacent hallway.

It wasn't until they were in the server closet that either of them dared to speak.

The tension snapped like brittle kindling when Joshua began rubbing his upper arms with his hands and shuffling back and forth from one foot to the other. "I'd've brought a sweater if I had known it was going to be colder than the vacuum of space in here," he mumbled once he came to a standstill again.

Alisha rolled her eyes and crouched in front of the nearest server, pulling Cleavon's dongle from her pack as she did. "Go keep watch by the door. Then it'll only be *mildly* freezing."

"Such a huge improvement," he deadpanned even as he moved toward the door. He opened it just a crack; just enough to see out into the hallway.

Behind him, he could hear Alisha on her communicator.

"It's plugged in. Everything working?"

"*Download in progress,*" Cleavon confirmed. "*It shouldn't take too long.*"

Perimeter of the Clawstock Building, Spire, Estaria

The truck was dark save for the scattered blinking lights of Cleavon's equipment. Even so, Rhodez pulled out his communicator. "What's visibility like, Hans?"

"*You're practically invisible,*" Hans assured them. "*I can sort of see the truck's outline, but I'm squinting, and I already know you're there.*" Rhodez was half a second away from sighing in relief when Hans added, "*I wouldn't underestimate the security around here, though. They've all been very well trained.*"

"Any recommendations?" Rhodez sighed, peering out one of the blackout windows. It was too dark for him to see anything, though.

"Seems like everything is going smoothly so far, so just stay alert and I'll let you know if I see anyone heading your way,"

Hans instructed. As a helpful afterthought, he added, "Relax. Tension slows your reaction time."

"I hate you," Rhodez informed him sullenly, though there was no heat behind the words.

"I'm a goddamn delight," Hans corrected him primly. Unwilling to encourage him, Rhodez let the line go dead after that.

Rhodez glanced around to see if he recognized any of Cleavon's equipment enough to check any of it, but it all seemed foreign to him at that moment.

"You're making me anxious," Cleavon informed him blandly, watching the progress of the download fixedly. "Stop acting like we're in trouble before we're actually in trouble."

Rhodez opened his mouth to protest, but Cleavon flapped a hand at him before he could get the words out, and he closed his mouth again with a click of teeth meeting teeth as he instead fell into a quiet sulk.

At least until his communicator activated again.

"We've got a guard heading in the truck's direction," Hans informed them. "Doesn't look hostile, but that could change if you don't handle the situation carefully."

"Need one of us to come back?" Joshua asked. "It's all quiet over here so far."

"You stay focused," Rhodez replied, almost scolding. "I've got this under control."

He hopped into the driver's seat and drew the barrier between the front and the back shut, so Cleavon and his equipment weren't visible from the front of the truck.

He tugged his goggles off the top of his head and stuffed them down behind the seat. Then he opened his holoconsole to a news site so it looked like he was just minding his own business by the time he could hear a fist hammering against the truck's driver's side door.

His face was a mask of befuddled concern as he found a security guard squinting back at him. "Uh...can I help you, officer?" Rhodez asked slowly.

The guard's eyebrows rose and he gave the truck a pointed once over. "No one's supposed to be back here," he stated plainly, irritation already edging into his voice. "Care to explain what you're doing here, sir?"

Rhodez offered a sheepish grin. "Sorry, officer. I'm part of a group of maintenance contractors." He gestured broadly with one hand, encompassing the entire cab of the truck in a single sweeping motion. "Playing chauffeur this evening to make sure we don't get towed. See, one of the team's got something of a bum leg and we wanted to minimize the walking he'd need to do. We figured we'd be done before it was a problem, but sometimes these things take longer than expected."

The security guard's mouth twisted to one side with skepticism. "If he's that bad off, why didn't he just take some time off?"

Rhodez's expression went flat, unimpressed. "Officer, if you can afford to do that on a whim, then I'm very happy for you."

The security guard recoiled a step, a disorganized spill of half-finished syllables stumbling out of his mouth before he cleared his throat and gathered his composure once again. He dropped his head down enough to pinch the bridge of his nose between two fingers.

"Look," he sighed, dragging his hand down his face and straightening up, "I'm going to keep moving. But if you're still parked here by the time I'm on my next pass, I'm going to have to write you up. Deal?"

Rhodez pasted a winning smile into place. "Sounds great, officer. I'll be out of your hair in no time."

The security guard didn't move for a moment, still watching Rhodez dubiously, before at last he slowly turned and continued on his way.

Rhodez watched him go for a few seconds, then he closed the window again. He shoved the divider aside so he could stick his head into the back. "About how much longer is this going to take? Based on his walking speed and what I saw of the map earlier, we've probably got…maybe thirty-five minutes before we have a problem on our hands."

Cleavon was silent at first, eyes narrowed at his holoconsole for a second before his eyes drifted up and to the side in thought. "It should be doable," he decided carefully, and he activated his communicator as he added, "But Joshua and Alisha are going to need to run like their asses are on fire on the way back to the truck."

"My favorite way to run," Joshua assured him dryly.

"We know, you told us how you failed out of track and field," Alisha pointed out.

"Hey—"

Cleavon turned his communicator off before Joshua could finish expounding on how offended he was.

With a drawn-out sigh, Rhodez climbed from the front of the truck to the back, slumping down in a clear space. "Hurry up and wait, I guess," he mused, and Cleavon hummed in agreement.

Server Department, Clawstock Building, Spire, Estaria

Watching the dongle wasn't going to make the download happen any faster, but Alisha couldn't quite keep herself from staring at it, as if it was going to spontaneously drop out of the port if it didn't have adequate attention.

She looked up when she heard Joshua tapping two fingers against the wall, though most of his attention was still focused out into the hallway.

"A guard is on patrol," he reported, voice low. "I just saw one pass the other hallway. Not coming this way yet, but I figure it's only a matter of time. Trying to explain why we're in the server room isn't going to be quite the same as explaining why we're parked nearby."

Alisha heaved a slow sigh, her shoulders rising and falling with the motion. All things considered, it had all gone surprisingly well, but she had still been hoping for a quiet, uneventful mission.

She cocked her head to one side to listen, and if she strained, she could make out voices elsewhere in the building, louder than they had been initially. She grabbed her communicator with one hand and wrapped her other hand around the dongle.

"Cleavon, we need to get out of here," Alisha hissed urgently into her communicator. "How's it looking on your end?"

For a horrible moment, the only reply was dead air, and then Cleavon's voice reported sharply, *"Got it! Download's complete. Get your asses back here."*

They didn't need to be told twice. Alisha yanked the dongle from the port and shoved it back into her pack as she moved, falling into step behind Joshua as they retraced their steps through the halls.

They were halfway back when Alisha turned on her communicator again. "Hans, we're coming back. We're in a hurry, so you need to be back at the truck by the time we're there."

"Copy that," Hans replied simply, and he let the line go dead.

Alisha and Joshua both picked up the pace.

Dutifully, Hans was back in the truck by the time Alisha and Joshua loped out the door. Alisha launched herself into the back of the truck and tugged the rear door closed, leaving Joshua to climb into the driver's seat.

With a quiet rumble, the truck started and pulled out of its impromptu parking spot.

Strata-Highway 473

The truck bounced like it was trying to break atmosphere, and Hans yelped as he toppled over in the back. "Who let him drive?" he demanded. "My granny is literally blind, and she could do a better job!"

Joshua paid him no mind, and Alisha shoved the front half of her torso into the cab to look out the windshield, unbothered as the truck bounced.

"Looking clear?" she asked, hands on the backs of the driver's seat and the passenger seat to keep her balance. "Nobody tailing us?"

"All clear," Joshua replied as he tried to see in the back. He wanted to glance into the back of the truck to see what everyone else was up to but someone was blocking him. "Alisha?" he called out.

Hans kicked the back of the driver's seat. "Eyes on the road, you goddamn loony toon!"

"I feel like I'm being kept out of the loop," Joshua pouted in return, though he dutifully turned back around to face the road. "What's going on back there?"

"I'm going to barf," Rhodez answered, one hand braced on the side of the truck. "Does that answer any of your questions?"

"Aim for Cleavon," Joshua advised. "Just not his equipment."

In the back, Cleavon opened his mouth to object, only to stay silent as Joshua added that last addendum.

Finally, the truck fell silent, and the path smoothed slightly as Joshua turned on cruise control and folded his hands over the top of the steering wheel. Cleavon used the quiet to his advantage, reading through the diagnostics his system was still running through just to make sure that the satellite servers hadn't given him a virus or any other unpleasant surprises.

"Well?" Alisha probed eventually, shuffling over to slump against his shoulder. "Did it work? We're all dying to know we didn't do this for no reason."

"It was good experience either way," he reasoned, and he ducked to the side before she could punch his shoulder. He straightened up and opened his holoconsole to start testing keywords to find any information related to their most immediate questions.

He cleared his screen and brought up an activity log, and started filtering it looking for any activity that seemed out of place.

"All right," he mused eventually, glancing up from his holo-console. "The signals are actually real; there's something out there. So, that wasn't planted, but..." He trailed off, eyes narrowing slightly as he scrutinized the activity log.

"Problems?" Joshua prompted after a moment of silence.

"The firewall logs show several unsuccessful attempts to breach them. Older attempts, I mean; not our initial try at it." Cleavon leaned to one side to let Alisha, Rhodez, and Hans see his console.

"So someone was trying to plant data," Alisha muttered, more to herself than to the group.

"It just didn't work," Cleavon confirmed. "The failed attempt to fake a signal and the recent actual signals are probably not a coincidence. Failing to fake it, to me it makes sense to assume that whoever tried instead just moved on to throwing an actual anomaly into satellite range."

"Ominous," Joshua observed, his tone deceptively pleasant. "Bates is going to flip," he added, darting a glance into the back again until Hans kicked the back of his seat a second time.

"That's not all," Cleavon butted in again before he began rapidly sorting through information until his console was filled with numbers and distance readings. "Our processing power is a bit faster than theirs," he stated dryly, singling out a specific set of readings and letting his console do the calculations for him. "So while they're still working on it, we already know definitively that whatever it is, it's heading right for us."

Hans whistled, long and low. "Well, shit."

"Anything else?" Alisha asked, leaning over Cleavon's shoulder to peer closer to his console.

"Still working on it," he replied, his tone distracted as he began sorting through the data again. "It's a lot of data to go through." Pitching his voice louder, he added, "Try to keep this thing steady, yeah? If Rhodez doesn't barf on my equipment I'm probably going to do it myself."

Joshua pulled one hand away from the wheel just long enough to flip off the back of the truck.

CHAPTER EIGHT

<u>Bates's Office, Special Task Force Offices, Undisclosed Location, Estaria</u>

"You're sure about this."

While it was nominally a question, Bates's tone left little room for it to sound inquisitive.

Cleavon nodded once. "Positive." It had taken some prodding from Alisha to get him to head the meeting, but he had taken to the role well after a bit of stumbling. "More importantly, my setup figured out what theirs hasn't yet: the signals are coming from ships in the outer system."

"Plural?" Philip asked, in a tone that suggested that he hadn't misheard but was instead simply hoping that he had.

"And heading our way," Cleavon confirmed with a brief nod of his head. "I'm just not completely sure how many yet; the signals are too close together to differentiate one from the others."

Carol settled more heavily in her chair and reached up to massage her temples with two fingers from each hand. She seemed very tired in that moment. But she allowed herself only a few seconds to absorb the information before she let her hands fall back to the top of her desk. "How long until everyone else knows about this?"

Cleavon shrugged, and then looked sheepish, unsure if that sort of gesture was unprofessional in the current setting. He didn't think about it long, though. "It depends on how much processing they allocate toward it. But it could be any time now, potentially."

"I imagine it will be sooner rather than later," Bates sighed, folding her hands together on top of the desk. "The safety of the planet depends on it; everyone is taking it very seriously."

"Yeah, we've all seen the news," Alisha grumbled, more to herself than to Bates. Rhodez patted her shoulder sympathetically. She straightened up, her expression growing stern as she asked, "So, what are we supposed to do? Should we try and stop them from figuring it out?"

Bates was silent at first, her gaze leveled at her desk though her thoughts were elsewhere. Finally, she decided in a low voice, "No. Despite the implications of it, and despite knowing that something else is ultimately going on, we can't corrupt the entire system because of it. The ramifications of it would be too far-reaching for us to feasibly clean up afterward." She lapsed into silence after that, but her expression was still contemplative, and they all knew she hadn't said everything that she needed to say. The room was quiet enough that a mouse walking across the floor would have sounded like a commotion.

"We'll let them figure it out," Bates decided at length, tenting her fingers together in front of her chin. "But we need to warn Molly about it. She'll need to know that something is going to happen."

She leveled a look at Cleavon at last, then at the rest of the group behind him, and she let the smallest smile slip. "You've all done excellent work today," she assured them. "You're dismissed."

One by one, they turned and filed out of the room, Cleavon

turning and taking up the rear of the line. The door slid closed behind them.

"I could make the call if you want me to," Philip offered quietly, sliding Bates a sidelong glance.

Slowly, she sighed and reached up to massage her temples again. "Thank you, but no," she answered after a moment. "I can handle it." She nodded her head toward the door. "Go on. I'll let you know if anything unexpected happens."

Philip paused for only a second before he nodded slowly, then turned on his heel and left. Bates waited until the door closed once again before she picked up her communicator.

Carol Bates hit Send on a holomessage to Paige about their findings. She thought for a second and then decided to relay the information directly to Molly herself as well. If nothing else she might be able to get a temperature read on their plan.

She connected a holocall to her daughter then waited, staring out of her office window onto the bullpen. Over her audio implant, a holding message thanked her for her call and asked her to remain connected while Molly was located.

No doubt it was something set up by Oz as he moved Molly's attention from one task to another, like the extension of her consciousness that Carol assumed he must be by now.

"Hi Mom," Molly answered. Her voice was polite but tired.

"Molly. I have news," Carol responded.

"Great."

"We've got confirmation on the satellite reading. Turns out that not only is it indeed moving our way, but it's also many objects. Probably ships from the size of them."

There was a silence on the line for a moment. Carol glanced down at her wrist device to make sure they were still connected.

"The good news is," Carol continued, "we still have at least a little time before the military stations get through crunching the data and figuring out what we already know. But if you're going to make a move, you'll need to do it fast."

More silence on the line. Carol pursed her lips, waiting.

"Ok, Mom. Thanks for the heads up. I take it we checked to make sure that this data is authentic... from the satellites themselves. Not planted?"

"Affirmative," Carol confirmed. "Although, it looks like someone had tried to plant it months ago but was unable to bypass their security protocols."

Molly snorted on the other end of the line. "Small mercies!" she exclaimed.

"Indeed." The team is running down the details. Seeing if we can trace it back to anyone in particular. I think it's safe to assume that the Northern Clan was behind it in some form or another."

"Yes, agreed," Molly replied.

"So speaking of you making a move—what exactly are you planning to do?" Carol could almost see Molly rolling her eyes, but with a lack of information she had no way to confront her on her suspicion.

"Well, if you must know... *Mom*," she replied with emphasis on the Mom, "I'm planning to head on out there and see what these folks want."

Carol didn't even pause. "Ah yes, with that secret technology that Lance gave you. Well, I'm not sure I approve of—"

Molly suddenly engaged in the conversation, her voice lifting an octave and a few decibels as if she had been trying to restrain herself up until this point. "Approve? Mother, I'm trying to save the system! Your approval is the least important thing in the whole equation."

Carol's voice rose in response. "You're running straight into a dangerous situation head first, with no backup and no idea what you're going to face. You always were a reckless child!"

"Actually," Molly countered firmly. "I *have* got backup. And if you get any more intel on what I'm walking into, then I'd be pleased to see it."

There was another awkward silence as both women contemplated their next move without escalating their relationship to nuclear.

"Now," Molly said, her tone dialed back a little, "is that all, Mother?"

"Yes. I suppose." Director Bates sighed, deflating. "I just don't know why you still feel you need to prove yourself."

Molly opened her mouth to respond, then changed her mind on what she was going to say. "Thanks for the intel Mom. I'll be in touch if anything changes."

Carol was clearly ready to start a rant, but quietly waved her daughter off before ending the call.

She sat back in her chair in her stark blue office, vaguely aware of the personnel in the office beyond.

She'd always wondered what it would feel like to be working with her daughter. Now she knew for sure, and it was far more anxiety-producing than she ever thought. Worry wasn't something that came naturally to her, after all.

Molly's Conference Room, Safe House, Gaitune-67

It was getting late on the asteroid, but the team were still abuzz with activity. Although it was going to take several days for the Zhyn fleet to get there, it seemed like the preparations were endless.

"Well, it sounds like bringing our blue warrior-friends into the mix was an especially good call… now we know what we're up against," Sean added.

Molly sat across from him, poking her fork into the curry in her takeout box.

"You know, that skill of yours might come in handy in that regard."

"What skill?"

"You know, your ability to push your will."

Molly frowned, contemplating the suggestion. "I guess," she said quietly.

"No I'm serious," Sean insisted. "Think about it. Let's say you're close enough to the ships to be able to force them to change their minds about firing on us... that would be useful."

"I think a missile has a longer range than my so-called ability. Anyway, I don't even know if I have it anymore... or if it was even real in the first place."

"Oh, believe me. It was real. I know my mind when it comes to tactical decisions, and you changed it... completely turned me around for a few hours after talking with you about it."

Molly sighed. "Well, if it's not even permanent I don't know how it's going to even help in this pickle..."

Sean bobbed his head from side to side, about to concede the point. "Ah... but what if it were enough to influence say... a vote. Like in the Senate, or something."

"You mean fuck with the very fabric of our political system?"

"No, I mean, make sure that those dumb asses make the right decision."

Molly shook her head at him. "Well, apart from the fact that goes against everything we stand for..."

"Apart from that," Sean smiled.

"I don't see us having a situation like that any time soon. That's all." She shrugged and stabbed her fork into a faux protein chunk before popping it in her mouth.

"Anyway, shouldn't we be thinking about fleet tactics for when our guests arrive?"

Sean finished his food and wiped his mouth with a napkin. "We should," he agreed. He reached to his holo and pulled up a few screens before activating one on the room's holoprojector. "We're still awaiting exact numbers and weight of the ships we're expecting but working on my estimates there are a few scenarios which would minimize our risk and give most of them a retreat protocol."

He hesitated. "Of course, we're the only ones with gate capabilities, and I don't think these guys can move faster than light… which means…"

"Say it," she said firmly. "Which means that if this other fleet has anything more advanced, our Zhyn compatriots are screwed."

"I thought they were mercenaries?"

"Just on paper. We think of them as friends. In each scenario. If we lose a single life out there it's one too many." Molly paused, dwelling briefly on the realization of what they were planning. She exhaled heavily and then moved on.

"What do those formations look like then?" she asked, getting down to the one practical thing she could think about.

Workshop, Base, Gaitune-67

Crash and Brock were taking a break from the heavy workload.

"You know," Crash mused, kicking back on the dust-bitten sofa they used for gaming, "I don't think I've ever met a Zhyn warrior."

"You know Ben'or," Crash responded, somewhat distracted by his console.

"Well, yeah, to say hello to. But it's not like we've kicked back and got drunk together. I don't know anything about his culture, or about him. I mean… I've no idea if he prefers meat or veggies only on his pizza."

Crash chuckled quietly. "Yeah. These are the important things to suss out about a person before you decide what kind of man he is."

Brock sniggered, hugging a cushion to his chest as he lay

back. "You know, we should make a point of breaking bread with some of these guys when they get here. Find out about them. What their hopes and dreams are. What makes them tick. What their world is like."

Crash smiled at him from his game of 3D chess against the console. "I think that's a good idea. Mind, just a hunch, I get the sense that Ben'or isn't particularly representative of the Zhyn warrior culture."

"What makes you say that?"

Crash shrugged. "He's just not very warrior-like." He paused his game as his eyes drifted off thoughtfully. "If I had to guess, I'd say in his position as a diplomat and being responsible for smoothing over situations so that they don't have to go to war, is probably a pretty big task. He must have an infinite capacity for patience and very little ego in the game."

Brock thought for a few moments. "So you think the role dictates his temperament? Or vice versa?"

"Who knows," Crash shrugged.

A voice boomed from the Daemon door to the workshop. "I can tell you categorically that my temperament got me the role!"

Brock nearly jumped out of his skin. Wide-eyed, his head appeared over the back of the couch as he sat bolt upright, heart pounding. "Ben'or! I... didn't see you there."

Crash looked like he was trying to catch his breath as well. "Man!" he exclaimed. "For a big dude you walk like a grasshopper on morning frikkin dew!"

Ben'or chuckled a hearty belly laugh. "I was just coming through the daemon door when I heard you talking about my brethren. I was interested to hear your thoughts... uncensored, as it were."

Brock responded quickly. "I'm sorry sir, we didn't mean any disrespect."

"Oh, I know. You didn't say anything that I could possibly take offense to." Ben'or smiled congenially. "And I'm sure the landing party would be delighted to join you for pizza and what-have-you when they finally get here."

Brock got up, his physiology returning to normal after the shock. "Great. I'll mark my calendar. But we still need to know the most important thing."

"Oh yes? What would that be?"

"Meat or veggie on your pizza?"

Ben'or chuckled and ambled off toward the stairs, waving his hand as if he wasn't going to answer.

Brock called after him. "You know we'll find out somehow!"

Ben'or chuckled some more as he climbed the stairs to the safe house.

"I'll ask Arlene!" Brock called after him.

Crash sniggered away shaking his head at the comedy playing out in front of him. His first impression of Brock when they met had never been disproven once: there was indeed never a dull moment when he was around.

CHAPTER NINE

Hangar Deck, Base, Gaitune-67

Orange flashing lights flickered rhythmically as Oz ran the announcement base-wide. "Alert, alert. Please be advised our allies are arriving at the hangar deck in t-minus five minutes and counting." His voice echoed through every speaker in the PA system.

Brock appeared in the workshop, frantically fastening his overalls. "I can't believe they're here already. I didn't have time to clean up around *The Empress*. They're going to be so judgy about the mess down there. Crash? Crash? Do you think—"

He looked around for Crash as if he should have been there already. A moment later Crash emerged from the daemon passage. "We've still got that oil spill to clean up underneath *The Empress!*" he announced.

For someone who was normally so subdued under pressure, he actually looked dramatically stressed out.

"I know!" Brock exclaimed. "That's what I was just saying. Except you weren't here to hear my panic."

Crash smiled sagely, picked up a sand bucket and a few cloths and headed back out of the door. "I've got it. You just get down there and represent us all in the welcome party."

Brock started to protest. "But—"

Crash turned back to him briefly. "I'm not a people person." Then he disappeared.

Brock exhaled quickly with mild humor, then busied himself trying to make sure that the workshop looked presentable. After twenty seconds of dancing himself into a dither, he fluffed a cushion, put it back on the sofa, rearranged it, then decided he was majoring in irrelevant details.

Seconds later he was heading out of the daemon door and down the corridor to the hangar deck. As he approached the overlooking walkway at the end of the daemon corridor, he slowed. Paige, Maya, and Pieter were already there.

"How did you guys get down here so fast?" he asked.

Paige flicked her long dark hair over one shoulder and turned to eye him in playful seductivity. "We walked," she told him, wiggling her eyebrows over her narrowed eyes pretending she had just told him the biggest secret in the world.

Maya slapped at her arm. "Stop it," she told her. "We asked Oz to give us a heads up when they were twenty minutes out." She nodded down at their high heeled shoes. "Needed extra time to get here what with all this foot binding shit!"

Brock laughed and slung his arms around the shoulders of the two girls, his right hand resting on Pieter's shoulder too. The four of them looked out over the hangar deck as Molly, Sean, Jack, and Joel emerged from the direction of the base conference room.

"This is an historic day," Brock told them, his eyes taking on a distant look and his voice suddenly more awe-inspired than panicked now. "The first time that Zhyn have been on this base. And we're here to witness it."

Paige glanced at him sideways. "Actually, we're here to welcome and entertain," she corrected him.

"And we don't know this is the first time," Pieter added. "Remember, we were the first ones on this base in fifty-something years... but who knows what went on before that. This whole base could have been operated by Zhyn before then."

Maya chuckled. "Unlikely. But we get the point," she agreed.

Brock sighed. "Oh, small minds." He patted the heads of the two girls. "History is unraveling before your very eyes and yet you jest about trivialities.

"And technicalities," Pieter added.

"And actual facts," Paige added with a grin.

Just then the hangar doors started opening, revealing the inky blackness of space behind them. The four waited, barely daring to breathe. They strained their eyes into the distant darkness, waiting for a glimpse of a ship that was going to escort them out into an area of space they had never thought of venturing yet, to meet what would likely be the most formidable opponent they had ever encountered.

A number of seconds passed before the darkness beyond was eclipsed by something huge and ship-like.

"It's not going to fit!" Maya gasped.

"That's what she said," Brock started, sniggering to himself. The others couldn't help but smile at the lame-ass joke.

Pieter pulled up his holo. "Oz wouldn't be guiding them in if they weren't going to fit," he told her, as if Maya were being ridiculous in her concern.

A few moments later the ship seemed to line up with the hangar doors and slip effortlessly into the space inside. A few more minutes later it gently touched down in the central open space of the deck.

"It's massive!" Maya gasped, her eyes wide and everyone else forgotten.

This time Paige sniggered at the obvious continuation joke which a quick glance to the others told her she didn't need to bother vocalizing.

"We should head down," Brock interrupted enthusiastically. Before the others knew what was happening Brock was already half-way down the first flight of stairs, boots thumping against the metal. Paige noticed the side door of the ship opening and a staircase unfurling. She was tempted to watch from her vantage point but didn't want to miss the introductions. She hurried after the others, carefully picking her way in her high heels and cursing her affinity to fashion.

They arrived on the deck just in time to see four large Zhyn heading from the stairs of their ship to the group of their leaders: Joel, Jack, Sean and Molly who had taken a few steps forward and were about to shake hands.

Paige caught up with Maya, grabbing her arm. "They're even bigger than Ben'or!" she gasped. "I can't believe Molly is going to do that human custom! She'll get her hand broken."

"I know," Maya agreed, wincing in anticipation. "I'm glad I'm not a diplomat or anything. All that touching and backslapping. Being a leader when there are guys like this around is a risky business."

Paige narrowed her eyes at her. "You're pulling my leg?"

Maya grinned and kept walking, stopping a few yards away, just next to where Brock and Pieter had felt it appropriate to stop.

Molly watched as the group of Zhyn dignitaries and representatives approached her welcome party. Now seeing the Admiral, she wished she had made more of an effort. Merely hoping that Paige would take care of details like the refreshments seemed like a massive oversight on her part.

She stepped forward and held out her hand, hoping that the human custom would be understood.

"Greetings Admiral," she said, addressing the warrior with the most medals on the front of his robes.

"Awww hawwww, Molly Bates, I presume!" the Admiral guffawed as he approached. He took her hand and shook it enthusiastically. Molly felt her whole body being shaken up and down as he shook her hand and then clamped her firmly on her shoulder.

She recovered herself and managed to wriggle free. "Admiral, welcome to Gaitune-67. We are most honored to have you here… and deeply appreciative of your efforts in helping us."

"Ah, speak nothing of it, Ms. Bates. We're glad to be here. And after everything you've done for our empire over the years, it is an honor to be able to repay the debt."

Molly felt the eyeballs of the team behind her, and when she turned she clocked Paige, Maya, Pieter, and Brock not a short distance away too.

"May I introduce you to my team, Admiral," she offered, stepping out of the way. "This is Joel Dunham, Sean Royale, and Jack Nolan."

She surreptitiously tried to rub her shoulder joint as they made their greetings. Interestingly no one else opted for stepping forward to shake his hand. Instead, they kept their arms firmly by their sides and bowed courteously.

Neat trick. Wish I'd thought of that before my shoulder was dislocated.

All in the days work for a leader.

Quite. But I bet these guys don't know their own strength.

I rather suspect they're used to handling people who have a similar resiliency to themselves.

I don't disagree.

The Admiral, looking very pleased, turned back to Molly. "Thank you for your warm welcome. May I present some of my crew members. This is my second in command, Fleet Sergeant Kitcher."

The Zhyn who was similarly dressed stepped forward to bow shortly to Molly. Having learned her lesson, she returned the bow. He made a similar gesture to the others and they introduced themselves again, helping one another to remember the new names.

Two Zhyn in flight suits stood back a few paces. Molly wasn't familiar with their customs but they looked as though they were standing at attention, and were probably of a lower rank. She was about to offer an introduction to them when Admiral Clor's gaze fell behind her, as if he were distracted. She turned to see Ben'or coming over to join them.

"Admiral Clor, you probably know The Right Honorable Ben'or—" Before she could get any further with the introduction Ben'or and Clor were embracing each other, slapping each other vigorously and enthusiastically on the backs.

"I guess you guys know each other?"

"That we do, Molly dear. That we do," Ben'or chuckled. He released Clor and turned to Kitcher. "Good to see you too, Kitcher. It's been too long."

Kitcher embraced Ben'or with a similar enthusiasm, but Molly noticed a slight resistance in his eye. "Ben'or. Not long enough. I still haven't forgotten how you tricked me on our final test."

Ben'or chuckled loudly as he waved an arm to the other two Zhyn warriors in the party.

"Now, now," Clor interjected. "Graduation was a long time ago now, Kitcher."

"Yes, not good to carry grudges," Ben'or added, tapping his nose and winking at what Molly deduced must have been an old rival back at some Zhyn training thing.

The decibel levels of the conversations had escalated since Ben'or arrived on the deck leaving the others mostly just spectators in proceedings now.

"How about we retire to one of the conference rooms where

we can have some refreshments, and discuss our plans?" Molly suggested, gesturing in the direction of the base conference rooms and labs.

"Of course, thank you," Admiral Clor replied. He and Ben'or led the way chatting between themselves. Kitcher held back a little, allowing the humans to go ahead of him, and then he and Molly brought up the rear. He turned back briefly to nod to the other two who hadn't yet been introduced.

Each of the two saluted him and relaxed their postures as if they'd been dismissed.

Paige took the initiative, delicately stepping forward. "Greetings of the day to you," she called to them, her voice raised as if talking to someone who might be deaf.

The pair glanced at each other, then grinned. "Greetings," they responded, stepping forward to meet with Paige's group.

"I'm Trev'or," the first said, waving a hand casually.

"And I'm Ruther."

Paige put a hand on her chest. "Paige," she told them.

Maya waved nervously. "Maya."

The pair nodded.

"Pieter," Pieter said, waving and then knocking his hair out of his eyes awkwardly.

"Brock," Brock added finally. He beamed at them. "So I guess you're also not invited to the private party?" he joked, nodding in the direction where the leaders had disappeared.

"Ah, nah," Trev'or replied. "Above our stripes," he added tapping the stripes on the arm of his jumpsuit.

Brock sniggered. "Ours too."

There was an awkward silence between the two groups as they each racked their brains for the next thing to say.

"So…" Paige ventured, "what do you guys do on the ship?"

Ruther shrugged. "Well, we're basically technicians that follow those two around and execute their orders."

Trev'or took over. "Means we could be flying their ship one minute…"

"Or communicating with the entire fleet the next," Ruther added.

Paige smiled at the way they seemed to talk as a unit.

"Actually," Ruther continued, "the boss thought it would be a good idea for us to come and meet with you. We're going to be helping coordinate the operation, so he thought us knowing each other would be useful."

Paige grinned, excited that though they operated worlds apart they still seemed to share a common thought process. "That was some good thinking!" she exclaimed.

"Plus," Trev'or added, "we were kinda curious. We have never seen any Estarians before. You're strangely more multicolored than we expected."

Paige giggled and nudged Maya who was also amused. "Oh… We're not all Estarian. I'm half human. Estarian coloring. Brock and Pieter are human…"

Brock waved, grinning. Pieter nodded awkwardly, flicking some unkempt hair out of his eyes.

"And you saw Molly and the others… They're also human."

"I'm Estarian though," Maya chirped up. Then she looped an errant strand of dark hair behind her ear and did a turn on her toes.

The two Zhyn technicians looked at each other and applauded at her twirl.

"Forgive us," Trev'or explained. "We don't mean to be rude. We're just fascinated. We appreciate you explaining the difference to us."

Paige wafted her hand. "No problem at all. We were kinda curious about the Zhyn people too. I think it's a great thing that we get to spend some time together."

Ruther piped up. "Hey, so, in the interests of learning what we can about your culture… what do you think you can show us?"

"Well, we could start with the tour of the base," Paige started.

Maya put a hand on her friend's' forearm. "I have a better idea," she offered in a slightly conspiratorial tone. "How about we show them something truly human?"

Paige frowned. "What do you propose?"

"Pizza," Maya said simply.

They all laughed.

Except for the two Zhyn. "What is this pizza you speak of?" Ruther asked.

Brock grinned inching forward into the conversation a little more. "It's a human specialty," he explained with a wink.

Paige clapped her hands and led them toward the stairs to the safe house. "Good thinking, Maya. And while we eat, we can talk and tell you anything you want to know."

"Food?" Ruther grinned. "Couldn't have thought of anything better myself." He rubbed his strong, over-sized hands together, clearly even more interested in the cultural exchange now.

The group moved across the hangar deck as a unit now. "Let's head upstairs then," Paige confirmed, "and I'll put an order in."

Maya and Paige led the way, the two Sarkian boys walking behind with their new comrades.

Base Conference Room, Gaitune-67

Mochas and teas were passed around, and several plates of hors-d'oeuvres were placed in front of the guests.

"Are you sure you don't want to rest before we talk?" Molly asked again.

"No, no... we're fine. We've just hopped down on the transporter."

Molly frowned. "You mean that ship you've just arrived on."

"Uh huh."

"So that's not your regular space-faring ship?"

"Oh no..." Clor chuckled, throwing Ben'or a knowing glance.

"That's like a little shuttle to get us from the flagship down to land here. Easier for dockings and landing on planets. Uses about one-millionth of the energy for takeoff... and landing."

Ben'or watched the realization of the relative ship sizes dawn on Molly, as if LEDs had just been activated in dark areas of her brain.

Molly nodded deferentially.

Fleet Sergeant Kitcher and Joel had been talking. They seemed to have worked out an order of business between them whilst the teas were being passed around.

Kitcher cleared his throat. "Well. If we're all ready..."

Molly motioned to give him the floor.

Kitcher acknowledged her with a bow of his head and then began. "Thank you again for your hospitality. Joel and I thought it might be useful to start with the resources we have available. So although we weren't able to bring the entire fleet, we have managed to bring twenty ships."

Sean nearly choked on his tea. "That's a whole fleet to some people!" he looked up a moment. "Well, some... Perhaps not the Empire."

Joel smirked, watching him recover himself. "Certainly in this sector," he agreed, a little more composed.

Clor gruffed from behind a pastry which looked smaller than miniature in his large hand. "Well, our fleets normally ride out a hundred ship strong on normal missions. But of course, this is a special case and we couldn't risk alerting other powers in the Federation."

Molly nodded quietly. "Of course. And we're grateful for any help."

Joel and Sean sat quietly, wide-eyed at the sheer firepower at the beck and call of these two men. If Joel had to guess from Sean's posture, he may have suspected that maybe Sean was even a little intimidated by their superior firepower.

Sean swallowed hard and found his voice. "So... just to be

clear. The ship you landed was a... transporter. How much bigger are your actual ships?"

The two Zhyn exchanged a glance as if searching for a number. Clor shrugged. "I dunno. Maybe a hundred?"

"Oh."

Sean sat back, his questions taken care of.

Jack leaned forward next, a perplexed look on her face. "Sorry... it's probably not super relevant. But if your ships are a hundred times bigger... how do you ever land them?"

Kitcher glanced at his boss and seemed to volunteer to take this next question. "Generally, we don't. We build them in a docking station, and when we decommission them we do the reverse. Dock them, and take them apart for parts. Most ships have never even been in an atmosphere."

"Oh," Jack managed, before she too sat back with no further questions.

Sean sat up again. "But your transporter had guns, and missiles! Big-ass missiles!"

Ben'or sat quietly the corner of his mouth now smirking.

Kitcher could see him out of his peripheral vision but managed to keep his own face straight. "This is true," he conceded. "Though they are nothing compared to the actual battleships."

Molly watched the team acclimatize to the new levels of fire-power in their mix. Seeing that their burning questions had been answered she leaned forward. "So. Erm... our plan?"

"Yes," the Admiral agreed, "what do you need us to do?"

Molly thought for a moment. "Well, mostly we need you there as a deterrent. A threat, so we don't just rock up and get ourselves annihilated. But if things should go south, then we need to have a contingency plan, so we can escape. Our primary goal is to try to avoid a confrontation and as we explained in the mission documents, it's highly unlikely that we would need to fire a single shot."

The Admiral nodded. "But if we do?"

Sean sat forward again in his seat, his composure regained. He tapped his holo and brought up some slides in the holoscreen at the center of the table. "This is plan A," he announced. The screen showed a formation of ships, and a sequence evolving over time.

Kitcher interrupted with a wave of his finger. "Of how many plans?"

"We have four contingencies. Let's go through them one at a time and make sure you're happy with all of them." Sean dug into the details, thankful that although he hadn't had any idea of the sheer size of the ships, at least he had been prepared for the numbers and how to arrange them.

Workshop, Safe House Basement, Gaitune-67

Several hours later Pieter sat in the workshop as Brock worked solidly on adapting their shields for an expanded frequency.

"I wish I'd know about this possibility sooner," he grumbled, pausing only a moment to rub his fingers into his forehead before continuing to fiddle with the control box.

"I know," Pieter agreed. "Giles only mentioned it as a possible gotcha the other day, and I didn't realize that there was anything we could do about it until earlier."

"I know. It's not your fault. It's not anyone's fault. It's just... all a little much, you know." Brock sat back on his stool, allowing his eyes to focus on the far wall for a moment to rest his eyes from the detailed work.

"It'll be fine," Pieter reassured him. "We'll all be fine."

Just then Trev'or came down the steps. "Ah, there you both are." He looked at Brock fiddling with the control box. "Still working?"

"Yeah," Brock grunted. "Trying to expand the range of our

shields in case these ARs have some kind of firepower that can penetrate our shields."

Trev'or slumped down on a stool at the same workbench as Pieter and Brock. "Hey man, it really is going to be all ok. We've got your backs. Those ARs fire one shot anywhere near you and we'll take them out." His fist clenched automatically as he spoke the words.

Brock took a deep breath and exhaled slowly. "I appreciate that, Trev'or." He smiled. "But I still need to make sure I do everything I possibly can to keep the team alive out there."

"Of course."

Bourne's voice suddenly chirped up over the workshop intercom. "You know... I'm good for more than just hologames!"

Trev'or looked startled and looked around to see where the voice was coming from.

Pieter chuckled. "It's ok. That's just Bourne."

"Bourne?"

"Yeah, one of our in-house AIs."

"AIs? As in..."

"Artificial intelligence."

"I prefer the term Advanced Entity," Bourne interjected.

"He's sentient," Pieter added rolling his eyes as if to elicit sympathy from Trev'or.

Trev'or's brow furrowed. "You have sentient AIs?"

Brock kept working as he spoke. "Yeah. It's a thing. Sorry... we should have warned you." He lifted his voice a little to reach the intercom. "Bourne, this is our new friend Trev'or. Trev'or, this is Bourne."

"Nice to make your acquaintance," Bourne said.

"Likewise." Trev'or looked a little unnerved still. "So, this is for real?" he asked Pieter quietly.

Pieter nodded, grinning now. "Yeah. We liberated him from a military base a while ago. Now he just mostly watches movies from the archives and hangs out playing holo games with us. And Oz... the other AI."

Trev'or took a deep breath. "Wow, this is... incredible."

"You mean, you don't have AIs in the Zhyn Empire?" Pieter looked confused. "I thought you guys were technological badasses?"

Trev'or's eye widened. "Heck no. I couldn't think of anything more terrifying. One of us would certainly destroy the other." He shrugged. "I guess it's kinda like your Estarians in the face of meeting a new tribe."

"Why do you say that?" Brock asked.

Trev'or shrugged. "Well, we've never seen AIs before. Our tech is good, and we have self-learning intelligent programs. But nothing alive. And I think most of our warriors would agree that another life form that has more capability than us would be a threat. And so they'd have to snuff it out. So I guess no one's bothered to think about inventing a fully sentient entity, simply because... well, what's the point?"

Pieter watched his new friend, fascinated. "That is truly incredible."

"I guess," Trev'or agreed. "But from our perspective it's just never been a goal we've sought. We figure that we're smart enough and complicated enough, without compounding our problems."

Brock suddenly sat back, a relieved look on his face. "Done!" he announced, pushing the box away from him and further onto the bench.

"Great!" Bourne pipped up again. "Game time!"

The holoscreen over by the old couch came to life, game music starting up in the background.

Pieter sniggered. "Come on, let us show you the advantages of having a friendly AI hanging about the base." He led Trev'or over to the gaming area and handed him a gamepad.

"I'll be back in ten minutes," Brock announced, heading out toward the daemon door. "Just have to fit this box…"

His words fell on deaf ears. Pieter and Trev'or were already immersed in the new world Bourne was creating for them as the game powered-up.

CHAPTER TEN

On Board Glock'stor Ship #597

As Supervisor Gultorra made his way toward the mess hall, he glanced out a bulkhead window. He fancied, for a moment, that he could see Gaitune-67 in the distance. As close as the ship was to it, though, he knew they weren't *that* close.

Perhaps one of the twenty Zhyn ships might have been, but not his. He spared the bit of whimsy only a moment of thought before he pulled his attention away from the bulkhead window and continued on his way.

The dome of the mess hall was abuzz with conversation. Every so often someone shouted from the main table up to one of the walkways above. It was lively and almost bombastic, and that, combined with the lingering smell of roasted zarther-beast, it was a bit like home.

"Supervisor on deck!" someone announced from down the table. As one, all eyes turned to Gultorra and everyone at the table saluted in nearly clockwork unison before turning back to their meals and their conversations.

Gultorra plucked his hat off of his head and took a seat at the head of the table, Kalvor to his left and Tulnok to his right.

Kalvor passed the zarther-beast platter and Gultorra plucked the bone from it. It had nearly been carved clean, but enough meat still lingered to be satisfying, and the bone was the best part, regardless.

As Kalvor set the platter down and shoved it back along the table. Tulnok turned his expectant gaze on Gultorra.

Gultorra paused with the bone raised halfway to his mouth before he sighed and set it back on the plate, the tips of his fingers instead drumming on the table. "Tulnok."

"Boss."

"Have you picked up the habit of thinking before you start speaking? I'm impressed."

Tulnok snorted and rolled his eyes. "Not quite," he returned wryly. "Just wondering, Boss, but what's up with this muttering I keep hearing about us being mercenaries now?"

Gultorra's eyes narrowed, just enough to take him out of the running of ever winning a poker match. "Who said anything about that?"

Tulnok waved it off with an unconcerned flick of his claws. "You know how it goes. Just some scuttlebutt."

"Uh huh," Gultorra hummed dubiously. "Well, it's not something I'm supposed to talk about."

Suddenly much more interested, Tulnok leaned closer on his elbows. "You don't say." While he didn't actually say 'I'm all ears,' the implication was there.

At last, Kalvor offered his own two cents. "Yeah, I heard about this whole 'mercenary' thing, too," he chimed in, lifting both hands to make air quotes with his fingers as he said the word 'mercenary.'

Gultorra shook his head in comic exasperation. "Put your hands down when you say that. You look like a cheerleader!"

Kalvor's hands dropped back to the table so quickly they nearly broke the sound barrier. As Kalvor scowled, Tulnok's eyebrows rose slowly and he wondered, "Why is he doing that?"

Gultorra simply arched one questioning eyebrow and finally started eating, teeth ripping at what little was left on the bone.

"The air quotes thing?" Kalvor supplied. He lifted his hands to do it again, just to see Gultorra glower at him.

"Yeah, that." Tulnok nodded once. "When you say mercenary."

Gultorra groaned and dropped the bone back down to his plate. "If I refuse to answer, are you going to drop it?"

"Probably not," Tulnok answered pleasantly. He grinned, showing his dinosaur-like teeth.

Gultorra dug at the corners of his eyes with two of his knuckles. "Of course," he moaned. "Just remember, I didn't tell you any of this." He punctuated his words with a lingering look at Tulnok, who looked only marginally offended about being singled out.

"We aren't supposed to be here," Gultorra admitted without any more evasion. "Not in an official, Empire-related capacity, at any rate. But Lord Ben'or, dipping into his infinite wisdom, found a loophole that means we're not breaking the Federation treaty."

Tulnok's eyebrows rose once again. "By letting people hire us out for money?"

"You didn't hear it from me," Gultorra offered by way of confirmation. Tulnok seemed distracted with his own thoughts after that, so Gultorra didn't bother waiting for a reply. Instead, he picked up the bone from his plate and resumed gnawing at it, until it was nearly clean and it cracked beneath his teeth.

"So," Tulnok mused slowly, slightly disconcerted, "we've been bought. We're being pimped out for cash. Like common whores!"

Gultorra didn't offer any sort of confirmation, instead taking a moment to appreciate the look of dawning horror on Tulnok's face…at least until it was very quickly replaced with elation.

"Cool!" Tulnok grinned broadly and turned halfway around in his seat to look at the next table over. "Hey! Hey, Georg'oh! We're mercs now!"

Georg'oh offered a distracted thumbs-up in reply. Whether or not he put any stock in the words coming out of Tulnok's mouth was up for some debate.

When Tulnok turned back around, it was with a slightly worrisome grin on his face. Gultorra felt a knot of dread rising in his chest.

"Sooo," Tulnok began casually.

"Don't you dare," Gultorra practically growled. He already knew where the conversation was going to go next.

Unperturbed, Tulnok asked, "Since you're in charge, does that make you our pimp?"

Gultorra heaved a beleaguered sigh. "It means you have four seconds to get out of my face before I shove my mercenary boot so far up your ass you're tasting shoe polish."

"Right, yeah." Tulnok got to his feet, grabbing his empty plate and Gultorra's as he did. "No one will know you told me, boss. Sounds like fun!" Notably, he didn't say that he wasn't going to mention it at all.

He got distracted just a few steps away, leaning against the next table over to talk to another friend.

"Aren't you glad I'm normal?" Kalvor asked, grinning as he watched Tulnok depart.

"Someone needs to balance you out," Gultorra replied dryly. "I like to think of you as a matched set."

Base conference Room, Gaitune-67

Molly glanced around the table of wide-eye attentive team members. Admiral Clor and Fleet Sergeant Kitcher sat quietly, with Ben'or on one side of them, taking it all in.

Molly turned to Crash. "Ok, how are the ships looking?"

Crash sat up a little straighter as he responded. "*The Empress* is ready to go and we've loaded up four pods as you asked."

Paige frowned. "Why just four?"

Crash looked awkward for a moment and glanced at Molly.

Molly signaled to him that she'd take the question. "Just in case. You might need them back here in the future if… anything were to happen out there."

Paige's eyes seemed to flicker with a horror that she quickly tried to suppress. She felt Maya look at her, probably with the same reaction, but she held her finger up discreetly from her hand on the table and Maya dropped her gaze to the table. She realized it wasn't the time to discuss the implications of Molly's comment.

Molly's eye caught that of the Admiral at the other end of the table before she quickly continued with her briefing. "And the *Little Empress*?" she asked Crash.

"Also on board and ready to rock," he said simply.

Molly turned to Sean. "And how are we looking in terms of weapons?"

"We've loaded up everything that we think is necessary and useful. Obviously, we want to keep the weight down as much as possible. And space is an issue what with the additional ships… but we've got more than enough for any of the four scenarios."

"Good. Ok. Joel?"

Joel stood up to take the lead on the team details. "Pieter, we'll need you to be monitoring all signals on all frequencies during the approach. We've no idea how the ships are going to be able to communicate with us."

Pieter nodded. "I've already adapted a couple of the receivers to pick up a broader spectrum than normal and hooked them up to my holo."

"Good," Joel confirmed. He turned to Arlene and Giles. "If you two are ok to join us, we'd appreciate any assistance in recognizing patterns or languages."

Arlene nodded obediently. Giles raised his hand though. "Yes, of course. We can bring *The Scamp Princess* along, in case you need us for evasive maneuvers or to create a distrac—."

"Actually," Joel interrupted him, "we'd need you on board *The Empress* with us, to interpret anything Pieter picks up."

Giles sat back, folding his arms, clearly disappointed to not be riding into battle on his own steed. "Very well," he agreed reluctantly.

"Jack, you're in charge of weapons from the cockpit. If we need to arm up personally, you'll also oversee that. You know the protocols."

She nodded. "Yes."

Molly frowned. "You've briefed her on the strategies, and not shooting to kill unless we have the code word."

Jack smirked. "Yes. I know the code word."

Brock became suddenly animated flicking his eyes from Joel to Molly to Jack. "What code word?"

Pieter grinned. "Need to know, Mate," he said, touching his nose.

Brock glanced at Crash. "Why are we being left out?"

Crash shrugged. "Speak for yourself…"

Brock started to protest. "Hang on—"

Molly held up a hand. "It's ok Brock. It's just a security measure to make sure there are no misunderstandings on opening fire. This is an incredibly delicate situation we're walking into. That's all."

Joel continued, nodding to their new allies who had been sitting quietly. "Admiral Clor and Fleet Sergeant Kitcher also know the code word and will use deadly force only if that code word is uttered."

"Maya and Paige," he said next, turning to them. "We need you to stay put here and hold the fort."

Arlene leaned forward. Joel clocked it and acknowledged her. "And yes, we should have Anne brought up from the surface to stay with Paige and Maya while you, Giles and Ben'or are on the mission with us."

Arlene nodded.

"Which brings us onto our friend Ben'or," Joel continued. Ben'or held Joel's gaze steadily. Joel smiled. "Who would you like to ride with? Us or the Admiral?"

The Admiral waved his hand in offering to Ben'or as if he didn't mind which ship he chose.

Ben'or paused for a moment, then without much consideration allowed his eyes to rest on Arlene. "My place is by Arlene's side," he said simply.

Joel noticed Arlene's eyes get a little watery as he moved the meeting on. There were a few minor details to iron out and then the meeting wrapped up promptly.

"Ok folks, we leave in twelve hours. Let's make sure we all get some good rest tonight. We'll meet at the ships at 0800."

The team got up and scattered, leaving Molly and Joel with Clor and Kitcher.

"I'm sure you have preparations to make, Ms. Bates," the Admiral said congenially. "Kitcher and I will head back to our ships and we'll look forward to accompanying you into battle in the morning."

"Of course. And thank you again for doing this," Molly responded. She started to move forward to shake hands with the pair, then remembering her damaged shoulder and bruised hand, stopped suddenly and bowed. Joel did the same before they accompanied their new friends out of the conference room and back to their transport ship where Trev'or and Ruther were already waiting with a stack of pizza boxes each.

The Admiral glanced at their strange packages.

"Gifts," Ruther explained simply. "From our new friends."

The Admiral raised one eyebrow.

"They're food. That's all," Trev'or explained a little further.

The Admiral sniffed at one stack, cocked his head approvingly and then beckoned for the two warrior-technicians to follow him on board.

"Until tomorrow, Molly Bates," he called over his shoulder as he climbed the ramp to their transporter ship.

Molly smiled as she waved. "You know," she told Joel, "I do believe Paige has just single-handedly established pizza as a new upcoming food in the Zhyn Empire."

Joel chuckled. "And to think, Giles missed this cultural transfer phenomenon completely."

She sighed. "Yes. I suspect his mind has been on other things recently." The pair waved as the transporter ramp retracted with the Zhyn crew on board and seconds later they were lifting into the air with a roar of their engines.

Molly and Joel ambled back across the hangar deck toward the steps for the safe house. "I'm sure it will all go well," he said reassuringly. "No one has anything to worry about..."

"I hope you're right," she replied, her voice clearly trying to mask the degree of anxiety she was actually experiencing.

"Of course, you know what the big question is in all of this," he added.

"No?"

"Whether those pizzas Paige sent the guys home with are meat or vegetarian..."

Molly sniggered despite the intensity of the situation that loomed ahead of them.

CHAPTER ELEVEN

<u>Bailey Residence, Estaria</u>

Arlene and Ben'or wandered into Arlene's apartment.

"That was a much longer day than I was expecting," Arlene admitted peeling her atmojacket off and sitting down on the sofa to untie her boots.

Ben'or stood, exhausted, in the middle of the living room, thinking for a moment. He glanced around. "Anne?" he called.

No answer.

He headed further into the open plan arrangement, looking around. "Anne?" He called again.

"She's probably got her music on," Arlene offered wearily.

Ben'or disappeared into the bedroom corridor, calling for Anne.

Arlene slumped back on the sofa. "How about I open a bottle of something?" she called through to him.

Ben'or came back through, his boots tapping heavily on the wooden floor. "Anne's not here," he reported, the concern weighing heavily in his voice.

Arlene hauled herself back into an upright position. "You're fucking kidding me!" She rolled her eyes in frustration. "That girl... She'll be the death of me."

Ben'or frowned. "You don't seem that worried."

"Oh, she's done this before. Turned up on the ship, no less. Only found her when it was too late to take her back." Arlene stood up with her hands now on her hips. She took a breath, her voice lower now. "You know," she said slowly, "I wouldn't put it past her to pull the same stunt again."

She pulled up her wrist holo and started typing.

Ben'or watched. "What are you doing?"

"Calling the base."

The call connected. "Hey, Paige. Bad news. Anne has gone missing. Yes, again. I think she may be trying to get on board one of the ships so that she can come with us..."

There was a pause as Arlene listened to the other side of the call.

"Yeah. That's a good idea. Tell me... did Brock end up finding a way to stop her from melting herself out of the camera images?"

Ben'or's eyes widened as he watched Arlene. He caught her eye. She shook her head at him as she listened.

Then she sighed. "Ok. We'll give it half an hour before we come back up. Goodness knows how she could have pulled this one off. Although... wanna put a tracker on the other pod we had down here? Yeah, I'll wait."

Arlene wiped her hand over her graying skin. Her eyes showed how exhausted she was feeling now. "They're tracking the other pod. The one we'd left down here. Won't take a second."

Ben'or nodded, perching on a nearby chair at the dining table, an expression of deep concern in his eyes.

"Yes, yes, I'm here," Arlene pipped up again. "Oh, well that kinda narrows it down. Yes, ok. We'll stay here for the time being then. Keep me posted? Thanks, Paige."

She disconnected the call and closed the holoscreen, before

slumping back down onto the sofa and covering her eyes with her hands.

"What's happened?" Ben'or asked gently.

Arlene took a deep breath. "By the sounds of it, it's most likely that she's headed up to the base. That pod is back on Emma's holodeck, so we can guess she's back there. Probably."

"Probably?"

"Well, it turns out the Zhyn transporter also went back out to rejoin the fleet. So it's possible she hitched a ride on that."

Ben'or chuckled. "Well, she is quite the adventurer."

"You have no idea."

Ben'or smiled. "So, what's the plan?"

Arlene sank back into the sofa she had perched on. "Paige suggested we hang here for now and try and get some rest. She'll see if she's on the base or any of the ships, and if they don't locate her they'll let us know and we can head on up to help. But she was keen that we take advantage of the downtime we have before we have to go."

Ben'or grinned. "Is she now? Well, in that case..." He wandered over to the wine rack and pulled off a bottle. "I think it would be irresponsible to ignore her suggestion."

Arlene shook her head smiling. "You're right. I'm sure Anne is fine. I'll get some glasses," she added getting up with a seemingly renewed energy now.

Safehouse, Gaitune-67

Giles was on his way out of the kitchen, mocha in hand, when he felt his wrist buzzing. Careful not to spill his mocha he glanced down and saw it was a group message from Oz.

ALL PERSONNEL BE ALERT. ANNE MISSING AND ASSUMED ON BASE.

...

...

...

YES. AGAIN.

Giles exhaled strongly, shifted the antigrav mug into his other hand, and then scrolled down the rest of the message to read the details of what they knew. Then he hit to connect a voice call with Oz.

"Hey, Oz."

"What's up G-man?" Oz replied through Giles's audio implant.

"Anne, by the sounds of it. Is anyone checking the ships?" he asked, recalling the last time she had disappeared, and thoroughly embarrassed him by stowing away on *The Scamp Princess*.

"Yes. Crash and Brock are down there already. They're going to check *The Empress* just as soon as they've finished what they're working on."

Giles nodded grimly. "Ok. I'll head down there and give them a hand."

"Ok thanks, Giles. I'll let them know."

"Sure. Anything I can do to help." He turned around with his freshly brewed mocha and headed back into the kitchen. No point in trying to carry it around with him. He'd have to warm it up later.

He placed the mug down next to the machine, and reluctantly turned and headed out again. Crossing the open plan common area through to the foyer he stopped suddenly and listened.

There was a faint muffled whimpering sound, like someone trying not to be heard.

His brow furrowed as he listened more closely.

"Neechie?" he called gently.

Nothing.

Then a sniff.

"Hello?" he called, spinning around 360 degrees to try and figure out where the sound was coming from.

There were a shuffle and a thunk. He glanced all around him trying to figure out where the movement was coming from.

"Anne? Is that you?" he called.

No answer. And then another faint thunk. He looked up. There was an air duct.

"Anne?" he called again. "Are you in the air duct?"

He waited, straining his ears. "Maybe," a little voice replied.

Giles stood up straight and stopped craning his neck. "Anne. Are you ok?"

No answer. Then another sniff.

"You're crying?"

"Maybe," the muffled voice replied again.

Giles's tone shifted. "Anne. For goodness sake. You've got the whole team looking for you." He tapped on his holo to alert Oz, then he softened his voice. "How did you get in there anyway?"

"Through the vent behind the common room."

Giles lifted his voice to the duct above him. "How about you come back down and we can talk?"

There was no answer, but he could hear a shuffling just a little further down the duct like she had begun moving.

He hit his holo. "Oz?"

"Yep."

"I've found Anne. She's with me. You can call off the search."

"Ok. Good. Thank goodness for that. Arlene and Ben'or were about to mount a search too. I'll let everyone know."

"Thanks, Oz."

The shuffling and thunking had become louder and moved along the duct into the open plan common area. Now the noise was sliding down the far wall, beyond the holoscreen and back sofa. Giles watched in anticipation before realizing that she was going to emerge from the vent somewhere on the other side. He rounded the common area to watch the dead space between there and the foyer. Sure enough, a few moments later a rather grubby and dusty-looking Estarian adolescent emerged from the vent. She dusted off her head and face, dropping big globs of dirt on the floor, then turned and bent down in front of the vent and replaced the cover she had kicked out of the way.

Giles stayed where he was so as not to crowd her. "So..." he said, by way of opening. "What's going on?"

She turned around and her face was all smeared with dirt and tears.

She had tried to stop herself from crying as she crawled out, but now, another tear escaped from her left eye. "It's all my fault. Arlene said this would happen. That I was a transmitter for something dangerous."

Giles was by her side in an instant, wrapping his arms around her now. She didn't try and stop him. In fact, for a change she moved in and leaned into the hug. "I'm sorry. I tried not to be bad. I didn't want any of this to happen. I'm..."

"Hey. Hey. It's not your fault. Not at all. Even if you were the antenna, you were only doing what we asked you to. And there is nothing bad about you. Your powers, your skills are incredible. They represent the next stage of Estarian evolution. You're a shining example."

"That just happens to get us all killed," she retorted. Her eyes were all screwed up and dirt streaked down her face.

"That would only be the case if those aliens are out to kill us... But I very much doubt they are. If my theories are correct these were the people who put us on these various planets. If anything, we think they're looking forward to meeting us. Think about it..."

He peeled her off him so he could look at her. "If they were intent on killing us they could have done that already. They could have completely wiped us out at any point in history. Instead, they planted clues for us to go out and *find* them. They gave us the tools and information only when we had people with specific skills and abilities. Like you. Like Molly. Like Bethany Anne.

Anne's crying had stopped, and now she was merely sniffing.

"Come on," Giles said, standing up. "Let's get you a tissue from the kitchen." He took her hand and led her back through to the safe house kitchen.

"Remember," he told her as they walked. "We went out looking for the talismans and put the puzzle together. We all made the decision to pursue this: Molly. Bethany Anne. Everyone was on board. You were just one small piece of the puzzle. And you did great."

"But why?" Anne protested. "Why are they coming?"

Giles shrugged. "I'm not sure. To see what we've become probably. To help if they can. To let us in on their secrets... maybe."

"So they're definitely not coming to kill us?"

"I very much doubt it."

Giles sat her down at the table in the kitchen and handed her some damp kitchen roll. He found a clean mug and started making her a hot drink from the machine, then he disappeared into the pantry for a moment. He returned with a big cheesy grin. "Marshmallows?"

Anne grinned and nodded silently.

Giles finished making the hot chocolate in silence, piled it up with marshmallows and dumped it in front of her.

"Now," he said, gently but seriously, "a bunch of us are going off to check out this new fleet. Say hello and all. But I need you to stay here and look after Paige and Maya. They have a tendency to worry. And to drink too much. I need you here to stop them from doing that, and to reassure them when they get all... well, you know. You think you can do that for me?"

Anne thought for a moment. She didn't have the energy to protest about being left behind. "Can I drink with them then?"

"Hell no. Unless you're drinking water or tea."

"That's not fair!" she protested, her teenage will and spunk slowly returning.

"I know. Life is incredibly unfair. But the last thing they need is you drinking and not being able to control your powers. Eh?"

"Yeah. Ok. But when you and Arlene get back can I have a drink?"

Giles grinned and patted her shoulder. "When all this is over I'll take you drinking myself," he said, picking up his own mocha. "Well," he added, tilting his head, "maybe we'll start you off with a beer in a confined space where you can't set anything on fire. Or surge the electricity. Or break anything."

Anne sighed, and rolled her eyes, already looking more like her old self as she sipped her liquefied marshmallow drink with hot chocolate in it.

Giles stood watching her carefully, a new thought formulating in his mind.

Molly's Conference Room, Safe House, Gaitune-67

Giles wandered back down the corridor from escorting Anne back to her room so she could get cleaned up and rest.

Something had been nagging at him about Anne. He wasn't sure. It was still a theory... but if it was correct the implications could be dire.

He strode down the corridor, his boots squeaking against the polished floor. He thought briefly about how loudly they announced his arrival. But most of the crew were out on the base, making things ready for their departure the next morning. But then he noticed a light on in the conference room. Molly's conference room.

And the door was slightly ajar.

He was about to walk past it when he hesitated. Then stopped dead.

Molly turned around from her normal seat, where she would have her back to the door to avoid distractions.

He should say something, he thought to himself. He should share his concerns before it was too late.

She smiled. She looked tired, like she had been working solidly. He moved toward the door. "Hey. You got a minute?" he asked gently.

"Sure," she beamed. "Come on in." She had been sitting on one leg, studying the data on several different holoscreens. Now with a visitor, she dropped her leg down and relaxed back in her chair as if welcoming the break.

Giles wandered around to the corner of the table and sat down, placing one arm on the table edge. "I'm... not sure how to tell you this Molly. But, I didn't want to wait until it was too late."

He searched her face for a reaction. Nothing. She was just listening patiently, from all he could tell.

"It's Anne." He paused. "I just found her hiding in a ventilation duct because she was worried it was her fault that The Ascension Race was coming this way."

Molly frowned ever so slightly. "Well, it's not her fault. But she was a part of it."

Giles nodded and waved his hand, trying to get to the point. "Yes. I've tried to console her, and she's ok for now. But while we were talking something occurred to me. How do the ARs know where to find us?"

Molly thought for a moment. And then smirked, with genuine humor.

Giles sat up, bewildered by her reaction. "What?"

"ARs? You're going with that?"

"Well, in the absence of a better idea. You have something better?"

Molly tried to put her face straight, and not mock him. "No. No. We'll go with ARs until something better comes up."

Giles took a deep breath. "Anyway, my point... They seem to know where we are. But how?"

"Well, we're assuming they remember where they dropped the samples that created the Estarians."

"Well, then we'd expect for them to have folks showing up at all the sites where they made DNA drops. Like Earth. Like Zhyn…"

Molly frowned more deeply now. She shook her head. "No. We would have heard about it by now."

"Maybe. Maybe not. But it begs the question; if they're locked onto us… how are they finding us?"

"Well, we're all together, apart from…"

"Bethany Anne and Michael. Yes. But we have no way of knowing where they are or what they're facing."

"True. Though if the ARs are able to track through the etheric I'm sure they'll have a lock on them."

Giles clicked his fingers. "Yes. If they're tracking through the ether. However… Remember what Arlene said about the antenna…"

Molly's mouth dropped open. She covered it with her hand. "You think they're tracking Anne?"

Giles sighed, slowly, bobbing his head gently. "That was what had crossed my mind."

Molly sat gazing at the table for a few moments.

"I don't think she's in danger," Giles added. "If anything, I think she's just the homing beacon to get them into the vicinity of the rest of us. They must understand that we're a social species and will keep our own close by. And if we're solving the puzzles and everything that was required of us in order to do that, they must be able to make certain assumptions about our desires to protect each other."

Molly closed her eyes and shook her head. "I was so fixated on all the other moving parts… the trouble on Estaria, having to speak to these aliens… I completely missed it."

Giles grinned his cockiest grin. "And that's why you keep the A-team close!" He winked at her playfully.

She snorted lightly, amused. "It's a good thing modesty doesn't suit you, anyway."

"Huh?"

"Never mind. Ok, so if this is the case, we want Anne with us on that ship tomorrow. Not out here, telegraphing the location of the population."

Giles took his glasses off and started cleaning them. "You don't think as a precaution we should send her away? Like to another system? Or dead space or something?"

Molly frowned. "Why would we do that? Like you said, these guys aren't looking to harm anyone, right? I just think our best bet is to have her with us... in case we need her to get their attention or communicate or something."

"But just in case?"

"Are you doubting your theory now? Now that it comes down to Anne's safety?"

"No, no... Not at all—"

"Besides, we've nothing else with gate technology so even if we did scoot her out of here we can't get her far enough away."

"Except we do have *The Scamp Princess*," Giles added quietly.

"With a newly evolved AI, who needs more monitoring and is by no means battle-ready at this point." Molly eyed him carefully. "Plus, if the AR's technology is anything like what we have already seen, they will have already seen the signs of the civilizations."

Giles bobbed his head and replaced his glasses. "Yeah. Right. I guess that's a fair deduction. Besides, I'm sure Anne will be happier about not being left behind."

There was a quiet in the room for a moment as the two brainiacs considered their options.

"You know... it's still entirely possible they're tracking yourself, Arlene and indeed Bethany Anne," Giles reminded her.

Molly took her finger from her lips. "You're right. I'll warn the General. Have him get a message out... just in case."

The pair talked some more, and decided to just have Anne come along without having to let the others know about the thoughts they'd been having about her role in it all. "After all," Molly concluded, "it's not as if we've any new evidence. This is all just conjecture at this point."

"True. I'll let Anne know she can come with us in the morning," Giles agreed quietly.

Sean stood quietly outside the door, pressed against the wall, listening to every word. He'd been coming back from the kitchen in his socks and had seen Giles disappear in to talk with Molly.

As he heard the meeting come to an end he crept back toward the double doors and came through them noisily, glass of milk in hand.

He waved as he wandered past, drawing a nod from Giles before he disappeared out of view down the corridor.

CHAPTER TWELVE

Senate House, Spire, Estaria

"Were we not in agreement that this was to be a joint decision?" Bulin asked pointedly, eyeing the Estarian senate warily from the Oggs' side of the table. "While we understand the inclination to get jumpy when presented with an external threat like this, the fact of the matter remains that we agreed to act as one." His tone was getting harder as he spoke. he paused, took a breath, and slowly let it out. "The agreement was not for the Estarians to decide to launch the fleet at the slightest provocation."

The Estarian Speaker lifted his hands in a placating gesture, and Bulin fell quiet reluctantly.

"Our approach is...unconventional," the Speaker acknowledged silkily, folding his hands on the table. "But we don't have time to debate this when there could be an invasion force on the outskirts of our system."

"There *could* be," Bulin stressed. "But we don't know. We know there are ships, but not why. If you go flying off half-cocked, you could inadvertently be declaring war and giving us an enemy we know nothing about."

Ekks watched them go back and forth and drummed his fingers on his knees.

"What would you suggest?" the Speaker asked, considerably less silken. "We can scarcely control our people at this point. They're all getting antsy, and a lack of action on our part isn't helping matters at all. If we don't do something, we're going to be facing riots in the street."

"Perhaps you shouldn't have gone out of your way to inundate them with the news," Bulin suggested, deceptively pleasant. "They've been surrounded by the news like a swarm of flies, and they've had nothing else to think about. Of course they're getting jumpy."

"Spelling it out doesn't actually do anything to remedy the matter," the Speaker reminded him flatly.

"No," Bulin agreed. "But it does make it clear that it was your fault and your mistake." He paused and sighed, head hanging for a second as he rubbed his forehead. "I'm saying this as your ally," he continued once he straightened up again.

Ekks's hands curled into impatient fists against his thighs.

"Making another mistake isn't going to fix the first one," Bulin continued. "You're acting rashly and trying to break an agreement that both of our worlds agreed on for good reason. I don't think you've thought through the consequences of this, and frankly—"

The room fell silent as Ekks got to his feet, slamming his hands down on the table. The sound reverberated through the room like thunder. Slowly, all eyes turned to him.

"This is a military threat," he stated, his voice low and terse. "It is a military decision. As such, we will be doing what we need to do to succeed, regardless of how much you would all like to dither and clutch your pearls."

He pushed himself away from the table then turned, and left the room, his steps hurried and purposeful. The door hissed closed quietly behind him, but it could have been as loud as a gunshot in the silence of the boardroom.

Aboard *The Empress*, Base Hangar Deck, Gaitune-67

Molly watched as Arlene and Ben'or escorted Anne onto the ship. It looked like Anne was over anything that was bothering her the previous evening as she chattered away as Ben'or listened patiently.

Giles had already boarded three times. Each time he had forgotten something, like a talisman, or a star map... and then something personal that he didn't explain in passing.

Now Molly stood talking to Paige and Maya as she watched the last checks being made.

"You're sure you're going to be ok?" she asked Paige.

"Of course," Paige told her, almost as if she were trying too hard to allay any concerns Molly might have. "We've run point from here a million times. We know what we're doing."

Molly sighed and looked her friend in the eyes. "Look, we're probably going to be back pretty soon.... And there's probably nothing to worry about, but I don't think I say this enough, and... I just want you to know..." She looked down at her feet. Despite all the progress she had been making with the emotional touchy-feely stuff, it still looked like she was struggling.

Paige held her hands. "Hey, Molly, it's ok."

When Molly looked up her eyes were watery and filled with concern. "But just in case... I need you to know... you've been the best friend a girl could hope for... And what with all your other things, and what you've done for this team... You're an inspiration."

Paige teared up too. "Oh, Molly. Stop. Everything is going to be fine. You're going to come back soon and we'll beat whatever the bad stuff is that's going down and then we'll kick back with pizzas and margaritas, just as we always do."

Molly nodded, her eyes down at their clasped hands. She squeezed them tight then hugged Paige. Then Maya. Without another word or any eye contact, she hurried off down the side of the ship to get on board too.

Paige and Maya stood watching, their arms around each other. "It will be fine," Maya said quietly. "This is just routine."

Paige gave her a sideways glance, her humor returning through the anxiety. "Now you've gone and jinxed it!" she teased.

The girls giggled and pulled each other back away from the ship that was about to take off.

Onboard there was a flurry of activity as the team stowed away the last of their baggage and took their seats. Brock and Pieter were in the cockpit along with Crash. Pieter was manning numerous holoscreens as well as a bunch of functions that he'd routed through one of the main control consoles from the back of the cockpit. Brock sat in his usual seat as copilot, mostly there just to back up Crash and Emma who tended to have everything under control.

Crash finished his pre-flight checks and with a quick look to Brock who returned his glance with a nod, flicked the open channel to the comms for the ship.

"Ladies and gentlefolk. Welcome to Zhyn Airways. This is your captain speaking. We will be leaving in just a few moments now. As you will see as we exit the hangar today's flight is being accompanied by our brothers-in-arms, a certain set of quote, unquote, 'mercenaries,' who may or may not be on loan from the Zhyn Empire... depending on who you talk to and whether they're a part of the Federation or not."

He paused, and there were mutterings and chuckled through the lounge area.

"We will be cruising at an altitude of a zillion feet, at a land speed of Light times three... or thereabouts. We will refrain from gating on this occasion on account of not wanting to leave our escorts behind, but if the need arises we will still have that capability intact."

The ship was already midair about to pass through the opening hangar doors. "Please keep your hands and arms inside the carpet... aaaaaaaand, we're out of here."

The ship whooshed through the hangar doors, slap bang into the middle of the waiting Zhyn fleet outside.

All of a sudden, the forward motion was arrested.

"Hang on," Crash muttered over the audio. It switched off, leaving the lounge in a strange silence.

Molly looked out of her window. Joel had moved and sat next to her. He peered out too. "You think he's got this?" he asked.

Molly chuckled lightly. "I hope so. It's not a complicated plan to fly in formation from here to the outer system."

Joel smiled. "Yeah. I might go and make sure everything's ok."

Joel shuffled out of his seat and headed up to the cockpit.

"Everything all right in here?" he asked arriving to hear Crash talking over the external comms.

Brock swiveled round in his chair. "Yeah. It's fine. They're playing at being Canadian," he joked, rolling his eyes.

Joel frowned. "Come again?"

Pieter joined the conversation. "It's an old human expression from Earth," he explained. "Basically, Crash was going to allow the Admiral to go first, and the Admiral's people - Trev'or and Ruther said, *no please, after you, friend*. They've been back and forth on it a few times," he added quietly as if confiding in Joel.

Joel scratched his nose disguising that he tried to wipe his face in despair. "And what did we decide?" he asked, a hint of sarcasm creeping into his voice.

Brock interjected. "Hey, this is an important piece of protocol. How we treat our allies is a reflection of who we are. We don't want to offend the Admiral... and I for one am extremely grateful that the Zhyn are here backing us up after no one else was going to!"

Joel sighed and glanced at Pieter for a real answer.

Pieter rolled his lips before answering. "They're going together. Side by side. We're just waiting for the Admiral's ship to adjust his course and we'll be going."

"Ok. Thank fuck for that," Joel muttered, turning on his heels and heading back to the lounge. "I was beginning to think we had a problem..."

His boots clunked down the stairs as he disappeared from the cockpit.

Pieter and Brock exchanged looks as if Joel was the crazy one, and then shrugged before returning to their checks.

Joel returned to the lounge to find Giles had taken his seat next to Molly.

He felt a flash of irritation but knew there was more on the line than anything that may or may not have happened between the two.

Besides, he rationalized to himself, *he's probably boring her to death about some talisman theory or other.*

He put his thumb up to tell Molly everything was ok, just as the motion of the ship seemed to shift and move again. Molly nodded to him and returned the thumbs up.

If she wanted him to rescue her, she was going to have to make it obvious, he decided, *sitting down on one of the chairs near the front of the cabin.*

"So, you think what?" Molly asked.

"Well, it's kinda threatening to show up with a whole army behind us, don't you think?" Giles posed.

Molly frowned. "It's not even a full fleet— twenty ships remember."

"Well, all I'm saying," Giles was looking agitated and nervous, "is that it's just a little overkill if we're expecting this to be a friendly coming together of two new species. I mean, if someone showed up to talk to you, with reinforcements and weapons out, wouldn't you think that there was something wrong with the picture. You know... that maybe their intentions weren't as pure as they were saying."

"Giles, it's just a bit of strategic backup. Just in case."

Giles took his glasses off and pinched his eyes. Then he sighed. "I... I guess."

Molly lowered her voice and leaned in. "Look. I understand. And if it were just you, me and them in the middle of a desert, I'd be all for showing up unarmed. But it's not. When they showed up at the edge of the Sark System they pulled the whole Estarian, Ogg and Teshovian alliance into it. That's three civilizations. And the Federation... which is goodness knows how many different species, jurisdictions and lives. You and I have our values, but there is such a thing as being responsible to other people."

Giles's shoulders slumped. "I just hope it doesn't telegraph to them that we want to start a war," he muttered as he slipped out of his seat.

Molly grabbed his arm, and he paused. "Look. I know you're anxious. I am too." She glanced around the cabin to see all her teammates sitting uncharacteristically quietly. "Everyone is. But this is going to go down fine. We just have to keep our nerve and stay cool, ok?"

Giles suddenly looked embarrassed. He ran his hand through his hair and glanced around to see if anyone was watching him. He nodded and Molly let go of his arm, allowing him to stand up and shuffle back to his seat.

Molly put her head back on her headrest and closed her eyes.

You're worried he's right.

Like I said, taking half a fleet to a meeting isn't my first option. But I don't know what else we should be doing.

Well, there's nothing to do now. As long as they keep to the plan, stay back and don't open fire, everything should be ok.

After all, that satellite data Mom sent over indicated they had several ships in the fleet.

Oz?

Yes?

She's not your *mom.*

Well, she is yours.

Yes. But you don't get to call her Mom. It's... creepy.

All right. Man... you're so...

I know.

Anyway, all I was saying is, I don't feel like we're bringing a nuke to a knife fight.

Good to know...

CHAPTER THIRTEEN

Aboard *The Empress*, Outer Sark System

"Molly, you're probably going to want to see this..." Crash's voice in her audio implant woke her from her own thoughts. She looked around the cabin. Everything was still quiet with a tension that was palpable.

"Ok, coming," she responded, hitting her holo to acknowledge his request before scuffling up and past Joel who was dozing next to her.

She headed through the lounge and into the cockpit to see Crash putting the outside view on the main screen ahead of them.

Her breath caught in her chest as a shot of adrenaline released into her system. "Wow..." she whispered under her breath.

Not quite like anything we've ever seen before.

You can say that again.

"Boss?" Crash asked her quietly without turning around. "We're in position. What do you want us to do now?"

Joel appeared at her right elbow. "Holy fuck..." he whispered under his breath.

"I know, right?" Brock chimed in, his eyes fixated on the

screen. Pieter was silent, his eyes also glued to the image ahead of them, as if entranced by some sort of magic.

A single AR ship filled the screen, almost overwhelming the cameras and the viewers.

"Is there any way to pan out?" Molly asked.

"Negative," Crash replied. "We're already panned out as much as possible. These ships are humongous."

"Makes you wonder why the outer satellites didn't get a better read on them," Joel muttered, almost to himself.

Molly logged the observation. "So how many of them are there?" she asked.

Crash shrugged. "We can't get a real count. But here's an image off the starboard side. He pulled up another screen showing a number of similar-looking ships, all strangely organic in shape, like slightly elongated eggs bent at the front end of their length."

It was difficult to see the surface detail. It was almost as if their eyes couldn't focus on it, or that it kept shifting and changing.

Molly squinted, trying to make sense of what she was seeing. "Can we clean up the image?"

Emma responded promptly. "I've been trying to. It's not straightforward. It seems the ARs have some kind of forcefield that is preventing us from getting a lock on any of the details... visual or otherwise."

Pieter, frowning, scratched his head and stood up. "ARs?"

Brock grinned. "Shouldn't it be T-A-Rs?"

Joel moved closer to the screen as if he were going to try and touch it. "Tars?"

Brock shook his head absently, his eyes still fixated. "*The* Ascended Race," he explained.

"Ah, yes, he has a point," Pieter agreed, also as if he were half distracted by what was in front of them.

Joel rolled his eyes. "You were saying, Emma?"

"I can't get a read on them," the onboard EI explained. "There are moments when their fields fluctuate where I find it difficult to even get a lock on them."

Molly found herself short of breath and then started to breathe deliberately. She realized she'd been so absorbed with the new information she had forgotten to breathe. "It's so hard to judge their size out here. There's nothing to measure them against… Emma… any clues?"

"I got nothing," she replied. "As I said… the fluctuations are almost as if they're designed to stop us getting a lock on anything."

"That explains the satellite having issues," Joel grunted.

At some point, Sean had joined them in the cockpit. "Is this going to interfere with deploying weapons?" he interjected, matter-of-factly.

"Most certainly," Emma responded quickly.

"We should alert the Admiral then," he announced, looking to Molly to relay the order.

Molly shook herself from her trance-like state. "No. Not yet," she said, taking a breath. "No need to cause panic. Plus, we don't want to be firing on them anyway."

Sean frowned, his chest puffing up already. "That isn't the point. They have the right to know."

"In a moment," Molly said, distracted again and taking another step toward the screen. "Let's just hail them and find out what the score is. They know that their first reaction is to retreat at the slightest hint of trouble."

Sean, stood back, arms folded. Karina appeared at the cockpit door and shuffled in next to him, looking concerned about the new development too.

Joel edged forward again, his hands now on the back of Crash's seat as he gazed up at the screen showing the enormous ships towering over them. "You know, we obviously don't stand a chance against these guys," he muttered looking back at Molly.

Molly glared at him for voicing his concerns and worrying the troops even more. "Good thing they're friendly," she said firmly, and almost defiantly. "Crash, open a channel with our pre-recorded messages. Pieter, cycle through them until there is something they respond to."

Joel glanced over at Pieter then back to Molly. "Let's hope that Giles and Arlene have this frequency thing correct and they're not accidentally insulting their mother or something."

Molly shook her head but stood firm, watching the screen, her arms folded across her chest.

Out of the corner of her eye, she could see Pieter deploying the various signals they had pre-agreed on. Nothing changed on any of the screens in front of her that Brock was monitoring.

After several minutes she shifted her weight finally and dropped her arms. "Emma? Are we getting any change?"

"No, nothing," Emma reported over the audio. "No response. No change."

Molly felt her heart sink. "Well, at least they're not opening fire."

Maybe they're not reading the signals, Oz suggested silently in her mind.

Well, what? We need to get closer?

And perhaps drop our own shields. Take out some of the noise, so they can see the signal more clearly.

Like GI Joel and Sean are going to go for that!

I don't know what else to suggest.

Molly thought for a moment. "Brock, let the Admiral know that he needs to fall back 50 km from us. We're going to head in a little closer."

Brock started to protest.

"Look, if anything goes wrong we can gate. They can't."

Brock nodded solemnly and opened a channel to the Admiral's ship to explain the situation.

"Hi, Trev'or... are you reading me? Yeah. We're getting

instructions from Molly. Could you guys move the fleet back by fifty klicks? Yeah? Good. Thanks, man."

A moment later he turned back to her. "Ok. It's done. They're falling back."

Joel eyed him suspiciously. "That's how we're communicating with the other ships?"

Brock smirked and shrugged. "They're friends now. No point in being all formal for no reason."

Joel bobbed his head once, still skeptical.

Molly ignored the exchange and continued with her plan. "When they're done, we're going to drop our shields and move in another fifty km closer."

Brock's eyes flew open. "You're kidding me?"

Molly sighed. "No. No, I'm not. What you must have already realized Brock... and everyone else," she said, spinning around to eyeball Joel and Sean to include them in her explanation, "is that before we even got here we were vulnerable to them. Whether we have our shield or not is obviously not going to protect us from them one iota if they wanted to open fire on us. But with our shields up we may well be masking the signals we are trying to send. So... If we have any hope of making this work then we're going to need to drop our silly illusions and just trust."

"Anyone got a problem with that?" she added, almost as an afterthought.

There was silence in the cockpit.

"Good. Brock, make it so... just as soon as the Admiral and the others are back at their holding position."

"Yes, ma'am," Brock muttered, his fear subsiding, and his courage returning to him under her explanation. He turned back to his console to carry out the instructions.

Sean and Karina quietly slipped out of the cockpit door to confer. Molly stood back against the back wall, watching everything that was going on, marveling quietly at the ships that still filled their screen.

Joel sidled up next to her. "Hey, look... I'm sorry I er..."

"It's fine," she muttered absently.

"No. It's not," he countered. He moved closer. "Look, I think you've got this. And I'm behind you 100%. More than 100%. But just in case anything goes wrong, I just want you to know... I wouldn't have changed this for the world."

Molly snapped her gaze to him. "You mean...?"

"All of it. Even if I could have had a longer life. Even if this is it. I'm glad I followed you. I'm glad I've been a part of this team, and I couldn't think of anyone I would have rather followed to the ends of the galaxy... or into a powerful alien trap."

His gaze was steady.

Molly felt the emotions welling uncomfortably in her chest. She wasn't ready for this. She opened her mouth, but words didn't come out. She tried to speak, but her voice caught in her throat.

Joel nodded as if he understood. Then he hugged her. "It's ok," he whispered. "It's all ok. No matter what."

Molly felt herself slipping into brain fog. It had been a while since she had felt her emotions overwhelm that part of her brain. She had thought she had this emotional, interpersonal relationship thing covered. She thought she had evolved, but at that moment, knowing that they all might die any second, she realized that actually she had just mastered it by avoiding it at a completely different level. She avoided getting close to Joel, then Sean, and actually she was secretly relieved when Sean ended up getting married. Giles... when Giles shut down, it also took the pressure off her.

"We're getting incoming," Brock called, his voice breaking through the emotional fog and distraction.

Joel released her, and Molly moved away quickly, swiping at her eyes.

"It's just a signal?" she asked, glancing at the readings on his screen.

Pieter interjected. "Yep. Interpreting it now, using Arlene's talismans program."

"What's it saying?"

"Give me a minute. It's going to take a few seconds to get a large enough sample and decipher it."

Molly glanced across at Joel, suddenly aware of the gravity in the immediate situation.

Sean and Karina stood close together in the corridor just outside the cockpit. Sean could see the tension on Karina's face. He wanted to alleviate it. To tell her it was all going to be ok. But he couldn't. There was far more going on than she knew.

"Look," he said in his serious, hushed operational voice, "I don't know how this is going to go down, but I don't like it."

She shook her head, glancing nervously at the cockpit door. "Me neither," she revealed. "This is all feeling very reckless. We should be getting out of here. A long way from here."

Sean paused for a moment. "Yes…" he said slowly, choosing his words carefully. "But not for the reason you think. Remember I told you I'd overheard Molly and Giles talking last night?"

"Yes."

"Well, I didn't tell you everything. It wasn't just that they were worried. They were concerned that the aliens are tracking Anne."

"Why Anne? What do you mean?"

"Well, you know she has those special abilities and stuff?"

Karina nodded.

"Well," he continued in a hushed, hurried tone, "it turns out that Arlene has long had a theory that she is some kind of antenna. She practically broadcasts a signal."

"How?"

A shuffle down the corridor momentarily pulled his attention. He glanced behind her, making sure no one was coming in from the lounge. "I'm not sure. It's a part Estarian thing. But I saw some stuff when I was in the Federation. Spooky shit. And I think Arlene might be right."

"So you think the ARs are following Anne?"

"Maybe. In which case, we need to get her well away from this ship, and the Zhyn fleet, and in fact the rest of civilization."

Karina's face set in determination. "What do you need me to do?"

"Go get Anne," he decided. "Bring her down to the cargo bay. We'll take *The Little Empress*."

"Is that going to be fast enough?"

"No. But it will give us a fighting chance. And may save hundreds if not millions of lives in the process."

"Ok." She hesitated. "If you're sure this is the right thing to do?"

"I am." She had never seen this kind of seriousness in his eyes before. Normally he was calm, collected and confident. But there was always a humor behind his gaze. A self-satisfied sense that everything was going to be fine and his cockiness wasn't completely unfounded. But right now, all that was gone. It sent a cold chill down her spine.

She nodded, using her shiver to zip up her own feelings and anxiety about the situation. Then she echoed it by zipping her atmosuit up to the neck. "I'll see you back there in a few," she said decisively.

Then she headed back into the lounge quickly and quietly. Sean waited a moment then turned on his heels and pushed through the narrow door that would take him down the stairs to the downstairs passage as a different route into the cargo hold.

He knew what needed to be done.

Karina glided through to the cockpit, moving as quickly as she dared without alerting the others to the fact that something was afoot.

She casually stopped a few seats further down the lounge from where Anne was sitting. "Hey Anne," she called over. Anne looked up from the holo game she was playing on Jack's holo.

Karina smiled. "You wanna come see the hot chocolate this ship can make?"

Anne glanced up at Jack. Jack gave her a nod, so Anne slipped out of her seat and handed the holoscreen back to her.

Anne quietly followed Karina.

"Hey, young lady!" Arlene called wearily after her.

Anne stopped and doubled back. "Yes?"

"Wanna bring one for me and Ben'or?"

Anne smiled. "Sure," she agreed then trotted after Karina.

Giles sat quietly on the other side of the lounge, the talismans out in front of him. He could see one of the enormous AR ships from the side window and as they approached he had felt the talismans in his case vibrating strangely.

Now with them out in front of him he started to feel a little heady and spacey. He glanced back and saw Anne disappearing into the back of the ship. She seemed to glow in a strange blue light.

He took his glasses off and looked out of the window again. The ships had the same glow around them. He squinted then pinched his eyes as if he could massage the weirdness out of them.

He looked again. There was definitely something going on. And Anne was definitely related to it. He checked the other people in the lounge for a glow. Arlene was glowing a little, but not as brightly. Jack was normal. So was Ben'or.

He shook his head and gathered the talismans up from the table in front of him. He needed to talk to Molly.

Moments later he was striding through the lounge to the cockpit.

Arlene noticed him hustling his way through. She's known him long enough to sense from his demeanor when he was onto something. Quickly she slipped out from her seat and followed him up to the cockpit too.

CHAPTER FOURTEEN

Aboard *The Empress*, Outer Sark System

Giles entered the cockpit, talismans held in his hands, struggling not to drop them.

"I say, there's something—"

Joel turned to look at him. "Not now, Giles. We're in the middle of making contact."

"But... I think this is an important piece of the puzzle" he said, carefully setting the talismans down on the empty console to the left of the cockpit.

Pieter turned his attention pulled. "Are they—"

"Vibrating. Yes."

Molly glanced over at them. "Well, that's not surprising given they're made of ether and programmed by the ARs."

"Hang on," Pieter called over, his attention back on his screen. "Something's happening. The signals coming from them have suddenly increased..."

His eyes widened, and panic rose in his voice. "Shit. It's like they're broadcasting and heating up our sensors... I think they're going to overload us..."

Joel was by Pieter's console like a shot, watching. "Molly, Molly? Should we withdraw?"

There was no answer.

He turned to see Molly standing straight upright and stiff, her eyes fixed on a point in space as if she wasn't even there in her body.

"Molly?" Joel rushed to her and was about to grab her by the shoulders.

"No!" Giles called out. "Don't. Don't touch her!"

Joel felt his hackles go up. He was about to lash out and tell Giles exactly where to go, but Giles talked fast. "She's in a trance. Probably some kind of psychic lock with our friends out there. The talismans, the shields, the frequencies they're communicating on... it's all related."

His speech fell away as he turned to see that Arlene had come through the door and was in a similar state, her body rigid and eyes fixed off in the distance.

"What's happening to them?" Joel's voice rose an octave, the color gone from his face.

"I believe they're communicating," Giles said, suddenly fiddling with his glasses as a crutch to deal with his own processing of the situation.

An eeriness descended in the cockpit as the rest of the crew turned and saw what was going on. Seeing their leader and friend somehow taken with the ARs made them feel instantly powerless.

What if they were being harmed?

What if they were being controlled?

Thoughts raced through each individual's head, each person looking to Joel to make the next decision.

But all Joel could do was stand and watch Molly in horror, her absence distracting him from any sense of rational thought.

. . .

Cargo Bay, Aboard *The Empress*, Outer Sark System

Sean appeared from the weapons room. He was geared up, carrying spares for Karina. He threw her a rifle as he approached, which she caught effortlessly with one hand.

Anne looked at them both. "What's happening?" she asked, her face suddenly tense.

Karina could see the panic in her eyes. She clocked the tension in her legs as she readied herself to run.

"It's ok," Karina cooed in her most casual, calming voice. "We just wanted to have a look at *The Little Empress*. Giles let slip they have the best hot chocolate pods on there."

Anne eyed her suspiciously.

Sean cocked his head to the ship, and the two started to move, ushering Anne along with them.

Suddenly Anne froze and turned to face the front of the ship.

Sean grunted, grabbing at her. "Come on. We haven't got time for this, girlie…"

Karina put a hand on his arm. "Hang on," she warned, looking more closely at Anne's expression. She waved a hand in front of her eyes. She didn't react.

"She's not reacting," Karina reported.

Sean huffed impatiently. "Let's get her on board, then we can deal with her."

Karina stopped him. "No, we can't. What if she's having a seizure? She may need medical help. We need to stay here."

Sean looked around anxiously. "Dammit." He exhaled heavily and shifted the rifle onto his hip. "Ok. Let me tell Emma," he muttered, pulling up his holo. "Emma - this is important. Something is wrong with Anne. She seems to be in a trance."

"It's not just Anne," Emma returned through his audio implant. "Molly and Arlene are in a trance too. Just make sure you don't wake her. There's no telling what might happen."

Sean took his hands off her gingerly. "We're not to wake her, apparently."

Karina sighed her arms folded. "Well there goes that idea then," she said, glancing back at *The Little Empress* that was powered up ready for them to board.

Sean set his jaw. "We're stuck. At least until she wakes up." He explained that the same thing was happening to Arlene and Molly.

Karina looked at him, her eyes wide now, tinted with a deep, knowing sadness. "We're too late. It's begun."

Molly felt her consciousness again as if waking from a sleep, but she was waking up into a dream. It felt familiar for a moment. Like she'd been here before.

And she had, she remembered vaguely: in a dream, not long ago.

Or was it when she was a child?

She couldn't quite recall the details. The feeling had no information attached to it. It was just a sensation that ebbed through her being, like a memory becoming more and more distant.

Then she remembered something else. She was about to face The Ascension Race: the creatures she had wondered about for so long. The ones she had connected with months ago on Giles's harebrained adventure. She remembered that now she stood in front of them... on her ship—in real life. Which wasn't where she was now.

They were huge. She knew that much, even if she couldn't see them. Her mind kept catching glimpses of what they might look like. But she wasn't sure. They had a nebulous, etheric quality and she wasn't sure if she was imagining it or not.

After all, this was a dream. Or a realm jump? Or something. It felt like a realm jump.

Then there was a voice in her head: uncharacteristic, like it was her own thoughts wrapping themselves around concepts and ideas in order to communicate with them.

She couldn't feel her body. She thought she had hands. She could move them… just with the thought of it. She pulled them up to her face… and tried to touch her face. Her head. But they didn't connect with anything.

Bewildered, she started to settle, aware that not only was she without Oz, but she was probably in some altered state. Like a dream, but not.

Her thoughts spiraled. One thing moving her to the next, linking her to another realization or an idea. It was like dreaming when she had been studying hard for an exam when her mind would dance through concepts in only a semi-lucid state, an equation leading to something seemingly unrelated at first but then morphing into a realization that in the waking world would only be classified as genius.

Time had no meaning here. There were no thoughts of others. Just concepts. Ideas. And nebulous realizations.

First she sensed technology. Technology beyond what she could feel her mind could grasp. Abstract ideas which she could understand the fringes of, but not the whole. She thought of harnessing zero-point energy from space itself to deliver free, clean power to their civilization. She saw devices that could teleport matter. She sensed she knew many things. Things that had previously been beyond her grasp because her brain lacked the capacity needed to hold and comprehend the complex ideas. But to try and memorize them all now seemed trivial.

All of it streamed quickly through her mind at once, like a fully sensory movie of what it would feel like to live in a world where all this was known and understood.

It slowed as her attention was directed toward something else. To the beings themselves. She felt like she was in a chamber, speaking with them, only without words.

She felt the presence of Arlene and Anne next to her. They were in awe of what they were experiencing too.

The ARs hovered before them, majestic and wise, but at the same time kind and gentle. And she felt enveloped in a peace and... was it? Could it possibly be love? That sense of complete acceptance for who and what she was? Was that even possible?

She felt them pull her awareness out of her own thoughts where she was getting stuck. They reassured her: *This is real. This is possible. And there is nothing wrong with you that you cannot fully accept this love.*

We have no intention of harming you, or anyone else. We have waited millennia for you to be ready. For you to work together to solve our puzzles and be able to contact us. And you've managed it. You and your family... you have brought us to you and we are grateful for this. We wish to bring everything you have seen to the rest of your people. You are our family. Our people. And we want to end your suffering.

Molly felt herself being released from their grasp and given the opportunity to process her thoughts and feelings lucidly.

"Our people aren't ready for another race," she told them. "They are scared. They want to fight everyone that is not them. They are afraid you're too powerful and you will subjugate them. Or destroy them."

This is why we have been waiting here. For you to come and collect the message: so that you can return to them and show them that we mean them no harm.

"But how am I supposed to convince them of that? Why would they listen to me?"

Because you are Molly Bates. You have helped them. You are known to them.

"I'm supposed to be dead."

You're supposed to be resurrected. You're supposed to lead them to a higher plane where they will one day be ready to receive us. You need to prepare them.

"Ok?" Molly felt her down-to-earth humor returning. She

imagined her teammates around her as a comfort, wise-cracking and being flippant in the face of the enormity.

Yes. Use your team, the ARs told her. She looked to her right and saw Arlene. She reached out her hand and she took it. Arlene nodded, letting her know that somehow it was all going to be ok.

Then Anne reached out and took her other hand. She displayed a look of sheer determination. For a moment Molly questioned how she could ever doubt herself, or the team. Of course, they could do this. Of course, they could make it happen.

We will wait for one hundred of your Estarian days. Then we will follow. You have until then to make them ready.

"Oooohhhhh, hell no!" Molly cried out in her mind, her courage evaporated. "It's too soon! We can't possibly."

You can. Because now you have to. Good luck Molly Bates. The ability is within you.

And with that the envelope of complete peace and comfort started to evaporate away. Molly felt the beings leaving. Withdrawing. She looked at her sides and Arlene and Anne were slipping from her again. She was truly alone.

Everything was becoming harsher and darker, but albeit more familiar.

She felt herself returning to wherever she had come from, her memory of the science and technology and everything she had seen, slipping away with the feeling of warmth that was going away, and leaving her behind.

Cockpit, Aboard *The Empress*, Outer Sark System

"What about Oz?" Joel suddenly blurted out.

Pieter tapped furiously onto his holo.

"Yes, I'm here," Oz reported in over the cockpit holo. "I was trying to reach her, but I can't. It's like I'm blocked out of her synapses. I'm operating only on mechanical pieces at the moment I think… although I'm collecting readings."

Giles's agitation turned to excitement. "Can you share them on screen?"

"Sure." Oz brought up some graphs and telemetries as well as an image of Molly's brain, color-coded and lit up in various areas.

Joel peeled his eyes from her standing body in order to look at the information on the screen. "What does any of this mean?" he asked.

Giles stepped in, peering closely at the data Oz had displayed on the main screen where the image of the alien ships had been just a moment before. "Well, as I understand it," he explained carefully, "Molly, Anne, and Arlene all have some part of their brain developed in such a way that they are ready to communicate with the ARs."

Joel frowned. "How do you mean? Ready?"

Giles took his glasses off cleaning them as if he were a doctor trying to deliver bad news. "As if they had the right hardware, almost. I suppose." He replaced his glasses. "Preprogrammed even."

Joel frowned and looked back at Molly, crestfallen. "What does that mean?"

Giles brightened a little, his intellect obviously taking over. "Well, it's fascinating really. I think it means that they have the mutation or the evolution to be able to communicate psychically. Or Etherically. Or whatever it is. Like Anne has these traditionally Estarian abilities... like Arlene has developed hers deliberately over the decades... and Molly... well, the only thing I can think of is that it's related to her pod upgrade and her housing Oz. We've known for some time that it affected her physiology in a different way, but we never imagined it would give her a direct link like this."

He peered more closely at the data on the screen. "It looks like they're dreaming," he observed. "See this here... this is REM activity - but this here is the cortex, which is lit up like a

Christmas tree."

Joel shook his head. "What does that even mean? What's a Christmas tree?"

Giles snorted lightly. "Sorry. It means that they are seeing things. And here, they're hearing things. And this here is the language center."

"You think the ARs are talking with them?"

"I don't doubt it," Giles responded now with an air of authority he would pull out for the lecture theater.

"Any way of telling what they're saying?" Joel asked.

"No more than if you were dreaming and we could see your dreams."

Brock looked panicked. He shifted around in his chair again. "Wait, that's not possible is it?"

"No, Brock. Not with any equipment we're likely to have," Giles assured with a smirk.

"Well, that's a relief."

Giles shook his head. "We're in the middle of an historic alien encounter and that's what you're concerned about?"

"But how are they controlling her?" Joel interjected.

Giles took a deep breath. "I suspect it has something to do with the field their shields are producing. And the talismans. She only dropped into this state when we brought these pieces of programmed ethe up here."

Joel scowled at him. "When *you* brought them up here, you mean?"

Giles put his hands up defensively and shuffled back half a step. "Hang on... slow down. She's been around these pieces before. A lot. But it's only now when we're trying to reach the ARs and we're in proximity to their ships, that this happens. It's hardly an accident. Plus... for what it's worth, I'm sure she's perfectly safe."

He gestured back at the screen. "None of these readings look like her brain is being overwhelmed... only, it's significantly more active in seemingly disparate areas. But remember, she has this altered physiology now."

"But you said it was lit up like a Chimney Tree?"

"Christmas tree. Yes, but it's ok. It's not enough to over-stimulate her."

Joel's expression softened from fury back to just worry as he turned his attention back to her suspended body.

Pieter and Brock buried themselves in monitoring their various screens, searching for any detail that might suggest they needed to flee... Or anything that might give them more insight into what was happening.

Giles glanced at the communications screens where Pieter was working. "I suspect the frequencies are what triggered the contact. We were trying to reach out to them, repeating back sequences of pulses we found stored on the talismans." His voice trailed off.

Joel frowned. "Frequencies of what? Not the Electromagnetic spectrum?"

"No..." Giles said slowly. "I can only think it's to do with whatever the spectrum is that carries the Etheric field. The same field that Bethany Anne and Michael and others have used with their enhancements. It's really quite fascinating."

Joel narrowed his eyes, noticing a hint of delight in Giles's voice as he relayed the information.

Brock turned around in his console chair. "You think their powers are related to TAR then?"

Giles shook his head. "No. But they're tapping into similar technology. They have to be. Which was why it was one of the hurdles in the talisman quests. They needed us to have acquired some knowledge and use of the etheric before we were ready to meet them."

"Good theory," Joel cut in, "but how does this help us now?"

"I've no idea. How long have they been like this now?" he asked, looking over Pieter's shoulder again.

"Just a few minutes," Oz reported. "Hang on... something's changing..."

Just then Molly's posture changed as if she were released from the trance. Her eyelids started flickering and her posture returned to normal.

Joel immediately held her arms to steady her.

Then Arlene reacted similarly, as if also falling out of the trace. In an instant, Giles was at her side, asking her questions. "What did you see?" he demanded. "What happened? What can you remember?"

Arlene took a few deep breaths and pushed him aside. "Give me a minute," she scolded him.

"Sorry." His voice softened as he realized his faux pas. "Are you ok?"

She nodded, steadying herself on him. He guided her to the nearest console chair and grabbed an antigrav water bottle from Crash's console to give her.

Molly was already relaying the information they had been given.

"It's ok," she explained to Joel and the others. "They're friendly. We need to call off the Zhyn ships. Tell them to head back to Gaitune. It's all ok. But we do have work to do."

She looked anxious. Not like someone who'd had an out of this world experience. But rather like someone who had just had the weight of the world placed on her shoulders.

Joel noticed her expression was similar to that of the last Estarian leader who had been appointed, not hours after the election. It was one of bewilderment and intense responsibility.

Molly couldn't respond. It took her a few moments to be able to hold her attention on what he was even asking her. Eventually she nodded. "I need to sit down in the quiet," she told him.

He nodded, holding her by the arm, and led her out to head back to the lounge while Brock, Crash, and Pieter tried to make sense of their next set of orders.

. . .

Cargo Hold, Aboard *The Empress*, Outer Sark System

Anne's body suddenly relaxed and she stumbled back a step as if her consciousness was released. She blinked her eyes a few times and rubbed them.

Karina, who hadn't been more than a few feet from her lunged forward to help steady her.

"She ok?" Sean gruffed from behind her.

Anne opened her eyes to find herself in the dim lighting, with Sean and Karina looking at her like she had been shot or something.

"What's going on?" she asked. "Where am I?" she asked, surprised to be using her mouth to form words again.

"It's ok honey. We think you were in some sort of Estarian realm-walking trance or something, according to Emma."

Anne frowned, her eyes conveying a sadness. A loss. "Ok," she said simply.

"What's wrong honey? Are you sad?"

Sean had already started moving off toward the *Little Empress*.

"I saw them. The ARs. They're friendly. It was so... pleasant being there. It's... just hard to come back. It's like I was in a good dream."

Karina felt her compassion taking over. She wrapped her arms around the little Estarian and hugged her tightly. "It's ok. You're safe. You're going to be fine. We'll take care of you."

Anne pulled away. "You were trying to take me some-where..." Her expression changed. "You were taking me off the ship."

Karina couldn't find her words.

"But why?" Anne demanded.

Karina held her shoulders firmly. "We have reason to believe that the ARs may have locked onto you. This means that the whole crew and fleet are in danger. We were going to take you somewhere away from them, to protect them. But also, to keep you safe."

Anne's stern confused expression turned to one of determination. "But they're friendly. They're not going to hurt us. They don't want to hurt anyone. Not the Fleet, not the system…"

Sean called from behind them, halfway up the steps to the *Little Empress* cockpit. "We just can't take that chance, little one. Come on. We'll keep you safe."

Karina had gripped Anne by the shoulders now and was poised ready to force her onto the ship.

"NO!" Anne shouted as loudly as she could. The cargo bay vibrated.

Sean glanced around nervously. "Uh oh," he muttered. The loose weapons on the racks and boxes seemed to hum.

"What's happening?" Karina called to him over the rumbling.

Sean exhaled forcefully, irritated but also more than a little anxiously now. "The kid's got superpowers, remember. She can fry circuits and make things explode." He started running down the steps to help Karina. "We've got to get her out of here before it's too late."

"Too late? I'm telling you… they're not going to hurt us!" Anne screamed.

Karina held up her hand as Sean approached. He stopped dead in his tracks, and the vibrations and rattling subsided. "Ok honey. Let's talk about this. Tell us what happened. Help us understand…"

CHAPTER FIFTEEN

Aboard *The Empress*, Outer Sark System

Brock finished up his call with the Admiral's lead ship. "I know man, it was nuts. But it seems like we're in the clear. Ok. Let them know and give me a shout when you're on your way. Thanks, Trev'or." He disconnected their holo line and sat back in his console chair his eyes resting in the distance for a moment as he took a deep breath.

Crash flicked a few more switches, holding the ship in a stationary position as they watched their Zhyn allies reform and head back into the inner system.

"You ok?" he asked quietly watching Brock in his peripheral vision.

Brock let out a low whistle. "Yeah," he said slowly. "Just getting used to my mind being blown. I mean, aliens, man... This is... trippy. And did you see that look in Molly's eye when she was under their thrall?" He glanced over at Pieter who was listening now.

Pieter was nodding but suddenly stopped. "I wouldn't say it was a thrall as such. I mean... it was more like she just wasn't there."

Brock tilted his head, conceding the point. "Yeah. I guess that's what the G-man was saying."

Crash quietly turned around and looked at where she had been standing. "The way Giles was describing it, it sounded more like she was in some kind of dream-state."

Brock's eyes widened as he sighed again, his focus softening as if he were replaying it in his mind's eye. "Yeah... I wonder what it would have been like. Not that I want to know about any of that shit. Scary enough just knowing about it now..."

Pieter smiled. "I'm sure it's not that creepy. It just feels odd because it's new to us. We're not used to communicating with each other psychically, and because she was unable to move around and talk to us we obviously perceive that as a lack of control."

Brock frowned at him. "Hey, when did you get all insightful and stuff?"

Pieter ruffled his hair, embarrassed, and turned his eyes back to his holoscreens. "Oh, you know... You can pick up a lot just from watching people. You know..."

Brock grinned, a glimmer of humor and camaraderie in his eye. He glanced at Crash who winked back at him.

"Well," Crash announced almost deadpan again, "we'll be hovering here another hour or so before we gate back. So we have time for a break. Who wants first shift?"

"I'll take it," Pieter said without missing a beat. "You guys go and stretch your legs. Chill out for a bit."

Crash didn't need telling twice. "Thanks, man," he said, standing up stiffly and stretching his back out. "Love the flying but sitting still isn't my idea of a good time." He ambled toward the door, and Brock followed a moment later.

"Thanks, Pieter," Brock responded. "Hey, can I get you anything from the cabin?"

Pieter shook his head. "Not unless a Yollin brandy is on the cards," he teased.

Brock sniggered. "I think we can do some of that when we get back for sure. It's been one hell of a few days..."

He disappeared through the door after Crash, leaving Pieter to man the monitors and controls.

On Board Glock'stor Ship # 597

The pilot and the navigator kept glancing over their shoulders to the command chair. The engineer on shift, rather than working, was instead simply prodding harmlessly at his workstation and listening to the conversation happening behind him.

The entire bridge was tense, as if the entire crew was waiting anxiously for the other shoe to drop and put them out of their misery.

Admiral Clor paced back and forth across the bridge, until he returned to his seat at the center and dropped into it. Only for a moment, though, before he levered himself right back to his feet and kept pacing. He said nothing, simply holding his communicator to his ear in silence. Any actual contribution from him was evidently unnecessary.

The look on his face suggested he would rather chew his own eyes out than listen to much more of the conversation that he was only nominally participating in. Whether he objected to what he was being told or was simply bored, that was harder to tell. Either one could be potentially alarming, considering a bored Admiral could be just as concerning as an angry one.

Across the bridge, technicians Trev'or and Ruther shared an uneasy glance, only to both duck back to work on their respective terminals when the Admiral shot them a glance, his eyebrows rising with irritated expectation. They didn't speak a word to each other, but it was clear enough that their feelings on the tension were the same.

Eventually, though, whoever was on the opposite end of the line decided to put the Admiral out of his misery and the conversation ended. Clor pocketed his communicator so quickly it seemed like he was worried it might escape, and with a sigh like he had just run a marathon, he dropped down into the command chair again.

"Ruther," the Admiral called after a moment, glancing at him sidelong.

The communications technician snapped to attention, turning his chair halfway around to look at the Admiral. "Sir?"

"Open a command team line," Clor instructed, his weight shifting to one side. "The full command team, across the fleet. It would seem that I have a fleet-wide announcement I need to make."

"Of course, sir," Ruther replied quickly, already turning to face his terminal again. He opened a communication line to the full command team, and patched it into the Admiral's personal communicator. Everyone knew not to ignore anything from the Admiral's communicator. "Ready, sir."

Clor pulled his communicator from his pocket once again. "Fleet Commanders," he began, "this is Admiral Clor. We will be beginning retreat procedures starting now. This is a fleet-wide decision; save for an emergency, there will be no exceptions. However, you are free to consider this the most casual retreat in Zhyn history. As such, there's no need to hurry the matter. In fact, I encourage you to take your time about it. If there are any obnoxiously thorough maintenance checks any of you have been putting off, now is the time to get them over with. That will be all." He hung up the call without waiting to see if there were going to be any questions about the matter, and he shoved his communicator back into his pocket.

Ruther cataloged a few requests for clarification, but on the whole, it seemed that the command team wasn't particularly interested in the 'why' of the matter. But it tallied with the concept of a Zhyn warrior being trained to never retreat, and yet having received their instructions.

"Trev'or?" the Admiral wondered after a moment, gaze panning casually across the bridge again.

"Yes, sir?" Trev'or peered over his shoulder.

"Are there any obnoxiously thorough maintenance checks that we've been neglecting?" Clor wondered, quietly amused as he asked.

"Uh—" Trev'or cleared his throat. "Probably, sir," he replied. "Should I get started on those?"

"You may as well," the Admiral answered. "And Ruther? Filter anything having to do with the retreat to the communicator in my quarters. I can deal with it later."

"Yes, sir," Trev'or and Ruther replied in accidental unison. They shared a slightly disgruntled glance with each other before they decided the moment of synchronicity had been a fluke.

They both turned back toward their terminals to get to work. It had suddenly become a rather busy day.

Cargo Hold, Aboard *The Empress*, Outer Sark System

Anne took a breath between explaining to Karina what had happened and how she'd experienced things. Sean listened intently, all the while trying to weigh the word of a youngster against all his years in military combat.

Glancing down at his holo he quietly tapped a message to Emma to get an update on Arlene and Molly.

Anne and Karina continued to talk. "It was amazing. I could see Arlene there," Anne explained earnestly. "I held Molly's hand. And Molly was worried that we wouldn't be able to tell the Estarians and that they'd start a war then the ARs gave her some more information and she changed her mind!" Her voice was breathy and eyes wide in awe.

Karina was crouched in front of her, looking up trying to understand what had happened. "What information did they give her?" she asked.

"I'm... I'm not sure. All I got was a sense of what was happening..."

Karina glanced up at Sean who was still buried in his holo. "What's happening out there?" she asked, jerking her head toward the door.

He shook his head. "Checks out. Arlene and Molly were both in a trance. They seem ok now. Both are recovering in the lounge."

Karina's brow furrowed. "Maybe we should take her through to the others," she suggested. "Are you sure you're feeling ok?" she asked again, touching Anne's forehead like a mother to a sick child.

"I'm ok. Just tired I think."

The door to the cargo area whooshed open, revealing Jack in a perfect silhouette against the corridor lights. "Ah. There you all are!"

Sean and Karina exchanged awkward glances. Karina stood up and spun around to face Jack.

Jack stepped inside and surveyed the scene. Then she nodded wisely. "You were going to make a run for it," she concluded simply.

Sean started to stammer. "Yes. Er... no. It's not what it looks like..."

Jack raised one eyebrow, her face otherwise motionless. "You mean, you didn't find out that Anne was a beacon and you weren't trying to get her away from the rest of the fleet as fast as possible?"

Sean scratched his head. "Ah, well, then it's exactly what it looks like..." He shifted his feet awkwardly and then looked up at Jack again. "You're er... not going to tell Molly, are you?"

Jack shrugged. "Tell Molly what?" she winked, holding the door open and motioning for Anne to come back inside. Anne trotted over obediently leaving Karina and Joel in the cargo hold.

Sean's hand was still on the back of his head. "Thanks, Jack," he called. Jack waved and allowed the door to close behind her as she and Anne disappeared down the corridor.

"Well, so much for saving the day," Karina sighed, her face relaxing in relief.

Sean dropped his hands to his hips and exhaled slowly. "Yeah..." he said, more than a touch bamboozled.

The ship behind them powered down. Emma came over their audio implants. "I guess you won't be needing the *Little Empress* right now either," she explained.

Sean shook his head. "Nope. We're good. Thanks, Emma."

"Any time," she replied before closing the connection.

"Come on," Karina said. "I think the hot chocolate from that machine really is meant to be the best." She headed toward the door and Sean followed behind her, still not knowing what to make of the situation.

Safe House, Gaitune-67

Paige glanced down at her holo and saw the call coming in. She and Maya were walking back up to the safe house after a long day in the base conference room.

"It's *The Empress*," she said, the weariness of the day evaporating instantly only to be replaced with a strange mixture of hope and anxiety.

She stopped and answered the call. Maya stood next to her watching intently for any hints for what was happening.

"This is Paige," she announced.

"Paige, greetings. It's Pieter. Thought you might appreciate a quick update."

He paused. Paige waited without saying anything. She didn't want to risk missing anything.

Pieter continued. "It looks like the ARs are friendly. They put Molly and Arlene in a trance and gave them information. Joel is debriefing Molly now, so we'll know more soon, but in the meantime we've turned the fleet around. We'll be heading back shortly once the other ships are well on their way back."

Paige clamped her hand over her mouth, her eyes relaxing. "That's… great news," she managed through her fingers. She took a deep breath. Maya picked up on her relief and felt the tension in her neck and shoulders instantly melt away.

Paige suddenly stopped. "Hang on… so what does this mean? Are they still coming this way?"

"I think so. I don't know the full details, but Molly muttered something about needing to get Estaria ready."

Paige's brow furrowed again. "Oh heck. Things aren't great down here. The news circuit is full of all kinds of nonsense and it's looking like that Fleet General Shit-head is going to launch the Estarian fleet no matter what anyone else says."

Pieter's voice sounded concerned. "That's… not good. Well look, hang tight. As soon as we have more details I'm sure Molly will put together a plan. I'll ping this info to Oz just to keep them in the loop and if you hear anything else…"

"I'll holler. Sure."

"Ok cool. Thanks, Paige. It's going to be ok," he told her reassuringly. "We'll see you soon."

The call clicked off.

Paige's concerned expression reappeared on her face.

"What is it?" Maya pressed.

"Well, the bad news is that it is aliens. The ARs, as we expected. The good news is that they don't want to kill us. The other bad news is I think they want to come visit."

Maya clamped her hand over her mouth as Paige had done a few moments before. "What hope have we got? This is going to cause mass panic."

Paige nodded solemnly and continued walking up the stairs to the daemon corridor. "You're telling me. At this point, I'm fresh out of ideas."

CHAPTER SIXTEEN

<u>Aboard *The Empress*, Outer Sark System</u>

Arlene and Ben'or loitered in the privacy of the corridor between the cockpit and the main cabin. Arlene hadn't got as far as the lounge before she started talking to Ben'or in a hushed whisper as he came through to see what had been going on in the cockpit.

Ben'or held her face. "Are you sure you're ok? My ancestors... I shouldn't have let you go up there alone."

"Oh stop," Arlene blushed. "I'm fine. And there was no way any of you could have expected what happened."

"Well, as long as you're ok. Joel said you were both 'taken' or something?"

"Well, yeah, our consciousness at least. I think we just went into a dream state or something."

"Fascinating."

"Yes. It is... and exciting. This was first contact with an alien race! How incredible is that? And I got to be part of it."

Ben'or noticed that as the trance wore off and Arlene realized what had happened to her, her excitement and enthusiasm seemed to build. Right now, as she stood before him he could see the color returning to her blue cheeks and the glow rebuilding in her skin.

She was still a little unbalanced and toppled onto her other leg. He caught her arm. "Are you sure you're ok?"

She tutted him. "I'm fine, you big lug. It's ok. Just a little trancy. Nothing I haven't done in my teenage years… albeit it was drug induced back then. But alien-induced trance… that's one for the books!"

He watched her carefully as if he were monitoring her every bat of an eyelash for any signs of trouble. He was about to lean in to give her a hug when the door to the lounge whooshed open and Giles popped out to join them.

Also full of exuberance.

"Can you believe it?" he gushed. "This is truly first contact! With a more advanced race!" His gaze flicked from Arlene to Ben'or and back again… like a puppy with two toys he wanted to play with but couldn't decide which.

"This new AR race has got to be even more advanced than TOM. I think I can tell Bethany Anne to well and truly suck it now!" His eyes darted off into the distance as if seeing a whole new scene for his life. "All those years, I wasn't a proper archaeologist because they were all class 5 and below civilizations I'd made contact with. How she would look down on me!"

Arlene frowned. "Erm, hang on. I still think that was in your head. She always seems very, well, respectful… considering."

Giles cocked his head. "Considering?"

Arlene had a glimmer of humor in her eye. "Considering you were a bumbling idiot on steroids!" she exclaimed.

Giles looked shocked. His mouth hung open. "I was nothing but smooth and suave, I'll have you know!"

Ben'or chuckled and placed one of his over-sized hands on Giles's shoulder. "I'm sure you were, old boy. I'm sure you were."

"But this is my big break!" he insisted. "Just wait till I tell Uncle Lance. Class 10 at least, these guys were. They have their own language and their technology... to pull off something like this. Absolutely fucking incredible! I can't believe it. Maybe I'm dreaming?" He played at pinching himself, almost on the verge of giggling.

Arlene chuckled to herself. "No, I think that was probably me."

"Well, yes," he agreed, suddenly becoming more serious. "Erm... are you feeling ok?"

"Fine."

"Excellent. We'll do a full debrief in a few. Just need to go and find out what's happening with the whole war on civilization... but then we'll get a full record on what you experienced. Oh, and tests. I'll need to get some tests... monitor your physiology."

"Erm..."

"Don't worry. I'll be back in just a few moments Arlene, then you'll have my full attention," he promised, before disappearing into the lounge to follow up with Molly.

Ben'or stood in the corridor with her looking a little bewildered. "Well, it looks like you've got your next six months mapped out for you!"

Arlene pursed her lips. "No way am I letting him use me as his lab rat again. I've been there before. It wasn't pretty. Come on... Let's go get a drink to celebrate. This is good news. The AR don't have any intention of harming anyone."

Ben'or laughed a hearty laugh. "Sounds like you have your priorities straight," he said following her into the lounge. "This is indeed the best news we've heard all week!"

Ekks's Office, Senate House, Spire, Estaria

The fleet had been launched and it had finally been confirmed for everyone else.

Ekks felt a petty urge to shout '*I told you so*' the next time he saw any of the senators, regardless of the fact that he had slightly extenuating circumstances. He was a professional, though. He would rise above such immature urges.

His holoconsole was active in front of him, just waiting for him to do something. He reached toward it, ready to key in a call when his intercom reminded him that it was there, his secretary's voice pouring from it cheerfully.

"*Commander Ekks, there's a Senator Romero Vero here to see you,*" she informed him pleasantly. "*Shall I let him in?*"

"Go ahead," Ekks returned, one hand still hovering in front of his holoconsole before he slowly lowered it to his desk again. He turned his chair just enough to face the door as it slid open, his eyebrows rising expectantly as Vero stepped in.

"Senator," Ekks offered by way of greeting. "How can I help you? I'm assuming this isn't a social call."

Vero gave the active holoconsole a wary look as if he already knew what was going on. Ekks supposed it was likely that Vero did have some idea.

With a brief shake of his head, Vero drew his attention back to Ekks's face. "Once it was confirmed that the anomaly the satellites picked up was ships, I knew you weren't just going to sit on the information," he replied, his tone faintly accusing. "The rest of the Senate may be content to throw up their hands and let you do as you please, but I thought I might make one last attempt at getting you to see reason."

"Reason?" Ekks wondered, with a patience reminiscent of someone humoring a precocious preschooler. "From where I'm sitting, I'm being perfectly rational, but you have the floor if you'd like to try to correct that assumption."

Ekks's tone was not lost on Vero, whose mouth twisted downwards in sharp distaste. He didn't waste any time bringing it up, though, and instead launched straight into his objections.

"We know it's a fleet of ships," he acknowledged, stepping closer to Ekks's desk and gesturing to the holoconsole. "But we don't know who or why. For all we know, it's not an actively hostile force but you could be launching us straight into war by launching the fleet. Or it *could* be a hostile force, but we still know nothing of their capabilities. For all we know, they could wipe our fleet off of the star charts, leaving us helpless for whatever they decide to do after that and any future threats that will undoubtedly come along."

He was pacing back and forth in front of Ekks's desk by the time he finished speaking, though he came to a halt as he finished saying his piece.

He looked at Ekks warily, waiting for a response. The resignation hiding in the furrow of his eyebrows and the tightening of his jaw made it clear he already had some idea of what that response was going to be. Considering that, Ekks supposed his determination was almost respectable.

Almost.

Ekks regarded him silently, then without a word to acknowledge any of what Vero said, Ekks lifted a hand and keyed in the call on his holoconsole. It took some time before every branch of the call went through, the screen segmented itself so Ekks found himself looking at every other member of the Senate.

"Good evening," he greeted silkily, folding his hands on his desk. "My apologies for such an abrupt call, but as the Commander of the Estarian-Ogg Space Fleet, I've come to a very important decision."

Vero slammed his hands down on the desk, intruding into the call as he hissed, "Commander! You have a responsibility to your people. Have you even thought about that at all?"

Ekks waved him off with a dismissive flick of his wrist, though he didn't bother to make a fuss when Vero refused to step back.

"I assure you," Ekks sighed, glancing at Vero sidelong but with the bulk of his attention on the call, "I have the system's well-being at the top of my list of priorities. Are you quite certain that's why you're so against this?"

The Speaker sighed, tenting his fingers in front of his chin. "We all know what it is you've been chomping at the bit for, Commander," he pointed out blandly. "You may as well just come out and say it already."

Vero's hands curled into fists. "Commander—"

Ekks didn't give him the chance to interrupt any further than that. "As the Commander of the Fleet," he began once again, pitching his voice just loud enough to drown out Vero's, "I have decided that it is within the system's best interest that I launch the fleet. I'm sure you all have your own thoughts on this matter, but just know in advance that my opinion will not be swayed."

Slowly, Vero stepped back from the desk, stiff as a wind-up doll. He dragged his gaze to the holoconsole, watching everyone else with slowly rising dread. Though Ekks tried to stay professional, he couldn't quite restrain the small, unpleasant smile that curled one corner of his mouth. Vero's expression grew only more pinched when he noticed it.

The Speaker drew in a breath until his shoulders rose, and he let it out. "You're certain?" he asked, sounding exhausted already. None of the other senators said a word. Once it was clear that no one else was going to speak up, Vero turned on his heel and stormed from the office.

"Quite certain," Ekks confirmed. "I've already put some thought into what I should say once it comes time for the press conference."

It felt so much better than simply saying *I told you so.*

Aboard *The Empress*, Outer Sark System

Hey, Mollz. There's something you should know.

What's up, Oz?

Pieter just called Paige to loop her in. He thought you should know that she mentioned that tensions are rising on Estaria. Something about launching the Fleet.

They're doing it?

Not yet. But there seems to be a mounting call for it in the Senate and the media.

Shit.

I know. Want me to do anything?

Not yet. I need to figure this out.

Sure. Take your time. Pieter has Paige in a holding pattern for now.

Cool. Thanks, Oz.

Molly collapsed into her seat in the lounge.

"Stay put," Joel told her as he ushered her in. "I'm going to get you some water."

Molly sighed, exaggerating. "I could murder a mocha right now..."

Joel smiled a quirky little smile at her. "You serious? Want me to get you one?"

She shook her head. "No. As much as I crave one, it won't do me any good, even in the short term."

He pressed his lips together, nodded once, and disappeared from view.

Molly took a deep breath. There was so much to process, and her brain felt like it had just frozen still. She tried to recall what had just happened and tried to organize the priorities but felt like her mind had rusty brakes that were preventing her from thinking.

You're overloaded Molly. Just relax for a few minutes. It's going to take time for the fleet to turn around in any case.

Ok. Just make sure you and Pieter are collecting all the data you can while we're in proximity to the ARs. There's no telling what kind of signals and messages they might be sending us... and we can work on sifting through it all later when we're back at base.

Roger that.

Molly closed her eyes and felt herself breathing. She paid careful attention to the air moving in and out of her lungs... just as Arlene had taught her. Her mind's eye flashed to the image of Arlene in her realm-jump with the ARs. She remembered the feeling of absolute confidence that she could do what was asked of her. And now, sitting here, knowing she needed to start doing something that confidence was just that: a distant memory in her mind.

"Here you go."

She opened her eyes. Joel was there with an enclosed antigrav mug of water for her.

"Thanks."

He sat down next to her. "So... you ready to talk about what happened?"

She shrugged, holding the water and not drinking it. "I don't know. I'm having trouble putting it all together. I'm kind of preoccupied with the enormity of what they told me I need to do."

"To prepare the Estarians for contact?"

"Yeah. I mean... they got it right. Logically. The Estarians are the threat. The Oggs are relatively chill and accepting. They'll resist launching the fleet as much as they possibly can."

"Except it's not just down to them."

"Exactly. From what I know of the politics I'm guessing the Estarians will force their hand, either legally or otherwise. Paige called and said it's pretty much a *fait accompli* at this point."

Joel's brow furrowed. "Shit. That's not good."

"No. It's not. The Teshovians haven't the means to get embroiled in any kind of decision-making or contact... so it's down to the Estarians."

"Well, that narrows down where we need to focus our attention."

"I guess so." Molly cocked her head. "Ok, so assuming the Estarians launch the ships, perhaps..."

She hesitated.

Joel turned to look directly at her. "Go on."

"Well, I'm wondering how much a deterrent our Zhyn Fleet might be. I mean, what if we just block the movement of the Estarians?"

Joel sighed. "It's risky. I mean we may end up dragging the Zhyn into a war that has nothing to do with them."

"Nothing to do with them *yet*," Molly countered.

"True."

"But you have a point. Plus, I have no idea how this will sit with the General. Hang on... let me see if Oz can do a bit of powwowing with Lance so we have an idea when we get back."

Molly's eyes took on a glazed look as she went into her own mind to talk with her other self.

Oz? What do you think?

I can ask him. Technically there are restraints on Zhyn military activity as it pertains to the Federation.

But the Sark system isn't part of the Federation.

That's what makes it a gray area.

Ok. See if you can get an answer on that.

Will do.

Molly's eyes refocused on the seat in front of her. Remembering her water she took a sip.

"Oz is on it?" Joel asked.

"Yes. That piece."

"You ok?"

She shook her head. "Honestly... no." She sighed.

Joel leaned back and put a hand on her shoulder. "What is it?"

"Apart from being in communication with a new alien race? And having to prepare the system for it?"

He grinned and exhaled poignantly. "Good point."

She lowered her head. She was too tired to cry. Too bamboozled to talk. Her head felt like a mush of confusion. "I just don't know how I'm going to do this... What do I tell the Estarians? How are we meant to convince them to stand down... and I mean..."

Her voice wavered and cracked with emotion.

"… Is standing down the right thing? They're scared. They should have the right to defend themselves against a new threat…"

Joel frowned. "You don't really think there is a threat?"

"No. But look at it from their point of view. What if it's not just a war-hungry few that are orchestrating this mobilization? What if it's really what the people want? And what if they're right, and I'm wrong about the threat?"

Joel took a deep breath and exhaled slowly, mulling her concerns carefully. "You know," he started, "I know what the military decision would be in the face of a potential threat. But all threat assessments need to be done with the maximum amount of intel available.

Molly sighed, tipping her head back against the headrest. Joel watched a single tear of frustration trickle down the side of her face and neck.

He continued. "Deliver the message, then they can make their own minds up."

"But who am I to take on this enormous responsibility."

"You're afraid of fucking it up?"

"Of course!"

He rolled his lips inwards. "You're not going to like this…"

She narrowed her eyes and looked at him sideways.

He was on a roll. "But if that's the thing that's stopping you from doing your duty and protecting the people with the information you have, I think you just need to pull up your big girl pants and stop being selfish. This isn't anything you aren't able to handle. You can do this. Everything over the last several years has *prepared* you for this. You need to man up as it were and make it happen."

Molly looked at him in disbelief. "Joel?"

"No, it's his alter ego Joem," Joel responded with a slight smirk.

Molly's lips started to smile involuntarily. "You've never been tough on me."

He shrugged. "You've never needed me to."

"Till now?"

"Exactly. Think about it," he explained some more. "We do everything in our power to make life safe for the people of the system. No matter what the cost to us personally. Even if it means we have to face our worst fears... or as in this case, feel a bit uncomfortable. It's just what we do."

Molly nodded slowly.

Joel held her gaze steadily. "You don't feel up to it? You don't think you're good enough? Tough. As I said, pull up your big girl pants and get on with it. Because this is who you are and this is no time to be pretending that you're not. You're a leader - whatever that role demands of you."

Molly sat in silence for a good long minute. Joel started to wonder if he'd taken the right tact.

Finally she spoke very quietly. "You're right." She started to stand up.

"Where are you going?" he asked, a bewildered expression creeping into his eyes.

She smirked back at him. "You make a compelling argument. I'm going to pull up my big girl pants," she responded heading out into the aisle and moving toward the front of the ship.

Joel watched her for a second, then realized he should probably be following. He scrambled up out of his seat and hurried after her. Whatever was happening, he didn't want to miss a second of it.

CHAPTER SEVENTEEN

Aboard _The Empress_, Outer Sark System

Molly arrived in the cockpit with a flourish. Brock turned suddenly, sensing a reinvigorated presence around her. Her face was set hard with a look of determination. A determination he had only witnessed on a couple of occasions when their backs had been up against the proverbial wall.

"Ok folks, listen up," she declared.

Arlene and Sean appeared behind Joel who had just managed to catch up to her as she entered the cockpit.

"Here's what we're going to do. Once the fleet is well on its way we're going to head back to Gaitune to regroup. The first outcome we must secure is stopping that Estarian fleet from heading anywhere near the outer system. If we can prevent it from launching, so much the better."

Brock started to say something, but it was Pieter who blurted out a question before he could contain himself. "How on Estaria are we going to do that? We're just one ship!" Molly recognized the timbre of his voice. He was scared. And perhaps just as perplexed by the situation as she had been just a few moments ago.

"We need to use our powers of persuasion," Molly said, turning to include Arlene and Sean in the conversation. She gave Sean a very pointed look. Sean acknowledged it with a nod.

"We have one hundred days," she continued. "We need to use them wisely. Oz is working on what we can do in terms of using the Zhyn fleet to stop them. But we still need to use every other avenue available to us... planet-side."

"What does that mean?" Brock asked.

Molly pointed to him. "You can get on the holo as soon as we're in range. Talk to Carol. She can use the graduate teams to find out anything at all that might help us. Any threads from the Northern Clan... track them down, find leverage. Lean on them. Undo whatever they've been doing. She's got some very smart people at her disposal. Time to use them."

She listed off other points of contact on her fingers. "Paige and Maya: get them to find out what's happening in terms of the Senate and what needs to happen to have them vote no to launching a fleet. They'll need to pull in their contacts like Garet and whomever else is around."

She turned to Pieter. "Pieter, you can look into what angles that fleet commander might use to declare a state of emergency or martial law. We don't want him pulling that card... not least because it will put those ships out into escalation, but because it will undermine the people's belief in democracy. If it does go to a vote, we need it to be fair, and truly the wish of the people."

He frowned, still perplexed. "How?"

"We'll figure that out. I've got some ideas formulating. Find out what is possible and what is likely in the meantime."

Ben'or, Jack, Anne, and Karina had shown up while she was relaying her instructions. The cockpit was packed with everyone straining to hear and learn what their plan of action was.

"We're going to stop this Estarian fleet, folks," Molly declared with such confidence that the others couldn't help but feel it was a certainty. "And then we're going to introduce the ARs to the

Estarians in such a way that all hell doesn't break loose. This is going to be the most peaceful first contact this galaxy has ever seen."

She paused, looking each one of them in the eye. "Do I make myself clear?"

There was a combination of "yes, Mollys," "yes ma'ams," and even a few "sir, yes, sirs" from the assembly in the cockpit.

Molly's face relaxed a touch. "Good," she said, finally allowing herself to smile. "Let's get to it."

There was a scramble as everyone who wasn't meant to be in the cockpit scattered back out to the lounge and Brock and Pieter got busy on the holocomms.

Joel remained next to Molly. He looked like he was searching for something smart to say. Molly didn't give him the chance. She just glanced at him with a knowing look, winked and then walked out of the cockpit, leaving him chuckling to himself.

Outside the Senate House, Spire, Estaria

The walk to the main door seemed long. Ekks's thoughts were far away and scattered, so it felt as if he was crossing a lightyear between one step and the next. As he got closer to the door, it was the level of noise that drew him back into the moment.

Ekks paused just inside the door that would lead out to the courtyard, taking a moment to compose himself. He had only a moment, though. It took only a few seconds before the crowd gathered in the courtyard realized he was standing there. The doorman and the security guards did their best to keep the crowd from swarming the door, but even so, a young woman with a holocamera bobbing at her shoulder still managed to squirm past them.

She was standing right in front of the door by the time Ekks stepped out. Though he didn't scold her, he ushered her back a few paces. With some reluctance, she retreated a few steps. When a security guard moved to pull her farther away, Ekks lifted a hand to stop him.

Ekks stepped closer to the crowd, waving the doorman and the security guards away as he did. He cleared his throat and straightened the front of his uniform before he linked his hands together behind his back.

"I will be saying this only once," he explained to the crowd of reporters, and there was a flurry of motion as they all started checking their equipment. "So if you plan on recording any of this, this will be your one chance to do so."

He waited just a moment for the activity to quiet down, and when he cleared his throat again he had all attention focused on him.

"I know everyone has been waiting for someone to do something about the satellite signals in the outer system," he began. His voice was calm but he projected it loudly enough for the entire crowd to hear him.

"I know how frustrating it has been, seeming as if no one intends to do anything. Seeming as if no one intends to tell you anything concrete." He paused for a second, and he could just barely hear some discontented murmuring from some of the reporters, before the rest of the crowd hushed them. He smiled, just slightly.

"At last, I am here to let you all know what is happening," he carried on. "The signals in the outer system are not simply dust or debris or asteroids. They are ships. We don't know what they intend to do. But we do know we can't simply wait to find out. Any time we spend just sitting on our hands is added time that something could go wrong. And so it is for this reason that we have decided to launch the fleet. If danger is lurking at the edge of our system, then we will not be caught unawares by it."

He could see them all champing at the bit to start asking questions, but he held up his hands to hush them before they could.

"That is all I have to say for the time being," he informed

them, lowering his hands to link them behind his back once again. "There are many preparations to make to launch the fleet, and it is not a fast process. I would like to waste as little time as possible. But you have my word that you will know if there are any important developments."

He started walking, and one of the security guards jolted back into motion, hurrying forward to begin clearing a path for him as he walked.

"You all heard it here," a young, chipper reporter informed the camera, the crowd still milling behind her. "That was Commander Richard Ekks, Commander of the Estarian-Ogg Space Fleet, confirming that the until now nebulous signals in the outer system are from ships. No word on who the ships belong to or if anyone even has that information, but we know the fleet will be launching. Sooner rather than later, I would expect."

Her image froze as she finished talking, and then shrank and slid to the side so it only took up a corner of the screen, freeing up the rest of the screen for the show's host and her guests.

The Estarian host's smile was too practiced and too bright for the topic at hand as she beamed at the camera. "That was from earlier this afternoon!" she reminded the camera, before she turned her thousand-watt smile on her guests. "Now that we've all had some time for the news to sink in, it seemed like as good a time as any to get some opinions on the matter." She gestured broadly to the side, to her two guests seated at the other end of the table. A Teshovian man with fine, almost pretty features and dark eyes, and an Ogg woman with long nails and an expressive frown. Both seemed less than amused by the theatrics.

"With me this evening, we have Rue Morov and Goro Tuva." The host folded her arms on the table and leaned toward them with an attentiveness that almost seemed fake. "Tell me, what are your thoughts on this latest development?"

Rue and Goro shared a glance, and Rue nodded once for Goro to take the lead.

Goro cleared her throat and drummed her fingers on the table, her nails clicking in rapid-fire succession. "It all seems rather hasty, don't you think?" she wondered. The host's beaming smile dimmed slightly, but only for a moment. Goro paid it no mind and carried on. "The Oggs and the Estarians are supposed to be in agreement on these matters. It's the *Estarian-Ogg* Space Fleet," she emphasized sharply. "Not the Estarian Space Fleet. And yet we weren't consulted on this; we were simply told it was happening." She turned a sharp glare on the host. "Is this how Estarians keep their word, then?"

The host stammered for a moment before she coughed delicately behind one hand and pasted a considerably stiffer smile back into place. "I'm quite sure it only happened this way because it seemed like the most necessary course of action. These are trying times, after all, and we can't afford to waste any time."

Goro rolled her eyes so emphatically she could probably see her own brainstem for a split second. "Good to know that the Estarians consider honoring their agreements to be a waste of time."

The host stammered for a few seconds, but before she could truly begin backpedaling, Rue sighed and made his own thoughts known.

"I suppose there isn't much I can really say on the matter," he mused, leaning his chin in one hand, his elbow balanced on the edge of the table. "Compared to everyone else, we have few ships. Certainly nothing that compares to the Space Fleet. Even so, the Commander has declared that he'll be sending the fleet right into Teshovian space. Whether we have similar resources or not, it would have been a nice gesture to let us know in advance that he'll be trying to wage war in our backyard."

Even if she hadn't come up with anything to say to defend herself, the host had at least gathered her composure by then. "I'm sure everything will line up soon enough," she insisted, too upbeat to be speaking about impending war and invasions. "This is just the beginning, after all."

If anything, Goro and Rue seemed all the more exasperated by the declaration, and the host hurried to move on from there. She didn't need another fight breaking out on air if she wanted to avoid another stern lecture from her producers.

She turned her attention from her guests to the camera after that. "Now, sit tight for a few words from our sponsors, and we'll be right back!"

Beaufort's Office, Senate House, Estaria

Voices chattered, loud and hurried, frantic with excitement and concern alike. It was too loud to simply fade into white noise, snatches, and snippets of the various conversations too audible to fully tune them out.

Worse still were the people who were simply talking to themselves, voices carrying over the rest of the crowd as they checked equipment and rehearsed potential lines for when the press conference would inevitably be broadcast.

A man's office was supposed to be a productive place. For the most part, though, Garet didn't feel very productive. Mostly he felt a migraine threatening to lay him on his ass. He dug the heels of his palms against his eyes until gray and black patterns fizzed against the insides of his eyelids. It didn't help with the headache or with the noise, but at least it was better than nothing.

The noise might actually drive him crazy. Garet groaned and heaved his window shut, but it wasn't particularly helpful. Muffled though it was, he could still hear the babble of the crowd on the ground floor.

"Why hasn't security chased them all off by now?" he grumbled to himself, peering out the window once again before pulling his attention away from it. At that moment, he had a very uncomfortable understanding of everyone who had ever chased someone off of their lawn with a stick. He, too, sort of wished he could chase them off with a stick, even if it wasn't *his* lawn, strictly speaking.

All he wanted was some peace and quiet to make a call. He was fairly sure he wasn't actually going to get it, though.

Resigned to the fact that the muffled rambling was as good as he was going to get, he opened his holoconsole and set up the call. As he listened to it ring, a familiar circle of dots chased themselves in circles in the middle of the console, the word 'waiting...' in the middle of them. He reached up to rub his temples with two fingers of each hand, eyes drifting closed as he did.

He wasn't aware his call was picked up until he heard someone talking to him, her tone light and lilting with amusement.

"Wow," Paige observed dryly, sitting at a table so strewn with files that the actual table was all but invisible. "Who pissed in your cereal this morning, Sir Grumpsalot?" She was looking at him with her eyebrows nearly at her hairline when he looked up again. "You look like you're contemplating murder in various creative ways."

Despite himself, Garet huffed out a quiet laugh. "You're not far off," he replied, gesturing loosely toward the window with one hand. "I'm assuming you can hear at least some of what's going on out there."

Paige leaned closer to her holoconsole and cocked her head to one side to listen, and her nose wrinkled slightly in distaste before she leaned back again, settling more comfortably in her chair. "Is someone throwing a party on your lawn or something?"

"Were it only that simple," Garet griped, and Paige's eyebrows shot up once again.

"Well, now you have to tell me what's going on," she informed him pleasantly, leaning forward just enough to lean her elbows on the table and prop her chin up in her hands. "So what's all the hubbub?"

Garet folded his arms over his chest and leaned back in his chair. "That is why I called, yes," he replied wryly. "Granted, you'll likely be hearing about it all over the news soon enough, but I can at least give you a bit of a heads up." He paused for a second before he took a breath and stated simply, "Ekks has officially announced that he'll be launching the fleet, right at the ships in the outer system."

Paige's eyes widened. "But no one knows what's even going on!" she exclaimed after a moment of stunned stammering. "Is he *trying* to plunge us right into a galaxy-wide diplomatic incident?"

"Probably," Garet answered simply, his voice low and soft. "Either he is, or whoever paid for him to have his position is." He reached up to rub his forehead before he dragged his hand down his face. "He called me some time ago to bring the topic to my attention," he admitted, slumping in his seat. "I tried to talk him out of it at the time. Maybe if I had been a bit more persuasive—"

Paige snorted incredulously, cutting him off. "Beaufort, come on," she scoffed. "Ekks does what Ekks wants. Short of locking him up or killing him, no one was going to change his mind unless they offered him a better deal."

"I know," Garet acknowledged, leaning his head back against the back of his chair, so he could stare at the ceiling. "Even so, I can't help but think that someone could have done something to keep it from getting to this point."

"Maybe," Paige sighed. "Or maybe not. Either way, we'll do what we can to stop it from getting any worse," she promised fiercely. "But that means you need to keep us filled in on anything you can."

Garet nodded once, his attention returning to the holoconsole. "Of course," he agreed easily. "I can't make you any promises about how much I'll be kept in the loop—matters in the outer system are a bit outside of my jurisdiction—but I'll be sure to pass on anything I hear."

Paige grinned. "Much appreciated," she assured him. Her expression grew slightly more serious after that, her smile melting away until it was just a subtle quirk at the corners of her lips. "And we'll...do whatever we can," she sighed, running a hand through her hair to push it from her face. "I'm not sure what that *is* just now, but it's still early."

Garet lifted a hand as if to toast with an invisible drink. "To nebulous plans, then," he offered dryly.

"To nebulous plans," Paige agreed, lifting a hand in a similar gesture. "I would say I'd like to hear from you again, but right now I'm pretty sure that would mean bad news." She hummed a low, slightly consternated note. "Vexing."

"I'll do my best not to be offended," Garet replied, good-naturedly exasperated. "I'll get in touch if I know anything."

"Later, Beaufort."

With that final goodbye, Garet ended the call and sagged back in his seat. Head tipped back to look at the ceiling again, he mused quietly to himself, "Interesting times we live in."

In his line of work, he supposed he should have expected it. And yet, as the jumble of conversations continued outside and he reined in the urge to throw a bucket of water out of the window and send the crowd scattering, he felt as if he wasn't wholly prepared for whatever was coming next.

CHAPTER EIGHTEEN

<u>Base Conference Room, Gaitune-67</u>

As the name likely implied, the conference room was supposed to be used for conferences and the holoscreen was supposed to be used for demonstrations. There were no rules against simply working in there, though. Maya, like Molly, liked having space to spread her files out from one end of the long table to the other.

She also liked knowing that Paige was right at the other end of the table.

Maya had been ignoring the news playing in the background. There were half a million different ways to stay up-to-date, after all, and she always worked better when it wasn't quiet, so the news was mostly acting as background noise. Something to fill in the gaps in the air that didn't require any participation from her to distract her. At least, that was the case until some aggravatingly familiar words started to play.

"I know everyone has been waiting for someone to do something about the satellite signals in the outer system..."

Maya looked up from the files she was perusing to squint suspiciously at the screen. "This can't be right..." she murmured to herself, trailing off quietly as she watched the screen. But Ekks's press conference, filmed from a bobbing holocamera and with glimpses of at least a dozen other people popping into the frame from every angle, continued to play uninterrupted. There was no cutaway with a station producer explaining that the repeat was a scheduling mistake. There was no banner on the screen to offer some insight into why it was playing again.

She glanced at the time on the nearest clock, and her suspicion ratcheted up a few notches as she realized that, on any other day, the *weather* would be on.

"So it's actively suppressing other things," she mused quietly before she picked up the remote and muted the press conference. She could only listen to it so many times before she had it memorized, after all.

"Something wrong?" Paige wondered from the opposite end of the table. "Or are you just talking to yourself for giggles?"

Maya flapped a hand at the screen, and Paige had to lean forward halfway onto the table to actually see it from her side of the room.

"What about it?" she asked after a moment, eyeing the screen in vague distaste. Without the sound to make it clear that he was talking, Ekks stood so still he may as well have been a statue. To call it uncanny was perhaps a bit extreme, but if nothing else, Paige was fairly sure she never wanted to be in the same room with him on her own.

"This is the third time I've seen this same press conference today, and it's hardly even lunchtime yet," Maya explained, folding her arms on the table and slumping down on them until her chin was resting on her folded forearms and she had to practically roll her eyes back into her head to keep them focused on the screen. "And I haven't even been paying that much attention to it. So who knows how many times it's actually played?"

Paige hummed a low note in acknowledgment, scooting her chair around the corner of the table so she could sit back down and still see the screen. "Weird," she agreed before she took a glance at the time. "Hey, shouldn't—"

"The weather, yeah," Maya cut in. "That's what I figured. And yet…" She gestured to the press conference on the screen once again.

"Wasn't it super unbalanced after that last big senate meeting, too?" Paige wondered. "I mean, I swear I saw that clip of Ekks basically saying 'no comment' like a billion times a day. Everyone started getting seriously freaked out."

"Of course, they did," Maya scoffed. "I mean, ever since this whole 'signals in the outer system' business started, that's all they've heard about. It's been playing to the exclusion of…basically everything else."

"No local news," Paige sighed. "Not even any planetary news. Just…the outer system. Of course, everyone started getting jumpy when they weren't even allowed to know what was going on in their own backyards."

"I don't think it's an accident," Maya stated cautiously. "It just seems a bit…much, to be an accident."

"And an accident would have been corrected at some point," Paige agreed. "Plus…" She picked up the remote and started scrolling through news stations. On each one, it was the same press conference. "It was like this last time, too. If it was an accident, I don't think it would be on every news station."

Maya reached out as she sat up, flexing her fingers open and closed expectantly until Paige slid the remote across the table to her. Maya kept scrolling through channels until her exasperation compelled her to simply shut the screen off. "It really is all of them," she groused, slumping back in her seat. "This isn't a network thing or a journalist thing. This has to be coming straight from Cyber Communications." Her voice got quieter as she spoke until Paige had to lean closer to hear her, as Maya very nearly forgot that there was someone else in the room with her and that she was not actually speaking to just herself. "That's the only source that would have access to all of them."

Paige cleared her throat and drummed her hands lightly the table, Maya's startled attention snapping back to her again. She offered a crooked, sheepish smile.

"Someone has to be futzing with the scheduling algorithms," Maya continued, sure and steady. "That's the only way every station would have the same footage and the same oversaturation when there was a whole crowd of reporters at the conference and there are other things that *aren't* being covered."

"Then we need to get a handle on this," Paige replied decisively, straightening up in her seat and turning to the side to get up. "I mean, you've done all...this," she flicked one hand toward where the screen had been until a moment ago, "before, so if you say it's Cyber Communications then I'm willing to put my money there."

With a final, decisive nod, she started toward the conference room door.

"Where are you going?" Maya asked, bemused, getting halfway to her feet.

Paige turned, walking backward for a moment as she replied, "I'm going to call to let Bates know. She'll probably want to do something about this."

Maya nodded slowly in agreement and sat back down. "Right. Let me know if anything exciting happens."

Paige flashed her a thumbs-up before turning to step through the door. Maya watched the door for a moment before reluctantly pulling her attention back to her work. After all, she doubted she would miss it if anything new came up.

Special Task Force Offices, Undisclosed Location, Estaria

The lights above the bullpen flickered. The bulbs probably should have been changed weeks ago, but they still had a few weeks left until they actually died, and so no one had bothered. Rather than finally dealing with it, Elroy simply watched them flicker a few more times before they steadied once again.

In the cubicle to his left, he could hear Dhashana organizing the hard copies of the last two weeks' files, preparing them to be sent down to the archives. In the cubicle to his right, he could hear Soraya tapping her stylus against the edge of her desk as she proofread a weekly report.

It was quiet until he heard Soraya jump in surprise, slam her knees into her desk, and start swearing profusely. Despite that, when she answered her communicator, her, "How can I be of assistance, ma'am?" sounded remarkably steady and professional.

Elroy slowly straightened up in his seat, getting ready to get to his feet as he listened. Soraya's end of the conversation mostly consisted of a series of hums and "uh huhs" until she finished it off with, "Of course. We'll be right up, ma'am."

He heard her chair slide away from her desk, and by the time she was standing in his cubicle, he was already on his feet and stretching his arms over his head. "Upstairs?" he guessed.

"Upstairs," Soraya confirmed before she turned to lead the way. As they passed Dhashana's cubicle, she nearly tripped as she stomped her feet back into her shoes before she fell into step with them.

They were admitted into Bates's office as soon as Soraya knocked, and they filed in one by one to stand in front of Bates's desk. Her holoconsole was still open, a call recently finished.

Without any preamble, she began speaking. "It seems safe to assume that you three have noticed how single-minded the news has been lately."

Soraya nodded once. "Of course, ma'am."

Bates hummed in acknowledgment. "It's been brought to my attention recently that this intense level of focus is likely not an accident. The odds are high that someone at Cyber Communications has been fooling with things to make sure that there is always coverage of the outer system debacle," she explained briefly.

"That is where the three of you come into play." She gave them a pointed look. "However you see fit to do so, I need you three to find the culprit and take them into custody. If we're going to straighten this mess out, then we need to start somewhere."

"You're leaving the details up to us?" Soraya asked slowly, caught somewhere between disbelief and double-checking.

"You know what you're doing," Bates replied, offering it as confirmation. "I expect to be kept informed of what's going on, but I have no intentions of micromanaging you."

"Of course, ma'am," Soraya replied, as if the words were simply habit whenever Bates spoke. "We'll get started immediately."

"See that you do." Bates waved them toward the door again.

The three of them trekked back down the stairs in thoughtful silence. When they made it back to the bullpen, rather than returning to their individual cubicles, Soraya and Dhashana instead dragged their chairs into Elroy's cubicle.

They started out with the basics, simply dredging up as much unclassified information on Cyber Communications as they could, until all three of their holoconsoles were a mess of tabs and windows.

The public information offered little to go off of. It was time to change tacks.

"Any new employees?" Soraya asked, idly twisting her chair just slightly from one side to the other. "This is a recent issue, so either someone new has been introduced or something happened with an old-timer. I figure Occam's Razor is at play here, so we'll check for newbies first."

Elroy hummed, the universal sound for 'give me a sec,' and it was followed by the rapid sound of typing. A moment later, six pictures popped up on screen.

"All of them have only been working in Cyber Communications for a few months at most," he offered, hands still poised over his keyboard.

Soraya wrinkled her nose slightly in distaste. "That's still a lot of information to check, though. I was hoping this would be quick."

"Hang on." Dhashana glanced over the information briefly, before highlighting two of them; a woman named Jennifer and a nondescript man named Ben. "These two are the only ones who would have the authority to tweak broadcasting to this extent," she offered. "The other four are interns or lower level workers."

"And everyone else has been established there long enough that we probably would have gotten trouble from them before this," Elroy added. "Should I try to see how much of their stuff I can get through without being onsite?"

"Hold on." Soraya held a hand up before she leaned closer to the screen. Slowly, she pointed to Jennifer's picture and the job title beneath it. "Didn't her predecessor *die* not that long ago?" she asked pointedly.

"Murdered, yeah," Dhashana confirmed. "She got shot. Sniped, if you want to be specific."

"A woman gets murdered, and now her successor is one of our most likely suspects," Soraya mused, head cocked to one side as she contemplated the picture. "Seems a bit too convenient if you ask me. Start with her."

"Got it." Elroy flashed her a thumbs-up before he started typing again.

It was only a minute later when he made a disgusted noise and leaned back from his console as if it had offended him.

"Problem?" Soraya asked blandly.

"Firewall," he grumbled before he cracked his knuckles and started typing again. "Give me a minute."

He pulled up a list of employees, glanced at it quickly, and kept typing. A few minutes later, he crowed, "Got it!"

"Already?" Soraya wondered, peering over his shoulder. "How'd you bypass it?"

"Didn't," he answered, tone distracted. "Interns' accounts have less security. Got into one of those and used it as a proxy so Jennifer's account thinks the intrusion is coming from within the local network."

The bullpen lapsed into silence after that, and after a minute Soraya settled back into her seat once it became apparent that watching Elroy work wasn't all that exciting in real-time.

Eventually, Elroy heaved an exasperated sigh. "She's a complete amateur about coding," he grumbled.

"You've said that about professional programmers," Dhashana accused. "Not everyone has standards as high as the moon."

"Well they should," he insisted primly, leaning back into his seat. He pushed his holoconsole over for Soraya to look at. "She tried to cover her tracks, but there are bits and pieces of her code left all over the place. I can piece it back together enough to get some idea of what she was doing. Leaving breadcrumbs is an amateur move," he insisted.

"Can we definitively say that Jennifer is the cause of the scheduling discrepancies?" Soraya asked before he could go off on an overly-involved tangent.

He nodded quickly. "I'd say so, yeah," he confirmed. "Like I said, she tried to cover her tracks, so I can't put all of the specifics together from here." He flapped a hand at his console. "But her accounts accessed the scheduling system way more than it should have, and I can put together pieces of her override for the system. I mean, I can't guess at her *intent*, clearly, but she's at least had something to do with it."

Soraya nodded slowly. "Right," she agreed, glancing over Elroy's holoconsole. She didn't understand his digital work to the same extent as he did, but she could grasp the gist of it. "I guess we know what the next step is."

"Time to bring her in?" Elroy wondered, already making

copies of everything on his console before he started closing it down. They were going to need the evidence later, more than likely, which meant they couldn't risk any of it being erased in the interim.

"Time to bring her in," Soraya confirmed, getting to her feet. "We'll need to be careful, but I don't think it will be a particularly dangerous gig."

"You mean waltzing into the Department of Cyber Communications won't be like a battlefield?" Elroy wondered wryly, feigning a look of wide-eyed amazement. "I never would have guessed." His antics got no response.

"I'll go let the boss know what we're doing. You," Soraya pointed a finger at Elroy, "go get a car ready. And you," she turned to point at Dhashana, "go grab the mockup badges and uniforms for us. We need them to actually let us into the building beyond the lobby if we're going to do anything."

"Cops, I'm assuming?" Dhashana asked, levering herself to her feet. Already, her thoughts were churning as she mentally put together a list of everything they would need for the disguises.

Soraya simply nodded in agreement and waved her on her way, as she got to her feet and headed toward the lift. She turned to call over her shoulder, "And both of you be quick about it. I want this all out of the way by the end of the night."

"Got it!" Elroy called, already halfway to the garage.

"Understood," Dhashana offered distractedly, back in her own cubicle and compiling the information they would all need for suitably convincing IDs.

The lift opened and Soraya stepped in.

CHAPTER NINETEEN

Department of Cyber Communications, Spire, Estaria

Jennifer knocked on the door and waited, standing patiently in the hallway until her boss called, "Come in." She keyed in her entry code and stepped through when the door slid open. It closed automatically behind her.

With a cheerful smile on her face, she came to a halt in front of his desk. "Morning, sir," she offered. "I have a few things I need to get your approval on."

He reached out an expectant hand, waiting for her to hand it over. "Well, let's see it."

Jennifer knew her boss already. She had studied how he ticked, even in the short time she had known him. It was a skill she had developed. She knew how long his attention span actually lasted, so when she handed him a stack of half a dozen requests that needed his approval, she knew exactly what he was going to do.

He read the first two, just as she expected him to. Once he got to the third one, he read the first paragraph before he skipped to the end and signed it. So long as the first paragraph seemed safe, he was basically guaranteed to sign anything after the first two requests.

Her goal was the fourth request in the stack, tucked into it after two requests to shuffle various interns around and a request to upgrade the screen in her office. From its first paragraph, it looked perfectly reasonable; a request to let her overhaul the Department's outdated, much-neglected social media presence.

She watched him scan over the first paragraph, and then he paused. Glancing up at her, he wondered, "Is this really necessary, Jenn?"

Though her smile wanted to crumble, she kept it in place as she nodded. She had known he might have questions. She had walked into his office prepared to answer them.

"Positive," she assured him, and if her voice sounded just a touch too chipper in that moment, her boss didn't comment on it. "The world is changing all the time, and so is the way that people interact with it. If we want people to trust that we're telling them the truth, they need to feel like they know us. We need to be more present on the XtraNET, or—"

She cut herself off, closing her mouth with an audible click as her boss held up a hand to silence her.

"I don't need the full sales pitch, Jenn," he asserted, looking down at it again. "If you're that set on it, I suppose it won't hurt."

He glanced over the first paragraph again. And, just as expected, he skipped to the end and signed on the dotted line before he moved onto the next request.

Within fifteen minutes, Jennifer was on her way back to her office with her authorized requests in hand. It couldn't have gone more according to plan if she had scripted it herself.

She leaned back against her door for a moment once she was in her office, holding the stack of requests close to her chest. Then she pushed herself away from the door and headed to her desk. She set the stack of papers down and cracked her knuckles.

"Moment of truth," she murmured to herself, opening her holoconsole as she did. Most of the work was already done, but she found herself scanning through her pet project's coding despite that. She tweaked it here and there, just to make it a touch more efficient, and proofread it three times before she decided it was good to go. The last thing she needed was to be foiled by a missing bracket, after all.

The entire time she looked over it, she listened with half an ear to everything going on in the hallway. Every footstep that passed her door made her jump, yanking her hands away from her keyboard each time just to make sure she didn't make any accidental keystrokes.

"Why is this so hard?" she groused to herself, practically whining the words. Immediately afterward, she was glad there was no one else in the room to hear her.

It wasn't as if she had never snuck around at work before. It should have been as easy as any habit by then. But she supposed her latest pet project was a bit more intense than simply altering the scheduling algorithms. It reached considerably farther than just her own office building.

She had been staring at the finished product for almost a full minute, and finally she took a deep breath, exhaling slowly, and started the upload to the holo network.

No turning back, she mused silently herself. Whatever happened…happened, from that point forward.

She watched the progress bar creep along until there was a knock on her office door. She nearly leapt out of her skin, turning her chair around so quickly she practically toppled out of it.

"Um—"

She turned back around again to look at her console with panicked eyes as if it was going to suddenly jump up and do a dance for her. At least until her common sense caught up with the rest of her, and she simply opened a few other tabs to hide the upload's progress bar. Within a few seconds, her console looked the same as it would on any other day.

"Come in!" she called, her voice slightly strangled as the brief panic of just a moment before faded. It didn't leave relief in its wake, but rather just a sense of vague unease.

She couldn't bring herself to feel even an ounce of surprise when the door opened and Andrew stepped into the office.

"Andy!" she greeted, sitting too stiffly in her chair, her grin too broad and her grip on her chair's armrests too tight. "How's your day going?"

He recoiled half a step at the greeting, brows furrowing in bewilderment. "Fiiiine...?" he answered slowly, with a level of wariness that was perhaps more appropriate for trying to decide if a snake was venomous or not.

Consciously, Jennifer toned her smile down and tried to relax in her seat, leaning back and sliding down slightly. Mostly it looked as if she was trying to hold herself into the seat for dear life, as if a rocket ship was taking off.

Andrew continued to watch her like he was waiting for her to explode for a few seconds before he cleared his throat. "... Anyway." He didn't step any farther into the office. She didn't notice that he held a stack of files until he set them down on the side table by the door. At the deer-in-headlights look that Jennifer gave them, Andrew's eyebrows rose slowly.

"You filed for a couple of intern reassignments," he reminded her carefully. "I'm bringing you the information on the interns that have shifted to your roster." He gestured to the files somewhat needlessly. "Are you all right?" He sounded less like he was asking for her benefit and more so he could decide if he needed to flee from a contagion or not.

"Great!" she assured him brightly. "Why wouldn't I be?"

His eyebrows rose again, nearly disappearing into his hairline that time. "You look a bit, uh…" He trailed off for a few seconds, before he settled on a careful, "A bit uncomfortable."

"Long bike ride the other day," she answered, and she had to fight back the urge to wonder why that was the first excuse she went with. "Sitting down isn't the most comfortable thing right now."

To say Andrew looked unconvinced was to put it charitably. He was quiet for a moment longer before he simply shook his head and started to turn away. He sighed as the door started to open again. "On second thought, I don't think I want to know."

He stepped out, and Jennifer all but sagged in her chair. Her hands went limp on the armrests, her legs splayed out slightly, and she tipped her head back against the back of the seat. She felt a bit like a marionette whose strings had all been cut with a blunt knife.

She wasn't even sure what she was so nervous about. After all, her boss had said she could do it; she had made sure of it. So really, whose fault was it?

She waited until the door closed and she could hear Andrew's footsteps retreating before she sighed and dragged a hand down her face. She turned her chair around again and slumped onto her desk, holding her full weight up on her arms. It took her a moment to regain her composure before she turned her attention back to her console. She cleared out all of the decoy tabs until she was looking at the upload's progress bar again, and she pulled her legs up onto her seat as she waited for it to finish.

It seemed to take half the day before the upload finally finished, but when she glanced at the clock, it had only been a few minutes. She huffed out an irritated breath, but she didn't think about it beyond that. She wasn't quite done yet, after all.

She grabbed her communicator and made a single call. It was answered with a slow, "Yes?"

"The ball is out of my court now, Sloth," Jennifer stated simply before she hung up the call.

· · ·

Outside the Department of Cyber Communications, Spire, Estaria

"It looks so generic," Dhashana mused, staring up at the building. "Hard to believe anyone here could be capable of committing any sort of crime."

"That sort of mindset means working here is probably a great idea for anyone who wants to commit any sort of crime," Elroy pointed out, before he loped ahead to open the door. Just in time to miss the eye roll that Dhashana aimed at his back.

Soraya took a moment to straighten her borrowed jacket before she stepped inside, making sure that not a button was out of place. Belatedly, Dhashana and Elroy followed her lead, until all three of them looked polished and pressed, as if they had been putting those same uniforms on each and every day for years.

The receptionist at the front desk glanced up only briefly when the door opened, and did a double take and straightened up behind her desk once she realized that the three people who had just filed into the building were all wearing uniforms.

"Officers," she greeted carefully, bemused and concerned in equal measure. "Can I help you with something?" She was fidgeting already, twirling her stylus between her fingers before she set it down and tried to look professional.

Standing at the front of the trio, Soraya made it to the desk first. "Good afternoon," she offered as she pulled the badge Dhashana had made for her off of her belt. She presented it to the receptionist just long enough for her to get a good look at it before putting it back on her belt. Behind her, Elroy and Dhashana both presented their own badges. As the receptionist's concern increased until it could safely be called anxiety, Soraya got to the point. They weren't playing dress-up just for a good time, after all, and there was no point in beating around the bush.

"We're looking for a Miss Jennifer Etang," she stated. "Could you point us in the direction of her office?"

"Is she in trouble?" the receptionist asked fretfully, even as she was already writing down the floor and the room number on a slip of paper.

"I'm afraid we're not at liberty to discuss that," Soraya replied, feigning regret as she said it. It was no surprise when the receptionist's worry increased.

Sliding the paper across the desk with one hand, the receptionist pointed down the nearest hallway with the other hand. "The first lift on the right," she explained. "Let me know if you need anything else."

"Thank you very much for your assistance—" Soraya darted a glance at the nameplate on the desk. "Miss Dreyers. If we need anything, you'll be the first to know." She took the slip of paper between two fingers, and as she began to walk away from the desk, Elroy and Dhashana followed her in nearly perfect sync.

"Have a good day," the receptionist offered faintly before she fell silent, most likely still fretting at her desk, though Soraya didn't look back to confirm the assumption.

The ride in the lift was swift and silent, and they walked quickly down the hallway once they got to the proper floor. A few workers peered out of their offices after them, whispering to themselves. There was a young man who, as concerned as he looked, didn't seem surprised to see them. He disappeared back into his office quickly, as if he was afraid he might somehow get involved if he lingered.

They could hear Jennifer talking from inside her office once they were standing outside the door. Faint and slightly indistinct, but not so incoherent that they couldn't pick out the words.

"The ball is out of my court now, Sloth."

"She's up to something." Soraya's voice was low and sharp. "Both of you, be ready."

Elroy and Dhashana loosened up behind her, getting ready for anything.

Soraya tapped in the override code that Elroy had acquired just before they left the base, and as the keypad flashed an angry, urgent red, the door slid open just in time for them to see Jennifer setting her communicator down on the desk. It slipped from her grasp at the last moment, instead falling to the floor as she turned her chair around. She fumbled after it for a second before changing her mind. Instead, she simply stared at the three of them with wide eyes, her jaw working soundlessly for a moment before she managed an incredulous, "What—? Who—?"

She gave up on coherent words after that, instead simply gaping. She looked as if someone had decided to slap her upside the head with a rancid haddock; as if something had sent her entire world reeling in a single moment.

"Miss Etang," Soraya began sharply, storming into the room, "we're officers Soraya, Dhashana, and Elroy, and you're going to need to come with us. You're under arrest for the breaking of the mass communication protocols."

Jennifer got to her feet unsteadily and stumbled back, away from her desk. Her voice was faint and far away as she wondered, more to herself than to Soraya, "Did Andrew...?" Her question trailed off before she could even finish asking it.

There would be plenty of time to figure out who Andrew was later, so Soraya ignored it for the time being. She caught Jennifer by the elbow and tugged her closer. As stunned as if the floor had dropped out from beneath her, Jennifer followed easily, and her hands were cuffed together behind her back in a matter of seconds.

Soraya stood in front of her, and when Jennifer simply continued to look rather lost, Soraya snapped her fingers in her face. With a startled jolt, Jennifer's attention snapped to Soraya's face.

"What were you doing when we walked in?" Soraya asked seriously, in a tone that brooked no argument. "We could hear you through the door; you were talking to someone."

"There was no one in here but me," Jennifer replied, finally getting her wits about her as the shock of the situation wore off.

Soraya arched one eyebrow and looked pointedly at the communicator on the floor. Before she could say anything, Dhashana bent down, picked it up, and put it into an evidence pouch.

"We can get the call log off of it, probably," Dhashana offered, tucking the pouch into her uniform jacket as she straightened back up to her full height.

"Good," Soraya sighed, paying no mind to the way Jennifer paled. "I suppose that will have to be good enough. Elroy?" She glanced over her shoulder at him.

"Already on it," he assured her, just before he took a seat in Jennifer's chair. He spent a second adjusting it to a better height before scooting it closer to the desk. He cleared away all of the extraneous tabs on her holo network console, pulled the keyboard closer, and started typing. "If I find any clues about what she did, I'll let you know, but I'm not making any promises about being able to undo it if she did anything huge."

"I understand," Soraya assured him. "Just scour everything. And if you can, see if you can undo the damage she did to the scheduling."

He waved loosely in her direction. He already had the console's terminal open, and he had started to type and was hardly paying any attention to her anymore. "Will probably need to guess at what the settings are actually supposed to be, but I'll see what I can do," he replied already distracted.

"Use your best judgment," she advised wryly, before turning her attention back to Jennifer. Soraya grabbed her by the elbow, but by that point the shock had worn off enough that some of the fight had returned to her. Jennifer yanked her arm out of Soraya's hold, only for Dhashana to grab her by the shoulders and start guiding her toward the door like an elaborately shaped shopping cart.

The door opened and Jennifer led the way out, being guided by Dhashana all the while. Soraya, just before she stepped out of the room, took a moment to quietly let Elroy know, "We'll fill Bates in and someone will send a car to get you later. Just keep up the police officer act until then."

"It's not like I planned on shouting 'surprise, it was a trick!' as soon as you left," he replied, his words laced with dry amusement. "See you this evening, then."

Soraya left him to it after that, stepping out into the hallway and letting the door slide closed in her wake.

After a moment of thought, Elroy tapped into the security camera feeds, bringing up the video on one side of the console's screen just in time to see Soraya, Dhashana, and Jennifer stepping into the lift. He cycled through the camera feeds until he was looking through the camera in the lobby. He could tell when the three of them stepped off of the lift because he could see the receptionist hop to her feet and start fretting so intensely he could almost hear it through the silent footage.

When they entered the camera's view, Soraya looked exasperated, and it was plain that Jennifer had started arguing at some point between stepping onto the lift and stepping off it. Elroy supposed he had lucked out if he didn't need to deal with her.

He kept an eye on the footage until the three of them walked out of the building, and then he closed it and turned his attention back to the task at hand. He had work to do, after all, and he wasn't going to waste any more of his time on idle distractions.

Hangar Deck, Base, Gaitune-67

The Empress touched down as gracefully as ever on the hangar deck yellow paint and a few moments later Paige and Maya arrived through the door from the daemon passage to greet them.

Maya had changed into her soft trainers, clearly having had

enough of clipping around in heels. Paige trotted behind her, contemplating her life choices briefly.

"I'm so glad they're back," Maya called back to her. "It's like a weight off me!"

"I know that feeling," Paige agreed, grabbing hold of the rail and making it clear she wasn't going to head down the steps only to walk back up. "How about I organize some pizza. You go down and meet them, and let them know, eh?"

Maya grinned and hugged her friend excitedly. "Sure thing. Thanks Paige." She trotted effortlessly down the steps and bounded across the deck to meet with the crew who were only just disembarking.

Sean and Karina were the first off the ship. They looked bamboozled and distracted.

"Hey, welcome home," Maya called over. She paused taking in their expressions. "You guys ok?"

The pair kept walking. "Yeah," Sean replied. "Just one hell of a trip," he explained.

Maya watched as he hurried off after Karina. Everything was not all right, Maya concluded. "Hey, Paige is ordering up pizza! Come back down to the kitchen in a bit!"

Sean waved to her. "Sure. Thanks!"

Brock and Pieter were the next off, then Joel and Molly.

"Hey, guys... Paige is organizing pizza. Kitchen. Twenty minutes."

Brock and Pieter greeted her and hugged her. "Cool bananas," Brock agreed. "Can't wait to have some proper food and a beer. That was one hell of a trip."

Maya watched Molly and Joel headed not to the stairs of the safe house, but the base meetings rooms, as if they were going to work.

She lowered her voice and leaned in to talk with Pieter and Brock. "What's going on there?" she asked.

Brock adjusted the bag on his shoulder. "Serious shit going

down. You heard we've got one hundred days to prepare the Estarians for the ARs heading in?"

Maya clamped her hand over her mouth. "No. I had no idea."

Pieter nodded grimly, then ruffled his own hair. "Heavy stuff. Suspect they're going to work," he mused, motioning to where Molly and Joel disappeared.

Maya sighed. "Well, maybe I'll take them some pizza and beer down..."

Brock started moving to take his bags upstairs. "Better they come out and join the rest of the crew," he said quietly with a wink.

Maya smiled, understanding. "I'll get Oz to summon them then." She touched her nose.

Just then Anne came bounding over to her and nearly knocked her over as she wrapped her arms around her.

"Hey, trouble!"

"Hey, Maya! You wouldn't believe what happened out there!"

"I have a feeling you're going to tell me though," Maya responded.

Anne looped her arm into Maya's and started walking her across the hangar deck, chattering away. Maya was vaguely aware of the others getting off the ship, but she'd already decided she would send them a group holomessage to get them out to the safe house for pizza before everything got too crazy.

Fifteen minutes later Molly was in her quarters sorting her gear out when a message flashed on her holo. It was from Maya.

"Hi, all. Pizza in the kitchen. Beer is cold. We have a hundred days to solve this. It's a marathon, not a sprint. May I suggest you take the time to replenish and socialize so as to alleviate the stresses we're going to face. Beer. Pizza. Kitchen. Five minutes. Maya."

Molly chuckled.

She's certainly got leadership qualities!

This is true. We probably underutilize that in her.

I think it's hard when Paige is just so capable and likes taking on so many projects.

But it's good to know she is there when things spill over.

Oz paused. **Are you heading down? I think the troops need to see you now more than ever.**

Yes. I will. Gimme a few minutes and I'll head over.

Ten minutes later Molly emerged from her quarters, showered and changed into her sweats. She headed down to the kitchen to find everyone already eating and breeze-shooting.

Joel pulled out a chair for her on the far side. She rounded the table and sat down. Joel passed her the pizza that clearly had vegetables on it.

"Thanks," she smiled, taking a couple of slices.

Joel nodded. "It's been a while since we've done this, eh?"

"It has," she agreed.

"I dunno man. What if they get here and they mind-control us all into being slaves?" Brock posited between mouthfuls of cheesy-goodness.

Crash raised one eyebrow at him.

Sean shifted awkwardly in his seat. "He's got a point. I mean, we have no way of knowing their intentions. We could just be making it easier for them to come and take over."

Karina glanced at him from across the table, but said nothing. She took another swig of her beer.

Molly noticed the conversation. Then noticed Joel watching her to see if she was going to interject or counter what they were saying.

"Hey look, guys..." she interjected. "I know this is all a bit... surreal. And I know it's difficult to trust something that you haven't experienced, but we're going to get through this. And we're not going to be mind-controlled or anything else. We just need to stop this system falling into civil war."

She paused, letting her words sink in. Everyone else at the table had fallen silent, listening to her. "We've got one hundred days. That's just over three months. A lot can happen in even a week. We've got work to do... and we can turn this all around. We can make a difference. But we've got to stay focused on the outcomes we want. Not our fears." She deliberately tried not to look at Sean accusingly. She wasn't trying to shame anyone. Just help them see.

She dropped her hand from her beer and continued speaking, looking each one of them in the eye now. "We need to be consistent. But we also need to be specific in our objectives. I have an idea brewing. Something that might be able to plug into the existing system which will give us a read on what the people want."

"And if they want to go to war?" Sean asked.

"Then, we need to give them the reality check of what that means. They're outmatched. They can't possibly survive. But there is no incentive to fight. They're not going up against anyone or anything that wants to hurt them."

"I don't know," Arlene interjected. "Those ships looked pretty formidable."

"Yeah, and if they wanted to take us out they would have done so already. That's got to count for something," Molly insisted.

Paige was leaning her face on her hand, fiddling with her beer bottle with the other. "It's almost like we need a way to communicate that to the people."

Maya nodded in agreement before taking another bite of pizza.

"I think I have an idea," Molly confided. "But it needs some work on it."

"Give us a clue?" Paige pressed.

"No. Not now," Molly smiled. "Now we have beer and pizza.

We can have one night off. Let's talk about it tomorrow when we're all fresh. For now, let's enjoy a bit of R&R..."

Giles, who had been sitting quietly taking it all in finally spoke up. He raised his beer. "To taking the night off!"

The group chuckled, then raised their beers too. "To taking the night off!"

CHAPTER TWENTY

Base Conference Room, Gaitune-67

In the hub of activity and everything else going on the team had barely noticed the absence of the diplomat.

Ben'or sat quietly in the low lighting of the base conference room, connected in a holocall with his Emperor.

"Our ships will be back in the inner system in a few days," he reported. His tone was sober, but not showing any signs of concern.

"And you're sure there is no malicious intent on the part of these ARs?"

"Absolutely certain that there are no signs of it, Your Highness."

"Well, that is something. So what is to be done about this Estarian fleet?"

Ben'or's jaw set. "I'm afraid that is the major problem." He paused, shifting his gaze to the table in front of him. "If we allow them to intercept the ARs, I fear this will have massive ramifications for the rest of the Federation. Even if the ARs only defend themselves, the Estarian fleet will be wiped out. There will then be no way of stopping other empires from following suit to try and stop an imagined invasion."

"How do we know they're not invading, though?"

"We don't for sure. But they have done nothing threatening, other than present themselves."

"It is our own fear that is the invader." The Emperor took a deep breath and slowly exhaled, contemplating the conundrum.

"This is true, Your Highness."

"Can we intervene?"

"We have to be careful," Ben'or explained slowly. "It's a delicate situation. We don't want to drag the Federation into it else that will end in all-out civil war."

"What options do we have?"

"I think we need to exercise patience and allow our friends here to do what they do best: save the day."

"You mean, leave it in the humans' hands."

"I think it's the best course. They've never failed us in the past."

"This is true."

There was a long pause between the two leaders.

Finally, the Emperor spoke again. "Ok. Well, you have the use of the ships that are already in the system. I'll be hard pushed to move more in your direction unless the landscape changes dramatically."

"I understand, Your Highness. Your patience and trust are most appreciated."

"Of course. Just... keep me posted. In the meantime, I'll have some of our Generals work up some scenarios, just in case."

Ben'or bowed his head. "Very wise, Your Highness. I'll be in touch."

The Emperor waved a hand briefly before disconnecting the call.

Ben'or found himself sitting in the very dim light in the absence of the holoscreen. He sighed, staring into the nothingness, churning the options in his mind. None of the scenarios he had come up with on the trip back or since had ended with an outcome where the Estarians didn't suffer massive causalities.

How hard it was to save a race from itself, he pondered in the silence.

FINIS

AUTHOR NOTES - ELL LEIGH CLARKE
MAY

Thank yous..

Massive thanks must first go out to my collaborator: MA, known to most of you now as Yoda. It is because of him that this series exists... and that I'm in this world of writing for a living. I sometimes wonder what life would be like if we'd never met. These books certainly wouldn't exist... and nor would my writing career, I'm pretty sure! So thank you Yoda!

Steve and the JITers

Thank you also to Steve Campbell and his team of JITers.

You guys add the confidence we need to make sure the book goes out with all the details attended to. Knowing that we're not going to get slated for bad punctuation, typos, gaps in the stories, or even downright blatant inconsistencies, is a huge help.

I'd also like to thank those of you in the Ellie slack channel who volunteered for helping with some beta reading on new series I'm working on... and for your help, sometimes at ridiculous times at night, when I can't remember the names of characters several books back. I have no idea how come you can search past books so fast... but either way, your assistance has been invaluable.

You're the best, and I'm forever grateful for your input and support. Thank you for everything you do!

Amazon Reviewers

As always massive thanks goes out to our hoard of Zon reviewers. It's because of you that we get to do this full time. Without your five star reviews and thoughtful words on the Zon we simply wouldn't have enough folks reading these space-shenanigans to be able to write full time.

You are the reason these stories exist and you have no idea how frikkin' grateful I am to you.

Thank you, from the bottom of my heart.

Readers and FB page supporters

Last, and certainly by no means least, I'd like to thank you for reading this book... and all the others. Your enthusiasm for the world, and the characters, is heart-warming. Your words of encouragement, and demands for the next episode, are the things that often stay in my mind as I flick from checking the facebook page to the scrivener file when I start each writing session.

Thank you for being here, for reading, for reviewing, and for always brightening my day with your words of support on the fb page. You rock my world, and without you, there really would be no reason to write these stories.

Thank you <3

That's What She Said

So this may come as a complete surprise to you but I've never seen an episode of The Office: the English version or the American version. So when one of my friends at poker showed up with a T-shirt that said the following I was a little confused.

"That's what," - She.

Apparently being a writer I should have understood it. Thankfully he was more than happy to explain the reference when the others weren't listening. Recently however it seems that this joke "that's what she said" seems to have been returning to at least a very small subculture of the poker game. Last week a few people said it and it started to make more sense to me now that I had some context.

Jason, the original T-shirt guy, sent me a YouTube link to all the "That's what she said" incidents in the entire show... Ever.

Here it is: https://www.youtube.com/watch?v=ClzJkv3dpY8

I laughed my ass off.

But was also very inspired by the next week I was able to participate in the joke. Never had I felt so liberated as to unleash my normal sense of humour onto the group. And they got the jokes as well, and I can tell you it went to some dark places.

Check out the link above and tell me you're not even a little bit amused.

You're welcome. ;-)

That's What She Said, Literally

We do have a giggle at poker.

If you can imagine, it starts off with about 30 people all sitting around playing the game and drinking beer. As the night goes on people get knocked out of the tournament, and a cash game gets started up while the others finish at the final table.

Last week when I got knocked out of the final table and went on to enjoy the cash game. This gave me the perfect opportunity to use my new arsenal of 'that's what she said' jokes.

But the game itself wasn't without drama. I can't remember the exact hands but one guy beat another guy in a really, really big pot. There were a lot of chips on the table! And because one of them had gone "all-in" they had to do some kind of counting to make sure it got divided up right in order to pay off the winner, or to make sure that he was covered, or something.

Anyway, after all accounting had been done the guy who had lost put his hands out and scooped the entire stack towards him.

Everyone looked on in amazement.

"Dude what you doing!?" they piped up...

Gerald looked at them bewildered. "I just won that hand, right?"

The other Jason (not the t-shirt guy): "No. No you didn't!"

Gerald's face was a picture. It was kind of a mixture between horror and amazement. He made an apology and scooped the chips towards the winning Jason. A few people sipped their beer awkwardly. Others giggled.

Gerald sat there the next hand looking like he was in another place. Eventually someone asked him if he was okay. He replied, "I've never gone from happy to so sad so quickly."

Ellie: "that was your happy face?"

The whole table erupted in laughter.

When the winning Jason posted about the episode on our private Facebook group I couldn't resist adding my little joke in.

Jason: Best line of the night, "I've never gone from happiness to sadness so quickly."-Gerald

"that was your happy face?"-Ellie.

Ellie comment: that's what she said. Literally.

(There had also been a running joke about the difference between how English people and American people say the word literally!)

MA and Snipers (revisited)

The other day MA and I were talking about what we were going to put in our author notes. As usual MA was giving me shit about various things.

Since we had just recorded the author notes for Rebirth certain things must have been in his consciousness. One such idea were his thoughts around my supposed passive aggressiveness.

For those who haven't read any of our Author Notes ever before it might be useful for me to mention here that in *every other set of Author Notes*(!) he mentions the one time where he said that I was passive-aggressive and I protested that I wasn't.

He then famously went on to say: **yeah in the way that a sniper isn't aggressive.**

You may believe that my saying this now is somewhat redundant.

<MIKE EDIT: A good comment needs to be savored...often.>

I would agree with you.

However, when I asked him about it this most recent time he refers to it, his comment was:

"It was one of my finest moments and that's why keep talking about it."

And then somewhere between me sniggering I heard him say something about William Shatner.

Ellie: what was about William Shatner?

MA: oh so William Shatner was famous for going on about how great he was until years later he realised what he did keep being and now we can laugh about it.

Ellie: oh. I see. That's really funny. (Continues to laugh hysterically)

One of the things I appreciate most about MA is his ability to laugh at himself (eventually).... ;-)

———

Ellie: I don't know what to write for my author notes.

MA: well you should write about things that are relevant to the series that were closing out, and things about the new series. You probably want to give people an insight into other things that are going on in Ellie's world...

Ellie: Can't I just talk about carrying the box of 12 bottles of wine and how they made my arms ache for days afterwards?

MA and Lip Pouts

MA has a resistance to being manipulated. It's a thing. He's probably had horrible past experiences with women manipulating him to get what they want.

<MIKE EDIT: Don't almost all guys have this?>

<<Ellie response: not to this extreme!>>

Sometimes this can cause him to think that someone is trying to manipulate him even when the thought had never even crossed their mind.

One such incident happened the other day when we were talking about something and I was typing and making a note. Subconsciously I must've pushed my lip out as I was concentrating.

MA: (trying to talk about it without accusing me) how far does that lip come out?

Ellie: (realising that she was pouting accidentally, and this is a no-no for afore mentioned reasons, folds lip away.) Oh you know it doesn't always mean that trying to get you to do something I want to do. And actually come to think of it it doesn't always mean the same thing.

MA: (recovering from his initial reaction) So is there a correlation between how far out it is and what it means?

Ellie: (thinking out loud)... I don't know....

This is me sad. (Ellie pouts with a sad face).

This is me wanting you to do something that I want to you to do. (Ellie pouts with her intentional pout).

MA:... Like when you want to name the character Merry versus Mary.

Ellie: (brightening) yes!

MA: actually since were talking about that, I changed my mind about it.

Ellie: so the pout worked?

MA: Yes. But no. I just thought about it some more. Plus, having seen it about a hundred times now in the beats it's kind of grown on me. I think it will be okay.

Background: In the new series I wanted to call one of our characters in this new series or working on Merry. MA said that readers weren't going to like it and that we should call her Mary instead. (eyeroll)

<MIKE EDIT: *Actually, I said that reading Mary as Merry was causing my mind to have a disconnect every time I read her name and pulling me out of the story. I asked Ellie why she did it and her answer was (effectively) "I wanted to."*>

<<*Ellie response: But it wasn't even meant to be Mary in the first place. Or ever!*>>

Ellie Gets A Movie Pass

In recent weeks I've gradually started exploring the local area. There are a bunch of cool bars and cafes around and there is also a cinema within walking distance.

One of my author friends here came over to hang out, (and drink wine, lots of wine), and noticed how close I was to the local cinema. One of our mutual friends has a movie card. She suggested I look into getting one because it's so convenient and, well... Free movies.

I looked into it. Turns out for 10 bucks a month I can see an unlimited number of movies-whenever I want. Being a full-time writer now, and also needing to take lots and lots of breaks, it made sense.

I've had the card for about a month now.

It's still yet to be used.

The thought does cross my mind occasionally though. I think what happens is that I get temporary agoraphobia as soon as I contemplate venturing out of the apartment to do something like watch a movie!

You will be pleased to know however that as I write this I have two movie dates lined up for the next week. The first we had to book the tickets ahead of time for though - so I *still* won't be able to use the movie card...

Oh well, the intention is there.

MA and Being Too Important to Talk

As you probably have gathered MA is super busy with important things these days. I think he feels guilty now and again for letting things slip through the cracks.

<MIKE EDIT: I do, that's true.>

MA: I'm going to be knee deep in a conference tomorrow. I can try and call you. But I don't what time will be. I don't want to make promises that I can't deliver on.

Ellie: (completely not bothered, but sensing weakness) oh I see how it is now. Just too busy and important to make time for your collaborators.

<MIKE EDIT: Note the 'sensing weakness' in her comment right there.>

MA: (protests, makes excuses, looks defensive) *Blah blah blah.*

Ellie: it's okay I'll do what I can and will throw it over to you and then we can talk when you chance.

MA: what about the day after tomorrow?

Ellie: sure no problem. Let me know. Mr. Busy-and-very-important!

MA: hey! If it were anyone else I might be bumping it until next week.

Ellie: I'm gonna put that in the author notes so that all your other collaborators can see this! Bhwahahahahhahaahahaha!

MA: (turns red and begs for mercy.)

<MIKE EDIT: I see that did a fat lot of good. To the back of the line with you, Ms. Clarke with an 'e'.>

Ellie and Acupuncture

The quest for perfect health continues.

Having had a relapse and being bedridden for a couple of weeks I thought it was a good idea to seek some help in Austin.

After all, though I've been feeling better, I think going back to kickboxing so soon might have been a mistake.

<MIKE EDIT: *Note how often strenuous kickboxing takes Ellie down after a bout with bedridden-ness. You would think that she might realize that KICKBOXING isn't the first or second thing one should do as one gets better.*>

A friend of mine who has similar symptoms had been diagnosed with adrenal failure. I still don't really know if this is what is going on for me but adrenal failure was always in the mix of suspected labelled from the beginning of this last year. The thing is she's had this problem for a long time now, and it seems to be getting worse. She's even ended up taking cortisol tablets in order to stay awake during the day. That worries me. It seems a bit counter-intuitive to overload the adrenals even more. Plus, I'm personally not a fan of blindly trusting drugs, not because I don't like artificial stuff necessarily but more because they can have a massive effect on the system and can cause more problems than they solve.

Anyway, in the early hours of one insomnia-ridden morning I was googling locally and found an acupuncturist nearby. Feeling like I had nothing to lose and having had conversations with a friend who specialised in Chinese medicine and acupuncture I booked an appointment.

When I got the appointment I mentioned in passing the possibility of adrenal failure, and the doctor said something about how the symptoms I was describing was very adrenal failure-y.

Sounds weird but having a label to put on it somehow makes it easier to combat. (It also makes it easier for other people to accept when I'm having to make excuses for not being able to go out or do things they want me to do!) He also seemed very confident that it was something he could help with so went ahead and I've had a whole bunch of sessions in the last few weeks.

So far what I've learnt about the models seem to make sense

with all the seemingly disparate symptoms that have experienced over the last year... and even going back to my teenage years as well. Also, because the main problems have been only in the recent months it sounds like it can be quicker and easier to treat.

I'm optimistic.

In fact, I think that I'm having more natural energy over slightly longer periods already. (Goodness knows I need more energy and focus especially to keep churning out the stories and word count in the way the lawn fairies demand!)

<MIKE EDIT: For the record, YOU are the lawnfaires ;-).>

Anyway, the other thing that I realised in my massive amount of downtime is that I've horrendously underestimated the effect that emotions, and emotional events, can have on one's physical body. I always assumed that I was resilient enough to deal with whatever emotional stressors came my way. And when things get bad, then with the right attitude and focus, as human beings we can just... well, bounce back.

But I think it has been for this reason that I haven't protected myself emotionally in the past. I've been way too cavalier in diving in headfirst with situations and people that I should have been more cautious about.

Now that I understand this there are definitely things that I would have done differently in the last year or two. But now I know better. I guess we just live and learn: when the cost to ourselves is just way too high, we (I) just need to walk away much sooner.

I think having been through this though, and having had to pay the price physically, it's given me an embodied sense of where not to put my energy. My focus going forward is very much on self-care and getting myself healthy again. And I think I'll spot anything and anyone that will take away from that a mile off. I hope!

The mental exercise that I found helpful is thinking of my energy like a bank account. Or a poker bankroll. If I invest in something there has to be a reason for it, and I need to be very clear on those reasons. If something is leaving me depleted I have to walk away from it. New rules.

Poker has been an interesting case to consider.

Not only does it take a huge amount of mental energy, but it also has me drinking actual coffee just before I go out for a game. I'll often play way into the night and not sleep until the early hours of the morning.

On the surface it's bad for me.

But the energy that I get back from being among friends, and doing something productive, and meeting new people, and having a good time joking around – seems to completely outweighs the cost to my energy. I wake up the next day revitalized and motivated.

Contemplating doing things or not doing things for reasons related to my own well-being is a massive shift for me. Nowhere in this new equation is there a consideration for what others expect of me or what I need to do in order to keep them happy or whatever. It feels very strange, but ultimately I think it's something that's going to prevent me from being an emotional doormat in the future. Time will tell!

Does Your Butt Hurt?

I was about to sign off the call with MA the other day when suddenly I remembered something I meant to ask him.

Ellie: you know when you set and work in bed, or just sit and work too long?

MA: yes

Ellie: do you end up with a sore butt? You know right at the base of the spine?

MA: yes

Ellie: okay well I guess that's what's doing it then. I've never had a sore back like this before.

(Not that I was expecting MA to have had this problem, but

he is the only other person that I know who doesn't do exercise and has to sit at a computer for long hours at home.)

<MIKE EDIT: I had all sorts (ok two) snarky responses to this before I realized "yeah, I deserve that.".>

<<Ellie response: Bring it on, Batman!>>

MA: you might want to start stretching. I find getting a massage helps too.

Ellie: I think I just need to not be in bed all the time. This is changing with the acupuncture.

[Aside: the idea of a massage sounds great, but I'm just so delicate at the moment. I can't imagine a massage therapist being able to touch me gently enough not to hurt. In the good and the fascinating news though this is perfectly explained through lack of yin or something in the Chinese model that I mentioned already. I'm hoping/expecting this problem to be short lived! I'll look forward to being able to have a massage in the not too distant future!]

<MIKE EDIT: This is when (I think) I had to ask all about her acupuncture and bloody needles.>

The End Of An Era

When we first started writing this series MA in his infinite wisdom suggested that we write it in sets of four books. The reason for this being that if we wanted to stop at any point - for whatever reason, sales related or otherwise - we can always close out arc at the next set of four.

As you can tell at Molly 11 we are now reaching the end of a book of four: Molly 12. Molly 12 will mark the end of this series. It remains to be seen whether we start up another series with Molly and her crew picking up where Molly 12 finished.

Personally, I love Molly and would love to continue writing for her. However, with the longer series it's difficult to maintain the sales volumes that we see at the beginning of a series through so many books. This is just the reality of writing in the environment that we do. The solution those are serious and start another one.

We'll see ;-)

MA suggested I say a few words about writing a 12 book series.

I'm not really sure what to say that would be interesting to you. When we started this MA had some serious reservations about casting a protagonist who was going to be so flawed. As you seen through this journey of author notes it was a fascinating revelation for the both of us to see how much you warm to her despite her insecurities and issues and cheered her on to overcome them.

Writing a series has been challenging and probably not for the reasons one would expect. As you know there have been issues of burnout and health challenges on my part. None of this was because Molly hasn't been fun to write for. And none of it was because we lacked ideas for interesting places to take her stories. It was more just a case of trying to get the words down on paper. I don't know if you can tell, but I'm actually dictating this to the computer - something that MA has been using to write beats for a little while now. He suggested I give it a try the other day. Figuring I had nothing to lose I installed earlier and here we go!

I've yet to see whether this is can be faster and it's taking a different type of focus but I'm hopeful that this may actually help me there be able to tell more stories, faster, and with less burnout.

I'll let you know.

Anyway as I'm writing this now - well speaking it - we've already started work on Molly 12.

(Shit I just realised that we still haven't got a title or a cover for this book, Molly 11... Facepalm).

<MIKE EDIT: We have officially made the cover for #12 specifica-tions and gave them to Jeff Brown, the cover artist. We finally get our

shit together right when we are finished with a TWELVE BOOK SERIES .>

>> Oh my god did you see how the dictation thing wrote realised in English. Yay! <<

Molly 12 is going to encapsulate the grand finale that MA and I envisaged when we first started working together year ago. In fact I remember the moment when we conceived of it when we were hanging out in a hotel lounge one evening during a conference here in Austin.

Having been through 200 photos to choose the shot for the front cover of book 1, MA said we should probably think about where we want the rest of the series to go. What followed was what I coined his Joss Weedon moment. It was like an upsurge of creativity. I hope you like the end product.

Interstellar Spy For Hire

You may have heard MA talking about our newest collaboration. Since the Molly series is fast coming to an end and while we may continue with the characters and story in the future, it will technically be a new series, starting again at book 1.

In the meantime, we have lots of new ideas and new worlds we would like to build for your story-reading pleasure. One such world is another sci-fi story with another badass as the protagonist. But this time we will be leaning more on the comedy and layering twists upon twists and turns upon turns.

MA asked that I don't say too much about it. I think we need to maintain some air of mystery around it as we pull the pieces together. Besides, often the specifics of the story change on a whim so what it looks like today may be entirely different by the time it hits your kindle.

It is also important to note at this point that we still have work to do on finishing the Giles series. Not to mention the Tabitha collaboration that is still in the pipeline and waiting for fingers to reach the keyboard. (I believe photography is at least booked if not shot. I know Nicky has pictures done... So I think we just waiting for Tabitha images.)

<MIKE EDIT: Photography is done.>

We've already started plotting out the new spy for hire series. The bits that I'm enjoying most about it are being able to make jokes that are a little bit lewd and more sexual in nature - and not worry about what Molly will think!

I'm also enjoying the fact that we have a dope smoking physics professor who joins our crew.

<MIKE EDIT: In this case, dope means 'pot' not 'fresh, cool or neat'.>

I'd love to say more at this point but I suspect I've already said too much. If I have some of this won't even reach your eyes.

Needless to say if you want to find out more keep an eye out for future announcements on the Facebook pages and of course you can follow us on Amazon as this is where the books will next appear.

You can, of course, also join the mailing list and receive updates from Oz.

I am pleased to report that Oz valiantly survived the new GDRP regulations and will continue to reach your inbox if you so choose. He'll be covering any and all future series - whether that be Molly's communiqués or those of our new characters and series.

To receive updates from Oz please visit: www.EllLeigh-Clarke.com

First, THANK YOU for not only reading this story, but reading to the back of this book and our author notes, as well!

So, I just edited Ellie's author notes, adding my own comments and for a lot of it, I had none. Usually, there are plenty and it is a bit worrisome.

Why you ask? Because it means I'm about to get run over.

Poker and Americanisms

So, Ellie is ripping up everyone's expectations of how fast (or slow) a person will take to learn poker. She is learning it so fast, it is causing the guys to (probably) make mistakes.

#ICalledThis-JustSaying

Unfortunately, it has had an undesirable secondary effect.

Ellie is starting to catch on to all of my Americanisms in our conversations and she isn't nearly as easy to kid anymore.

This is a bad thing.

Ever since she read the lobster whitepaper (which is what I credit for the start of her 180-degree turnaround) she has caught up to understanding the stupidity of humanity (and less important in the big scheme of things but perhaps more important for me) she has started to figure out *guys in general.*

This makes it a very uneven battle when we engage in a battle of wits.

Or, in some cases, wit.

Either way, I think that my ability to confuse her just went the way of the dinosaurs…

#SoScrewed.

<<Ellie – hahahaha. I had *no idea* this was on your mind. I'm so glad we get to do author notes! Also – I hadn't noticed any change in the battle of the wit… ;-) >>

Book 12

As Ellie was mentioning, we worked on this series and the general concept at the SmarterArtists in Austin in 2017.

The general premise of The Ascension Myth was a play from the Kurtherian side, sure. However, more important was the play with Ellie's knowledge and understanding of how to deal with life and how to deal with the @#!%!% life throws at you.

Believing that there is something 'higher' than what humanity is feels almost genetically built in to humans, at times.

Otherwise, why do we question?

So, we knew where we were going with this twelve book series, we merely didn't know how to get there.

It reminds me of a joke I was told decades ago that if you were doing algebra and you knew both the question and the answer you would start with the first part of the equation and try to figure it out, then start with the answer and go backwards… where the two met, you would lick your thumb and smear the graphite.

(Get it? Anyone get it? Did I just fuck up the joke?)

<<Ellie edit: huh? I don't get it. You'll have to explain it to me…>>

We knew where we were starting with Molly, and we knew where we would end with Molly…we just didn't know the middle.

<<Ellie edit: oh, smearing the graphite would just be a blur in the

middle that the teacher didn't need to read? Or do you still need to explain it to me?>>

I sure hope you have enjoyed this story, and I encourage you to stay with us for the *DRAMATIC* conclusion in Book 12 of The Ascension Myth!

(See Ellie, I pronounced *Ascension* correctly!)

<<Ellie edit: I don't think the problem was in text... You have spell checker in word!... Ouch. Was that too harsh? ;-P >>

Austin

So, Ellie has moved to Austin, Tx and it fits her personality MUCH better than LA did. I'd like to say that is part of the equation for the name of our new protagonist in our next series, **Interplanetary Spy for Hire.**

(We keep arguing over the series name. I started with Interstellar, then Ellie went with Interplanetary, so I acquiesced and agreed to Interplanetary and she is now saying it's Interstellar... You can't keep some collaborators happy no matter how often you agree to their requests...<SIGH> - hehehehe.)

<<Ellie edit: yeah I just kept forgetting what we agreed on... It's not deliberate!>>

At some point, Austin, Tx. is going to claim Ell Leigh Clarke as their own bad-ass Sci-Fi writer no matter her accent.

England will just be shit-out-of-luck.

;-)

Sex and the Protagonist

Ellie and I were discussing the protagonist for ISH and I was placing beats into the story that were a little sexier than what we were doing in Molly's story.

Ellie was confused.

E: "Didn't you say we shouldn't be so forward with the sexiness in Molly's series?"

M: "Yes I did. However, this is another series – Think James

Bond in Space...as a female... and then think about the sex factor...

There was a pause... (As I was trying to remember if she ever commented on those movies. So, I now have to ask a question I've never had to ask other collaborators...)

M: "Wait, did you ever watch James Bond?"

<<Ellie edit: did you just make that up? I don't remember any of this...!>>

Other Movies

Every once in a while, I have to ask Ellie if she has seen a particular movie, as the 'vision' of what I'm trying to do is exemplified in those movies.

Recently, I asked if she had seen "The Fifth Element" – *She had not.*

I think I also asked if she had seen Blade Runner (another no I believe...I'm sure she will correct me in the author edit pass she is about to do if I'm wrong.)

<<Ellie edit: both statements are correct. I don't watch anything that might be a thriller. And I don't do post-apocalyptic, or scary future. They upset me. (for context: this is the girl who cried for a week when Doctor Who lost Rose. It took me several months to get over it.)>>

And while I'm at it, have you seen the latest version of Judge Dredd, Ellie? If not, you probably will want to. Plus, you will get to enjoy watching Karl Urban ;-)

<<Ellie edit: huh? And huh?>>

Oh SHIT Moments...

It seems I forget every damned time when I write Author Notes, that eventually Ellie and I are going to be recording these notes together for the Audio Books. So, in about a bazillion weeks (or less) I will have to say whatever I wrote out loud...

Providing Ellie another chance to hash it back out with me after she has been provided WEEKS to ponder it.

<<Ellie edit: yes, because I spend a portion of my cognitive capacity on important things like pondering how to get you back in between writing and recording them...>>

And this is after her chance to edit my author notes which SHE started (editing the author notes)... *Well, that might be a stretch,* but anyway...

Us hashing it out happened most recently on our latest audio book (read Ellie's notes, she goes into it with the passive-aggressive comments) and I think to myself (when recording) "Why do I give her so much ammo?"

It's like giving ...

Well, this sucks. I can't think of a proper metaphor here. Ellie is too different from most women to use the typical female stuff,

<<Ellie edit: Awwww...>>

and it would be improper to associate her with a guy...

<<Ellie edit: narrows eyes suspiciously...>>

Well, damn. This went no-where.

Awesome sauce!

I want to take a quick moment and let you, our fans and supporters, know that working with Ellie is just as fun as it looks to be. She is humorous, smart and freakishly fast understanding shit.

She truly is the next generation Albert Einstein and I'm happy to be her collaborator!

(Now, while this is absolutely true, I know how she will react on the audio when we say this – she will go 'Awwwww' and I'm giggling already.)

<<Ellie edit: Awwww... Crap, am I that predictable??!>>

We love you, folks! Stay tuned this coming month for the resounding *FINISH* to The Ascension Myth!

Ad Aeternitatem,

Michael Anderle

<u>Giles Kurns: Rogue Instigator (2)</u>

The Second Dark Ages
with Michael Anderle
Darkest Before The Dawn (3)
Dawn Arrives (4)
Deuces Wild
with Michael Anderle
Beyond The Frontiers (1)
Rampage (2)
Labyrinth (3)
Birthright (4)

BOOKS BY MICHAEL ANDERLE

For a complete list of books by Michael Anderle, please visit:

www.lmbpn.com/ma-books/

All LMBPN Audiobooks are Available at Audible.com and iTunes. For a complete list of audiobooks visit:

www.lmbpn.com/audible

CONNECT WITH THE AUTHORS

Receive updates from Oz by registering your holo/ email address here:
ellleighclarke.com

Facebook:
http://www.facebook.com/ellleighclarke/

Michael Anderle Social

Website:
http://kurtherianbooks.com/

Email List:
http://kurtherianbooks.com/email-list/

Facebook Here:
https://www.facebook.com/TheKurtherianGambitBooks/

www.ingramcontent.com/pod-product-compliance
Lightning Source LLC
Chambersburg PA
CBHW050306110726
47899CB00007B/2125